"What brin... the tracks, ...

"Uh, I…ah…" Jessica could not look at him and think straight.

"You must have a good reason for coming to a grimy police station weight room. I can't recall seeing you on this side of the street before."

She glanced at Doug, then quickly away. He was right. She rarely came to a station. Her job was at the courthouse. Though they were technically on the same side of the law, their jobs and their outlooks couldn't be further from one another. Had she made a mistake in coming here?

"Listen, Judge, I had a lousy night, thanks to you. A cold shower didn't do me a damn bit of good, but an hour in here was getting my head straight—until you showed up. I'm not in the mood for an argument, so if that's why you're here, you can just use those great legs of yours to take that sensational little tail of yours out of here."

Dear Reader,

Welcome to another month of the most exciting romantic reading around, courtesy of Silhouette Intimate Moments. Starting things off with a bang, we have *To Love a Thief* by ultrapopular Merline Lovelace. This newest CODE NAME: DANGER title takes you back into the supersecret world of the Omega Agency for a dangerous liaison you won't soon forget.

For military romance, Catherine Mann's WINGMEN WARRIORS are the ones to turn to. These uniformed heroes and heroines are irresistible, and once you join Darcy Renshaw and Max Keagan for a few *Private Maneuvers,* you won't even be trying to resist, anyway. Wendy Rosnau continues her unflashed miniseries THE BROTHERHOOD in *Last Man Standing,* while Sharon Mignerey's couple find themselves *In Too Deep.* Finally, welcome two authors who are new to the line but not to readers. Kristen Robinette makes an unforgettable entrance with *In the Arms of a Stranger,* and Ana Leigh offers a matchup between *The Law and Lady Justice.*

I hope you enjoy all six of these terrific novels, and that you'll come back next month for more of the most electrifying romantic reading around.

Enjoy!

Leslie J. Wainger
Executive Editor

Please address questions and book requests to:
Silhouette Reader Service
U.S.: 3010 Walden Ave., P.O. Box 1325, Buffalo, NY 14269
Canadian: P.O. Box 609, Fort Erie, Ont. L2A 5X3

The Law and Lady Justice

ANA LEIGH

Silhouette®

INTIMATE MOMENTS™

Published by Silhouette Books

America's Publisher of Contemporary Romance

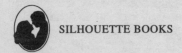 **SILHOUETTE BOOKS**

ISBN 0-373-27300-2

THE LAW AND LADY JUSTICE

Copyright © 2003 by Anna Lee Baier

Visit us at www.eHarlequin.com

Printed in U.S.A.

ANA LEIGH

a Wisconsin native, has three children and five grand-children. From the time of the publication of her first novel, in 1981, Ana successfully juggled her time between her chosen career and her hobby of writing until she officially retired in September of '94 to devote more time to that "hobby." In the past, she has been a theater cashier (who married the boss), the head of an account-ing department, a corporate officer and the only female on the board of directors of an engineering firm.

This *New York Times* bestselling author received a *Romantic Times* Career Achievement Award nomination for Storyteller of the Year in 1991, the BOOKRAK 1995–1996 Best Selling Author Award, the *Romantic Times* 1995–1996 Career Achievement Award and the *Romantic Times* 1996–1997 Career Achievement Award for Historical Storyteller of the Year. Her novels have been distributed worldwide, including Africa, China and Russia.

This one's for you, Don, in celebration of our big 50.

Chapter 1

"Good afternoon, I'm Sherilyn Matthews, speaking to you from outside of the Milwaukee County courthouse where, in an interesting turn of events Judge Jessica Kirkland has released LeRoy Gilbert, suspected murderer of his girlfriend, stripper Cindy Fires."

Jessica stood just inside the courthouse entrance, safely out of sight of the human vulture with huge hair, several loose strands whipping dangerously in the wind. The reporter proceeded to caw into her microphone, sensationalizing the latest disaster in Jessica's courtroom.

"Many of you will recall how Judge Kirkland, less than a year ago, released another murder suspect. Elected to the bench on a record of championing victims' rights as a prosecuting attorney, it would appear that Judge Kirkland has left those days behind her."

Jessica took a step forward, causing the police guard at the door to frown and shake his head. She sighed, knowing he was right. She was a judge. She did not have to explain herself to anyone—least of all blondie of the big hair and bigger mouth.

Just as she turned to leave, she saw him. Lounging against the courthouse wall, listening to Sherilyn as if he had nothing better to do in the world than look too good in a rumpled suit and loosened tie. How many times had she seen him in her courtroom looking just like that?

Tall and dark, he appeared just a bit dangerous, despite the well-trimmed hair and ever-present suit. She knew he wore a Glock 23 automatic beneath his jacket, which added to that high-powered energy he emanated. Although they'd rarely spoken beyond heated arguments, she'd been close enough to him to know that beneath those mirrored sunglasses his eyes were blue, and he smelled like a titillating blend of summer sunshine and midnight memories.

An obvious break in Sherilyn's cawing brought Jessica's attention back to the reporter, whose smile reminded Jessica of a cat with canary feathers hanging out of its mouth. Sherilyn had seen something she wanted, and she actually licked her lips in delight. Her cameraman barely had time to blink as he hurried after her when she made a beeline for the man still lounging against the courthouse wall.

He didn't retreat, remaining motionless as the reporter rushed at him, microphone waving like a talisman.

Shoving the microphone into her quarry's face, Sherilyn kept on talking. "Detective McGuire, you were the arresting officer on this case. What are your feelings on the matter of Judge Kirkland and her unfortunate habit of releasing your suspects back into the population at large?"

Jessica bit her lip. There was little love lost between her and homicide detective Doug McGuire. Though she might privately think he had the best pair of buns that ever graced a witness chair, in public, well—

"I wish just once a judge would put aside concern for the rights of the guilty and consider the rights of the victim."

Anger propelled Jessica forward, and she now stood in the open doorway of the courthouse, her gaze focused on the scene playing out only a few feet in front of her. When the guard approached, Jessica's glare halted him.

Raising his hands in surrender, he shrugged. "It's your funeral, Your Honor," he mumbled as he retreated, which only added to her frustration. Why did everyone but the judge get to have *his or her* day in court? Why did everyone, including the guilty, get to have his or her say on television?

McGuire looked straight into the camera, expounding his viewpoint to southern Wisconsin as Sherilyn gazed at him like a teenage girl salivating over Ricky Martin.

"What do you mean, Detective?"

The reporter bobbed her head and her hair tilted at a precarious angle. Jessica hoped the mass would fall off and hit McGuire between those sensuous dark blue eyes of his; but luck wasn't with her, and Sherilyn's hair appeared to do nothing other than whiplash his face with a few wayward strands.

"I mean," McGuire said, "this man got away with murder! I know it. You know it. The judge knows it. The guy's lawyer probably knows it for sure. So why is that man back on the street?"

"Because there's such a thing as an illegal search, Detective."

Jessica's outburst fell into a silence so loud she could hear a siren wailing down Interstate 43 behind them. She hadn't realized she'd stepped out of the shadow of the courthouse and into the bright June sunshine. All eyes turned toward her—so did the camera. The microphone nearly hit Jessica in the teeth as Sherilyn dove in her direction.

"Judge Kirkland, would you care to elaborate?"

Jessica ignored Sherilyn, for the moment concentrating on McGuire. She continued to glare at McGuire as he stopped lounging and stood up straight, seeming to tower over her even though a distance of several feet separated them. Slowly he removed his glasses, giving her an uncommon view of his eyes. She wished he'd put the shades back on. For once his eyes didn't spark with annoyance or anger, instead they looked—interested. That difference disconcerted her.

Jessica pulled her gaze away as Sherilyn waved the microphone dangerously close. "Would you care to elaborate, Your Honor?" the pushy reporter repeated.

"If I allowed the case in question to go to trial it would only be thrown out. The search of the suspect's premises was illegal. That is the law, not my opinion. My hands are tied."

"So were the victim's." McGuire had crept up on her, startling her.

The man moved too fast and too quietly for someone of his size. "Excuse me?" she said in her best judicial voice. She could not allow him to see how much his nearness rattled her. She was a tall woman, with confidence to spare, yet McGuire always made her feel tiny.

"You said your hands were tied, Your Honor. Well, so were the victim's. Do you think she'd want her murderer to go free over a legal technicality?"

Her mind flooded with memories, and she blinked at their vividness. The sun seemed to beat hotter; the voices around her buzzed louder—her temples pounded. Sweat trickled between her breasts, down her back, and she felt the silk blouse beneath her jacket sticking to her skin. She stared into McGuire's angry blue eyes, forced the past back where it belonged, and then she got mad, too.

She understood about victims…pain…and the need for justice in an unjust world. She'd spent the past fifteen years of her life working for what she believed in. She'd given up any hope of a husband, a family. Heck, she had no life at all, because she searched for one thing—justice.

How dare McGuire question that?

"I'm sure the victim doesn't care about the law. But I have to. If I don't follow the law, I'm no better than the ones I presume to judge. And neither are you, Detective. Do the job right next time, and we'll have no further problems."

"I did the job." He stepped closer, crowding her. "I got the warrant."

"With false information." She took a step forward, determined not to be the one to back off.

"I didn't know it was false at the time."

"That doesn't make it right."

"Well, this is very interesting," Sherilyn interrupted, her microphone separating the two of them, who were nearly nose-to-nose. "If you two could answer a few questions for our listeners…"

Jessica flushed. She'd forgotten she was on television. McGuire made her forget a lot of things. She glared at him and turned toward the camera.

"I just want the people to know that something has to be done to stop criminals from being set free on technicalities before the case reaches the courtroom. If anyone has a solution, I'd be glad to hear it."

She turned on her heel and marched back into the courthouse, ignoring the shouted questions and the scent of that man, which she knew would taunt her long into the evening ahead.

She spoke directly to me, begging for help. She has such a strong sense of justice and tries so hard, but the legal system—what can she do? It's her job—no more, no less— even if doing that job allows the guilty to go free.

I have a solution. I'll make her so happy. She won't have to be sad any longer. Since she can't do it, someone has to.

That someone will be me.

* * *

"Judge Kirkland, wait up."

The low-pitched command resonated with a feral undertone that suggested menace, while at the same time plunked sensuously on her backbone with the potency of Pablo Casales strumming a Takamine guitar.

Jessica halted, took a deep breath, and turned. "What is it, Detective McGuire?"

He pulled up, enveloping her again with the force of his male energy. "Just what in holy hell do you have against me?"

She raised her head in the hope of getting the full stature out of her five feet nine inches. "I don't understand what you mean."

"You know damn well what I mean. Hours and hours of investigative paper and legwork goes up in smoke in the couple of minutes it takes for a judge like you to throw a case out of court. First you did it with Bellemy, now Gilbert."

"Detective McGuire, you and your partner are quite aware that Sam Bellemy's admission of guilt would never have stood up in court."

"He confessed, didn't he?"

"Before his lawyer arrived! Why didn't you halt your questioning the moment he asked and wait until one was present? Instead, your partner made matters worse and beat the confession out of him."

"He didn't *beat* him. So he shoved him around a little bit. You can't blame Vic. He has an eight-year-old daughter. Any parent on a jury would have done the same if they'd seen what that sick pervert did to that little girl."

"I have no doubt you're right, but, unfortunately, Mr. Bellemy was spared the jury process because of Detective Peterson's actions—and yours for not restraining your partner."

"I had all I could do to restrain myself. My mistake was stopping Vic from killing the bastard!"

"Oh right, Detective, that would make Peterson a condemned murderer and he'd be the one who would end up serving a life sentence."

"Not if he came up before you, *Your Honor*. Seems like murderers get an easy walk in your court."

Jessica watched him storm off with that panther stride of his.

When Jessica entered the office, her distress must have shown on her face. Liz Alexander glanced up with a sympathetic smile. "I watched it all in living color. I see he got to you again, honey," she said, in reference to Nemesis-Detective Douglas I. McGuire.

Liz had been Jessica's secretary when they worked together in the D.A.'s office, and had come with her when Jessica had been chosen to fill a sudden vacancy on the circuit court. She had toiled tirelessly to help get Jessica elected to that seat when the temporary term had expired. But Liz was more than a secretary to her. The fifty-year-old widow had become her confidant, her counselor, the sympathetic ear to her tribulations—the joyous smile to her accomplishments—a shopping companion, or the one to share a pizza and gabfest over a current novel or show. Mother or sister, whatever the moment called for, but above all—best friend.

Whether one liked or resented Jessica, everyone in the courthouse loved Liz: police officers, detectives, bailiffs, sheriffs, court reporters, clerks, maintenance crews—even the media. They gravitated toward Liz's desk, and she mothered them all. The consensus among them that Liz could probably be a better counselor to the prisoners locked behind bars than the lawyers who defended them or the clergymen who attempted to offer them spiritual guidance.

Sighing deeply, Jessica shook her head. "That man drives me wild."

"You and probably every other woman he knows. He's one sexy hunk."

"I meant he makes me so angry I want to scream."

"Oh yeah, right."

"You don't believe me."

"I don't believe you haven't noticed he's sexy."

"Too much for his own good. That's probably why he's so arrogant. God's gift to womanhood!" She headed for her chambers. "I pity his poor wife, if he's married."

"He isn't," Liz replied.

Jessica halted and turned around. "Really? How do you know?"

"His partner told me."

"Ex-wife?"

"Nope."

"Well, I'm sure he's got a live-in girlfriend."

"Nope. No wife, ex-wife or live-in girlfriend."

"Boyfriend?" Jessica asked, hesitantly.

Liz rolled her eyes. "You've got to be kidding!"

"Well, obviously, no woman can tolerate him. He's arrogant, overbearing, short-tempered, foul-mouthed and…" She stopped and bit her lip to cut off her words.

"And what?" Liz asked.

Jessica expelled a deep breath. "The sexiest man I've ever met." Both women giggled.

"I never heard you say that about Dennis Wolcott in the whole seven years you went with him."

"We're not exactly comparing apples to apples here, Miss Elizabeth."

"In fact," Liz tapped a fuchsia-tipped finger against her chin, "I don't remember you even mentioning poor Mr. Pomp and Circumstance from the time you broke your engagement to him six months ago. I think I've just figured out what the problem is here."

"And just what would that be?" Jessica asked.

Liz leaned back in her chair, folded her arms across her still firm and very trim breasts, and poked her tongue in her cheek. "You're horny, Judge Kirkland."

Still steaming from his talk with the judge, Doug waited outside of the courthouse for Vic. Thankfully, Sherilyn the shark had left and had taken her microphone, camera and rawhide hair with her. Normally, he didn't blame anyone for trying to make an honest buck—but making money off of other people's misfortunes left him cold.

Too bad Sherilyn didn't have the class of the judge— or her legs. Those legs of hers! His thoughts immediately conjured up one of his favorite images—Judge Jessica's long legs. Keeping them hidden under that black robe was criminal.

A dark blue Crown Victoria pulled up. Doug walked over and opened the car door. Vic Peterson grinned at him from behind the wheel.

After removing his suit jacket, Doug climbed in, then tossed the jacket into the back seat. "What kept you?"

"I was watching the *Judge Jessica Meets The Wolf Man* show. It's a sure bet for renewal in the fall."

"She's something, isn't she?"

"You talking about the judge or the blonde?" Vic asked. When Doug threw him an exasperated look, Vic said, "You've really got a thing for her, don't you? Since when are you the shy type? Why don't you just ask her out?"

"I'm preserving my virginity for when Bev dumps you," Doug said. "Besides, Judge Jessica can't stand the sight of me, and she's engaged to that prick lawyer Wolcott."

"Boy, partner, you're really slipping. Don't you read the paper? They broke up six months ago."

Doug's pulses shot into overdrive. He grinned with pleasure. "No kidding?" Knowing Vic would spare no mercy if he suspected Doug was serious, he quickly tried to cover up. "I didn't think you read anything but the sports section."

"I don't. Her secretary told me."

Vic wheeled his way through the traffic to the House of Correction, where the criminals with minor offenses were incarcerated.

After signing in, and handing over a carton of cigarettes, they sat down in a small, private room. In a short time, they were joined by one of the convicts, his skinny five feet two inches decked in a bright orange jumpsuit of the Milwaukee County penal system.

"Hey, McGuire. Peterson." He nodded his head, sparsely covered with strands of dank, dark hair. His wide grin revealed a mouth of nicotine-stained teeth in an advanced stage of decay.

"How ya doin', Paulie?" Vic said.

"Good. Grub's real good here," he said.

"Must be. You're sure eager to come back often enough," Doug said. "What're you in for this time?"

"Just passing some checks," Paulie said. "I got a bum rap."

"Right," Doug said.

"You bring the smokes?" The little man nervously threaded his fingers through what was fast becoming a receding hairline.

"Yeah," Vic said, "you ought to give 'em up. They're gonna kill you."

Paulie chuckled. "Naw. That's why I smoke filter tips."

"So, what have you got that's so important?" Doug asked.

"I wuz talkin' to this fella who wuz jest brought in today. He told me somethin' you guys oughta know."

"That's what we're here for," Doug said to the snitch.

"I figure it's worth a sawbuck to ya."

"We already brought you a carton of smokes. It cost a damn sight more than a sawbuck."

"You sure they're filter tips?"

"Get on with it, Paulie," Doug said impatiently. "If you've got something good, we'll throw in the ten dollars."

"Okay, okay. This fella lives in the Third Ward and said the word on the street is that someone's lookin' to hire a hit man."

Paulie paused to let his words sink in as Doug and Vic exchanged a long look.

"Who's the target?"

"He didn't know."

"Who's putting out the contract?"

"Didn't know that, either. He only heard it involved a case McGuire and Peterson had handled."

"Which case?"

"He didn't know."

"You're saying he doesn't know the case, the victim or who put out the contract," Doug said. "You wouldn't be holding out on us, would you, Paulie?"

"No, I swear, fellas, that's all he told me. Ain't I always been up front with ya?"

The guy was clueless. Doug headed for the door. "If you hear anything more, give us a call."

"What about the sawbuck?"

"You'll get it when you give us something more," Vic said. "The name of the game is names, Paulie. We need names."

On the way out, Doug stopped and added a ten-dollar bill to the carton of cigarettes.

Vic shook his head. "Under all that skepticism, you're a real marshmallow, McGuire."

Chapter 2

Vic maneuvered the Crown Victoria into their parking space and killed the engine. He glanced at his watch, then at Doug. "You going home?"

Doug had already gotten out of the car and retrieved his jacket, shrugging into the sleeves, despite the late-afternoon heat. The captain frowned on detectives walking around without jackets in public. No displaying your weapon in front of the citizenry—probably wasn't a good idea for the criminals to see it, either. Like nobody knew they were wearing Glocks. Right!

"I think I'll go in for a while." Doug's gaze met his partner's across the top of the car, just in time to see the flash of concern in Vic's eyes. "What?"

"Why don't you come over for dinner? You've got to eat."

"Thanks, but no. I was over twice last week."

"Bev loves to have you—and the kids do, too. Andrea has a crush on you a mile wide. Right now it's cute, although I will have to kill you in about eight years. Justin and Brandon would love to toss the ball around.''

Doug ignored the stab of envy for his friend. Vic and Bev had been married twenty years. They had two teenage sons and an eight-year-old daughter—who was going on twenty-five. Vic was lucky. He was one of the few cops who had a marriage that had survived. His children were healthy, happy and thriving, and the Peterson clan always welcomed Doug with open arms. But lately he'd started to feel just a bit sad when he was there, and for the life of him he couldn't figure out why.

''I've got paperwork.'' He slammed the car door. ''See you in the morning.''

''Just don't stay here until all hours drinking coffee and skipping dinner.''

''Yes, Mother.''

''I mean it, McGuire. You're turning into an old man before my eyes.''

And since Vic was too close to the truth for comfort, Doug forced a grin and a lighthearted wave. ''You should know, old man.''

He headed for the station without looking back. The buzz of voices, calm against angry, swirled about him as soon as he stepped inside; the scent of cigarettes and stale coffee hit him like a punch to his empty stomach and set it to churning. Flickering florescent lights over his desk made the entire office seem like a surreal episode of *Star Trek*. Sitting down at his desk, he stared at the scene before him. Cops, perps and a couple victims.

''Welcome to my life,'' he muttered.

He'd asked for this; planned for it by taking Pre-Law courses and joining the force immediately after he finished college. For him solving puzzles was what was important. And there'd never been a puzzle he couldn't solve—unless you counted women.

Women!

Doug sighed. He just couldn't figure them out. Take Judge Jessica. Boy, would he like to take Judge Jessica!

Doug groaned at his wayward thoughts, and libido, forcing himself to pick up a pen and get to work. But within minutes his mind wandered once more. Name, address and crime just didn't measure up to smooth skin, the scent of sin and a body he'd like to get to know from the tip of what he was certain would be great toes to the top of that too-smart head of hers. How long was that hair she pinned up so primly? And was that red-brown color for real?

"Hey, McGuire!"

"Huh?" Doug blinked at the desk sergeant. "What?"

"I was calling your place. Don't you sign in anymore?"

"Sorry." His mind was not where it should be today. "What do you want, O'Riley?"

"You know that creep Judge Kirkland let go today?"

Doug sighed, the image of Jessica's hair trailing to her waist dissolving at the reminder of what had happened to the case of which he'd been so proud. "Gilbert? What about him?"

"They just pulled him out of the Milwaukee River at Michigan Avenue with a plastic bag over his head."

Doug gaped. "What?"

The sergeant shook his head and gave Doug a strange look. "He's dead, McGuire. Peterson's on his way. Meet him there."

Doug nodded and the sergeant retreated, still shaking his head. Doug sat at his desk and stared at the phone. Wouldn't Judge Jessica just love to hear this? He couldn't resist. He had to tell her, he thought, reaching for the phone.

Sounding rushed, Liz Alexander answered after several rings. "I'm sorry, Detective, you just caught me on my way out. Judge Kirkland isn't here. She was so upset about what happened today that she left early. I suspect she wanted to take a walk before her dinner meeting so she could clear her head. She does that sometimes.''

"Dinner?"

"At Water Street Bistro. Do you know it?"

"Fancy. On the Riverwalk. Prime real estate."

"That's the one." Doug could swear he heard a smile in Liz's voice, although he couldn't figure out what was so funny. "Would you like to leave a message?"

Doug grunted, annoyed that he'd given in to the impulse to call the judge. It had been childish. Even more childish was his irrational disappointment to find that the judge wasn't waiting to talk to him.

"No. No message."

"Detective?" Though Liz's voice was unfailingly polite, he just knew she was smiling. He could see her grinning from ear to ear, and he gritted his teeth to keep from saying something he'd regret. Doug McGuire might be a smartass, but his mother never raised her son to be rude to a lady.

"Yes, Liz."

"Jessica should be at the Bistro by six-thirty. She has dinner there every Thursday night."

"Thanks, Liz." He hung up.

Water Street Bistro would be her style, he thought. Candles and silver, white tablecloths and wineglasses on every table. Hovering waiters, a wine steward and a maître d'. He could see her in a black dress, single strand of pearls around that throat he'd love to taste, sipping champagne with some dude in a black tuxedo.

Doug growled and stood up. He had work to do. Places to go. Dead bodies to see. And it would have to snow in hell before he'd step foot in the Water Street Bistro.

Jessica always kept a pair of walking shoes beneath her desk. Often before work, and sometimes during the day, she would put on the shoes and walk off her frustration.

Without her robes she was just another career woman in a suit and tennies, hoofing it down Wells Street.

By the time she returned to her office, changed into her low-heeled taupe pumps and grabbed her briefcase and purse, she had no time to go home and change. So it was that she ended up at Water Street Bistro for her weekly dinner with her father wearing the same mint-green business suit she'd put on that morning before leaving her condominium on Lake Drive. She would have preferred just to go home, but her father would be crushed if she missed their dinner date. Every Thursday night the two of them got together and shared their lives. And she had to admit their dinners together always made her feel calmer and saner for a little while—just knowing that there was someone who loved you always, no matter what, could get a person through the toughest of times.

Since her mother's death ten years past, her father had thrown himself into his work, starting restaurants then selling them once they became well established. His latest venture, Water Street Bistro, was more successful than any of the others, and thus far he had given no indication he would sell. She hoped this meant he was beginning to get over her mother's death, as much as it was possible to get over the death of the woman he had adored.

Because of the importance of their weekly ritual, Jessica was surprised to arrive and find their usual table deserted.

"Your Honor." Bruno, the maître d' from Austria, bowed. "Your papa, he will be here soon. Please to sit down and order the wine."

Though Bruno was ever so serious, Jessica often had a hard time not laughing when he spoke. He sounded like Arnold Schwarzenegger, though Bruno was only five foot five and weighed a hundred pounds soaking wet.

Jessica nodded her thanks as Bruno pulled out her chair. "Where is my father, Bruno?"

"I do not know. He is everywhere. Here, there, gone

and back. And after he sees you today on the television, ach! The man he is a crazy person.'' Bruno threw up his hands. ''He marched out of here and he does not come back.''

Jessica frowned. She didn't like the sound of that. She took the wine list Bruno pressed upon her.

''Do not worry, he will be back soon, Your Honor. He would not miss this night with you for all the tea in his coffee cup.''

Jessica blinked. Bruno had a way with a cliché. Sometimes it took her several minutes, or days, to figure out what he meant. This one was easy. ''All the tea in China, Bruno.''

Bruno lifted his nose. ''That is what I said.''

With great dignity he left her alone and went to greet the gathering dinner crowd.

Jessica stared at the wine list, but she did not see the choices. Instead she frowned, reflecting. Though her father had never been late for one of their dinners before, she had noticed an increasing absentmindedness on his part. Now that she thought about it she could name several times she'd called the restaurant, or the house, when he should have been at one place or the other, only to have to leave messages on an answering machine. She was embarrassed to admit her job consumed her so completely she thought of little else, and had not put the disturbing incidents about her father together until now.

Could something be wrong with Daddy?

''Hey, baby girl, sorry I'm late.''

The object of her concern kissed her cheek before slipping into the chair opposite her. Jessica's smile felt stiff as she took in his disheveled state and flushed face. Ben Kirkland never looked unkempt. That would be bad for business. Yet here he sat with the top buttons of his shirt askew, his tie loose, and his salt-and-pepper hair looking as if he'd just come through a wind tunnel.

Jessica glanced through the wall-to-wall picture window that overlooked the river below them. Bright and shiny sunlight reflected off the still water. Not a breeze stirred. Her smile turned upside down as she narrowed her eyes upon her father. "Where have you been, Dad?"

He paused in the midst of tightening his tie. Was she wrong, or did he look just a bit guilty? What on earth could her father be hiding from her?

He smoothed his hair and raised an eyebrow in her direction. "Am I under oath, Your Honor?"

"Of course not. It's just…" Jessica sighed. She did have an abrupt manner when she questioned people. She couldn't help it, that was her way, her job. "You've just been different lately, Dad. I wondered if anything was wrong."

"Wrong?" He reached for the wine list, and crooked a finger at the wine steward who hovered nearby. "Why would anything be wrong?"

Jessica frowned. His voice was too high, his color too pink despite the healthy summer tan of his face, and he wouldn't meet her eyes. "Dad?"

Her voice wavered in the middle, sounding like a child frightened by the bogey man in the middle of the night. Her father, who had heard her cry out in the dark often enough and had always come to her rescue, glanced up in surprise. Their gazes met and he hesitated just long enough for her to wonder if he told her the truth with his brusque words. "I'm fine, baby. Leave it be."

He turned away to greet his steward, ordering wine with practiced ease. When he returned his attention to her, he was once again the man she knew, the man she loved more than any other. "So tell me about today."

The words were not a request but a demand. Jessica had known she would have to discuss her day, but she'd dreaded it. When things happened that she could not control, she wanted to crawl into the sand, bury her head and never pull it out.

"You heard what happened. Bruno told me you were upset."

Her father snorted. "Bruno! He doesn't understand our legal system. As he always says, 'I came to America for freedom, but sometimes your freedom is just too free.'"

"He's right." Jessica paused as her father performed the wine ritual with his steward, then she nodded her thanks as the accepted selection was poured into her glass. She picked up the crystal and swirled the ruby liquid about, tilting the glass just enough to catch the setting sun and turn the wine the color of blood. Then she put the wine down, untasted. "I had no choice, Dad."

"Of course you didn't. No one knows better than I how hard it was for you to let that creep go."

Their eyes met, and they shared a moment of silence for the tragedy in their past. Once there had been four Kirklands living happily in a house in a Milwaukee suburb. Jessica's sister, Karen, had been two years her senior, and though they had fought like sisters, they had loved like sisters, too. When Karen went away to college at the University of Wisconsin at Madison, Jessica had visited her often, counting the days until she could join Karen and experience the swirl of life in Mad City, as it was known to Wisconsin Badgers.

"Jessica?" Her father's voice brought her back to their table. He held his wineglass aloft, waiting for her to join him. She picked up her glass and tapped the rim to his. "Here's to getting past the past and moving on," he said.

Jessica took a sip, then set the glass down with deliberation. "I wish I could, Dad. But every time I have to let someone go whom I know is guilty, I remember Karen and…" She stopped and took a deep, ragged breath.

Her father's hand covered hers where it rested on the table. "And you feel like your heart is being ripped out of your chest and stomped on.'' She nodded. ''What happened to Karen was unspeakable, honey.''

Jessica stared at his large, blunt, sun-browned hand covering her smaller, thinner, paler one. ''Mom never got over it.''

''I doubt we will, either. At least until we can have some closure.''

She looked into his eyes and recognized the never-ending pain. ''I thought that if I put away the guilty, I'd feel better.''

''Don't you?''

''Sometimes. But every time I have to let one go, I remember *that* one, and not all the guilty ones I've sentenced.''

''Why do you think that is?''

''Because no matter how many I sentence, I'll never know if he's the one who murdered my sister.''

Her father winced.

''I'm sorry.'' Jessica turned her hand and intertwined her fingers with his. ''I shouldn't have said that.''

''It's the truth. Maybe we don't talk about Karen enough.''

''I doubt that. You know sometimes I can't remember what she looked like? I know she had lighter hair compared to mine, and she wanted to be a veterinarian. Sometimes, I can almost hear her laugh, but I can't remember her face.''

''Look at her picture. I always do.''

''Her picture isn't her, Dad.''

He squeezed her hand. ''We'll never forget Karen, never forgive what happened to her, but both of us need to get past it and move on with our lives. Especially you, Jess.''

Jessica straightened, pulling on her hand, but he wouldn't let go. ''What's that supposed to mean?''

''It means you need to do something other than worry about the bad guys all the time.''

"I thought you were proud of my career."

"I am. I'm bursting my buttons whenever I can work into the conversation that my daughter is a judge. But you're starting to worry me." Jessica scowled and took a gulp of her wine with her free hand. "Don't glare at me like that, young lady. You need to get a life."

"Pardon me?"

"Find a man. Have some fun. Live a little."

"You were the one who broke out the champagne when Dennis moved out."

"Dennis Wolcott was a wimp. Face it, girl, you need a man."

Jessica rolled her eyes. "Honestly, Dad!" But his gaze, no longer on her, was fixed on someone near the door. "Dad?"

"Here comes one now," he murmured, his mouth curving into a welcoming smile.

Jessica glanced over her shoulder to find Doug McGuire bearing down on them. Bruno chased after him, flapping his hands like an agitated bird.

McGuire stopped at their table, his dark blue gaze touching on the wine, then lighting on their joined hands. He frowned and lifted an icy stare to Jessica.

"What do you want, Detective McGuire?" She removed her hand from her father's, then picked up her wine when her hand suddenly felt too empty and vulnerable. McGuire always made her feel—nervous.

"We need to talk."

Jessica raised her eyebrows and lifted her glass. She sipped, ever so slowly, watching McGuire heat toward slow burn. Damn it was fun! "I think we talked enough today, Detective, don't you?"

Her father turned a laugh into a cough. Her gaze flicked toward him, and she remembered what he'd said just before McGuire descended. She needed a man. Well, McGuire might be a man, but he was not for her. She had to get rid of him before Daddy started matchmaking. And from the look of his grin and the sparkle in his eyes, she didn't have much time.

"I'm having dinner, Detective. You can make an appointment with Liz."

"No chance. The boyfriend will just have to eat alone tonight. I need you to come with me."

She narrowed her eyes, then carefully set down her wine before she made a scene by throwing it into McGuire's face. Then she sat back and looked him up and down. "This sounds interesting." She ran her tongue over her bottom lip, tasting the rich, red flavor of the Merlot her father had chosen. "What do you have in mind, Detective?"

His gaze, which had fixed on her lips, snapped to her eyes. The heat there made her want to pull at the suddenly tight neck of her blouse. "Lose the date," McGuire ordered.

Her father snorted again. She cast him an annoyed glare and stood up. Shouldering past McGuire, she bent and kissed her father's cheek. "Excuse me, but the detective is quite insistent." She patted his cheek. "I'll make it up to you, sweetheart."

Her father grinned at her obvious ploy and winked. "Good night, Jess."

Jessica turned and nearly bumped into a scowling McGuire. She moved past him and out the door.

Once outside, out of the range of too many listeners, she turned and demanded, "What's so important you dragged me away before I had a chance to eat?"

"So I'll buy you dinner." He took her arm and started to hustle her along at a rapid pace.

"Where are we going?"

"Where we can talk. I think we need a level playing field and that fancy jacket-and-tie joint ain't it. I know a good place to eat just a couple blocks from here. Do you mind walking?''

''Not at all, it's a beautiful night for a stroll. So why are we running a marathon?''

''Oh, sorry,'' he said, slowing his steps. ''Your boyfriend's sure the understanding type.''

She feathered a smile. ''He's very secure, because he knows how I feel about him.''

''He called you Jess. I like that. Heard you broke your engagement to Wolcott. You went with that guy a long time, didn't you?''

''Yes, seven years.''

''Sure didn't take you long to find a replacement.''

''Is that what you wanted to discuss, McGuire?'' she asked with a rise of anger. ''As much as I value your opinion, it's a poor substitute for a gourmet meal. This could have waited until morning.''

''Just wanted you to know that you got your wish.''

''My wish? I don't recall wishing for anything, except maybe your transfer to Anchorage.''

''Very funny. Figured you'd be interested to hear that we pulled your friend Gilbert out of the river a short time ago. Very wet—and very dead. Congratulations, Judge, justice has been served.''

Shocked, she stopped abruptly. Then had to hurry to catch up with him.

Chapter 3

By the time Jessica got over the initial shock of Gilbert's murder, they'd reached the restaurant. But it wasn't a restaurant. From the outside, the place looked like a sleazy, rundown, enter-at-your-own-risk dive. Big bold, black letters painted on the window identified it as The Precinct, and a smaller line below read Bar and Grill.

A cloud of gray cigarette smoke greeted them at the door along with Patsy Cline wailing "Crazy."

I must be, too, to allow myself to get maneuvered into this!

The moment she entered, Jessica recognized a dozen or more faces in a glance—she'd seen them in court time enough. Good Lord, he had brought her to a cop bar!

Doug would have to have been blind not to notice that Jessica drew the curious glances of most of the men in the room.

"Hey, Your Honor, you slumming?" one of the men standing at the bar asked good-naturedly.

"Well, Detective Slocum, what a pleasure to see you

outside of court. You look much taller now that I'm not peering down at you from behind my bench.''

"And if I might say, you look mighty good out from under that black robe.''

"Say it! Say it!'' she teased. "It's music to my ears, Detective.''

"How ya doin', Judge?'' another asked.

"Just fine, Tony,'' she said, slapping him on the shoulder in passing.

When she spied a heavyset man at the end of the bar, McGuire followed her over to him.

"Detective Bronowski! How are you? I miss seeing you in court.''

"Heck, Judge, call me Ski. We ain't in court now.''

"What have you been doing since you retired?'' she asked.

"Jerry and I bought this place,'' Ski said.

"So you and Jerry are still partners. Good for you.''

Bronowski nodded to Doug, then said, "If McGuire gives you any heat, just let me know. Jerry and I can handle him for you.''

That's a laugh! If anyone needed help, it was him, Doug thought. She was the one giving off the heat. He got hot every time he looked at her—and it sure wasn't from anything she said. He took her arm and steered her over to a corner table that offered a modicum of privacy.

"So this is where the long arm of the law comes to unwind,'' she said, once they were seated.

"One of them. There's a couple more in the city—Fuzzy's and Coach's on the south side. A couple sports bars on the north side. Mostly the guys like to hang out in the sports bars.''

One of the men playing Sheepshead at a nearby table yelled, "Hey, McGuire, when are you and the judge gonna put on gloves and sell tickets?''

"We've been considering it as a fund-raiser toward promoting your early retirement, Novack."

"I hear they pulled Gilbert out of the river tonight." Doug nodded, wishing the loudmouth would shut up and concentrate on his card game instead of them. Novack looked at Jessica. "Too bad, Your Honor. That walk you gave Gilbert got him a short swim instead. You the one that whacked him, McGuire?"

"Yeah, right."

"Novack, you gonna deal or shoot bull all night?" one of the men in the game asked. To Doug's relief, Novack shut up.

"Don't think you'll find too many Gilbert mourners in this crowd," he said.

"Well, I'll be honest with you…I'm not sorry he's dead. As a judge, I abhor violence, but the citizen in me is glad to know there's one less murderer out there tonight."

"I tried to get that scumball behind bars where he belonged." When she glanced around, he asked, "Who are you looking for?"

"Your friend Sherilyn and her Mr. Microphone."

Doug chuckled. "Yeah, she's a real piece of work, and the lady sure has got it in for you."

"I think she's one of those insecure women who look upon every other woman as her natural enemy." She made an appealing sound that might have been a giggle. "I suppose it didn't help when I beat out her boyfriend in the election."

Doug's approving gaze lingered on her face as he wondered how she'd look with that auburn hair tumbling around her shoulders. "She's not even in your class, Judge Jess."

The waitress approached with pad in hand. "How're you doin', Doug?"

"Real good, Kate. How's Danny?"

She drew a deep sigh. "About the same. He has some

good days and some bad ones. He told me he saw you on television today arguing with some dumb female judge who let your collar go.''

Doug threw Jessica a quick glance, but she showed no reaction. ''Be sure and give Danny my best.''

Kate nodded. ''So what'll it be tonight?''

''A couple of beers, burgers with the works and some fries.''

''You got it, honey.'' Kate came back instantly, put down a pitcher of beer and two glasses, and then took off again.

''Sorry about Kate's remark,'' he said, filling her glass.

''Think nothing of it. I'm getting used to those kind of comments.''

''You can't blame people for resenting how these criminals get off, can you? But don't be misled by Kate's remark. She's one of the great women of the world. Do you remember reading a few years back about this hopped up junkie who shot his girlfriend, set the house on fire, and before shooting himself put a bullet into the young police officer who came into the burning building to rescue an infant in a crib?''

''Oh, yes. That was so tragic. If I remember, they all died.''

''Not quite. The baby died…the woman died…the perp died, but the police officer wasn't that lucky. He sustained first-degree burns over his face and hands, and the bullet severed his spinal cord. The doctors say with continued therapy he *might* be able to sit up in a wheelchair in another year. In the meantime, they've been working on plastic surgery to cover up the burns on his face. He was pretty maimed. That young police officer is Danny Harrigan— Kate's twenty-one-year-old son. Her husband, Jimmy, had been shot and killed five years before that incident, when he stopped a car on a routine traffic violation.''

''That's terrible! I'm so sorry, Doug.''

"Yeah, we're all sorry. And poor Kate. Bad enough she lost a husband—and son—but she has to work her butt off to pay for the medical bills that the insurance doesn't cover. Any woman dumb enough to fall in love with a cop ought to go to a shrink first before marrying one."

"It sounds to me like you really mean anyone who chooses to become a police officer ought to pay a visit to that shrink. Why did you go into law enforcement, Doug?" she asked.

"I can tell you it wasn't for truth, justice and the American Way. I like solving puzzles. Every crime leaves some kind of clues. The challenge is to recognize them. They're like pieces of a picture puzzle. You keep moving them around until they all fit, and the whole picture is laid out before you."

"I would have thought the FBI would hold more of an appeal to you."

"They did try to recruit me when I finished college, but I come from a long line of cops, so I opted to join the Milwaukee Police Department. I put in the required five years in uniform—which had seemed like fifty at the time—counting the days until I could take the promotional exam for detective."

"Is your father on the force?"

"Not here. He's the police chief of a small town in Northern Illinois. What about you, Your Honor?"

"Jessica or Jess. We're not in court now."

"Okay, Jess. How come a beautiful young woman with brains and beauty to boot chose to become a felony judge?"

"I know you won't believe me, but I became a judge in order to see justice done."

"Yeah, but whose side are you on?"

"Doug, I don't take pleasure out of seeing criminals get off scot-free, but until the arresting officers play by the letter of the law, it will continue to happen. Not only in

my court, but also in courts all around the country. There
are too many defense lawyers out there today who know
every loophole in the book. Why blame the judges for
upholding the same laws you've sworn to protect?''

Fortunately, Kate arrived with their food, thus preventing what might have become another argument.

Jessica looked at the hamburger heaped with onions,
pickles, cheese, mushrooms and catsup dripping down the
sides. "I should have brought my calculator."

"Dinner's on me," he said.

"You're darn right it is, McGuire. You pulled me away
from a perfectly good meal. I just need a calculator to add
up all the fat grams we're about to eat. Looks like choles-
terol heaven."

Doug took a chomp of the sandwich and wondered why
a woman with a body like hers would worry about a few
extra calories. He wasn't supposed to think about the body
beneath that proper suit, but sitting across a table from her
sharing a meal—instead of a murder case—made him
more aware of the woman instead of the judge.

When they finished eating, they paired off in a shuffle-
board game against an engaged couple on the force. Then
they sat down and finished off the pitcher of beer—and
discovered that they both liked old movies, old torch
songs, Ella Fitzgerald singing jazz and Sinatra singing anything.

He also discovered she had a sense of humor, was easy
to talk to and fun to be with. So what was missing? Why
hadn't some lucky guy nailed her with a marriage license?
There'd had to be a better reason other than she couldn't
cook. The puzzle solver in him wondered about the missing piece. "You ever been married, Jess?"

She shook her head. "Dennis Wolcott and I were engaged, but we never got around to setting a date. As it
turned out, it was just as well we didn't—we weren't in
love. At least what I consider being in love. I'd never settle

for anything less than what my parents had together. What about you? Have you ever been in love, Doug?''

"A babe in Sheboygan got a gold watch out of me once. The next day she returned it to the jeweler for diamond earrings. I figured we weren't on the same wavelength, so I lost her phone number.''

"Just because the *babe* exchanged the gift you gave her.''

"I figure if someone you love gives you a gift, it ought to mean more to you than a damn pair of earrings!'' She was tapping into feelings he couldn't explain. Feelings he didn't want to deal with—much less talk about.

She must have sensed that, because she grinned at him. "Maybe she just couldn't tell time.'' Glancing at her watch, she said, "But I can, and it's getting pretty late.''

It was midnight by the time they returned to the parking lot of the Water Street Bistro to get their cars.

Jessica began to pull the pins out of her hair. "You'll have to excuse me but I have to let my hair down. These pins are beginning to drive me crazy.'' She raised her hands like claws. "I have a driving urgency to get my hands into it!''

They had another thing in common.

His stomach flopped over when she shook her hair out and the length dropped past her shoulders. "You ought to wear it like that more often,'' he said, spellbound.

"I'm afraid that would make me look more woman than judge.''

"Is that so bad?'' He couldn't take his eyes off her face.

"I'm afraid you're prejudiced, Detective McGuire.''

Detective McGuire. A few minutes ago, he'd been Doug and she'd been Jess. Come midnight, the ball had ended and Cinderella turned back into a felony judge of the Milwaukee County Circuit Court.

Except for that hair—that gorgeous long hair hanging past her shoulders.

After unlocking her car, she turned back with a smile. "Thank you, Detective Doug. I must admit I had a good time." She stepped closer and kissed him on the cheek.

"Yeah, right," he said, with a twisted smile. There was no way he was going to settle for a peck on the cheek like the old codger. She must have guessed his intent, and she stepped back abruptly, but not in time to avoid his arm that snagged her waist and pulled her against him. He swallowed her gasp as their mouths found a fit. Her lips were soft but tasted delicious—and he began to gorge on them, and on the smell of her…the feel of her in his arms. For the briefest of seconds she stiffened to resist, then she settled into the kiss, and slipped her arms around his neck. Her auburn hair drew his hand like a magnet, and he dug his fingers into the thickness. It felt like sliding between silk sheets.

They both gave as much as they took—jockeying for dominance—challenging, dueling and savoring, until they broke apart breathless. She looked him straight in the eye, her chest heaving, and her eyes twin pools of seduction beckoning him to jump in. His loins were on fire, and he was so hard he couldn't move. Even his hands itched so badly to touch her that he had to clench them into fists. He wanted a lot more than a kiss, and wondered what she'd say if he suggested going home with her. Then he thought the better of it—she wasn't the kind that hopped into the sack with a guy after one kiss. And one kiss was all he dared—another one, and he'd be pulling her into the back seat of the car. The sooner he put cold metal between them, the better. So he opened her car door and stepped aside for her to enter.

Her fingers trembled when she inserted the key into the ignition. He hoped the Park Avenue wouldn't start—a sign that they'd stay together and let nature take its course—but the damn engine turned over and purred.

She smiled up at him and for several seconds his gaze held hers as curiosity darkened her brown eyes.

Say it, McGuire! Even if you choke on it, get it out now before you have any more time to think about it. "Good night, Judge Jess." He slammed the car door.

As she drove away, he stood and watched until the taillights disappeared around the corner. Then he headed back to the precinct.

His lips were hard, urgent, against hers. How could he make her insane for more with just the touch of his mouth? Then he touched her with those big, hard hands, and her body came alive as it had never been alive before. She wanted to touch him, too, but for some reason she couldn't reach him. She moaned his name and opened her eyes.

"Doug?"

The word echoed in an empty room. Moonlight silvered the Belgian lace curtains that shrouded her windows. Jessica lay alone in her bed, sheets tangled about her legs, hot despite the coolness of the night. She rolled onto her side and looked at the clock—3:30. Gee, a whole hour later than she'd awoken after the last erotic dream of—

"McGuire," she muttered.

Why on earth had she let the man kiss her? Now she couldn't stop thinking about their first embrace.

If they hadn't been in full view of everyone on the street, she'd probably have yanked his clothes off right there. Heck, why not be honest? She hadn't been thinking about the public eye, or anything else while he kissed her. Her dreams proved that. All she'd wanted then—all she wanted now—was all of Doug McGuire.

Liz's words of that afternoon came back to her. Was her dissatisfaction with her life a result of too much work and too little sex? Would a torrid affair with the delectable detective make everything better? She would certainly sleep better tonight if she wasn't sleeping alone.

By the time the sun peeked over Lake Michigan, Jessica had given up trying to sleep. She took her coffee onto her terrace and had a stern little talk with herself.

You're an adult. He's an adult—or so he professes— though you wouldn't know it from his behavior. Her words sounded peevish, even to herself, but she was so tired. Her skin felt twitchy, as if it didn't belong on her body. A scalding hot shower had done nothing to relieve the feeling. Too much coffee, too early in the morning was making her head buzz.

I want him, and from that kiss last night I'd say he wants me. What could be simpler? That sounded better. Definitely more mature. If she could manage to sound like that when talking with McGuire there would be no problem. Of course talking wasn't the problem—wanting to put her hands all over him was the problem.

Jessica dumped the last of her coffee into the sink and glanced at her watch. Just enough time to stop at the police station on her way to the courthouse and have a heart-to-heart with Detective McGuire.

Though her reception at the front desk was far from welcoming, Jessica had little trouble being directed to her quarry. She walked through the station, head held high despite the stares and whispers. She had not gone into the law to be popular—she'd gone into it to make a difference. Although on some days—like yesterday—she thought she was losing the battle, but most days she figured she'd win her part of the war.

The desk sergeant had directed her to the lower level, third door on the right. Taking a deep breath in the hallway, she steeled herself against her usual libidinous reaction to McGuire. She was here to… Jessica dropped her hand from the door. To what? Offer herself on a platter? She gritted her teeth. With McGuire it wouldn't do to seem so eager. He was a competitive man. She was a competitive woman. He wanted her, but she didn't think he liked her very much. So then, why had he kissed her that way? There had been more than desire in that kiss—and she wanted to know why.

Jessica shoved open Door Number Three and nearly swallowed her tongue at the unexpected sight that greeted her.

McGuire, wearing baggy gray sweatpants and nothing else. She'd have thought he had a good butt, she hadn't gotten a look at his chest. She stood in the doorway and watched the man work.

He was doing bicep curls if she remembered correctly from the single time she'd allowed herself to be tortured in a weight room. The muscles in his upper arms flexed and released, rippling beneath bronzed, smooth skin. Her gaze traveled over the light dusting of hair covering equally defined pectoral muscles and a flat, ridged stomach. The sweatpants rode low on his hips, a drawstring hanging down the front, enticing her gaze to the easily distinguishable bulge despite the looseness of his clothing.

"See anything you like, Your Honor?"

She swallowed and met his eyes. Amusement filled his gaze and she flushed, mortified to be caught ogling him as if she wanted to slip a dollar bill beneath his waistband.

Realizing she stood in an open doorway, Jessica shut the door and leaned back for support. McGuire turned around to replace the free weights in their stand, giving her an excellent view of the backside she liked so much, with the added bonus of naked and rippling shoulder muscles. Her skin began to hum again, and her palms itched to touch that back.

She wished for a moment she hadn't worn her suit jacket. They kept this place far too hot for a workout room. Sweat prickled her brow.

McGuire turned and began to walk toward her with the loose-limbed, confident grace that was so much a part of him. Suddenly the door at her back no longer supported but confined her. He stopped—too close—invading her space as he always did.

She could smell him, and amazingly the scent excited her: heat, and salt—and man. Mesmerized, she watched a drop of sweat slide down his neck, and she imagined how it would feel to catch the droplet on her tongue, put her lips to that chest and learn the ridges and valleys of his body with her mouth.

"Judge?"

"Hmm?"

"If you're going to keep looking at me like that, I'm not going to be responsible for what happens."

She straightened, the ridges of her spine grinding against the door. "Like what? I don't know what you're talking about."

"You don't, huh? Fine, we can play it your way." For some unknown reason he seemed annoyed with her already. He stalked away, grabbing a water bottle from a nearby bench and taking a long drink.

Jessica lost her train of thought as she watched his throat contract and release. Water ran out of his mouth and down his neck, streaking across glistening muscles. Her head began to buzz, and she put her fingers to her eyes, rubbing against the dry, gritty sensation caused by too little sleep and too much McGuire in the night.

"What brings you to my side of the tracks?"

"Uh, I...ah..." Jessica dropped her hand and pushed away from the door. She could not look at him and think straight. Instead she fiddled with her purse, moving items around as if she were in desperate need of finding some hidden treasure within.

"You must have a good reason for coming to a grimy police station weight room. I can't recall seeing you on this side of the street before."

She glanced at him, then quickly away. He was right. She rarely came to a station. Her job was at the courthouse.

Though they were on the same side of the law, technically, their jobs and their outlooks couldn't be further from one another. Had she made a mistake in coming here?

"Listen, Judge, I had a lousy night thanks to you. A cold shower didn't do me a damn bit of good, but an hour in here was getting my head straight—until you showed up. I'm not in the mood for an argument, so if that's why you're here, you can just use those great legs of yours to take that sensational little tail of yours out of here."

Jessica was too interested in the fact that he'd been up all night and needed to take a cold shower because of her to get insulted over his chauvinistic assessment of her body. She abandoned her purse to look his way, startled to find him too close once again.

Their eyes met, held. Her lips parted and she whispered, "Why did you kiss me last night, Doug?"

His gaze dropped to her mouth and he inched closer. Excitement flooded her as he aligned his body to hers; his thin sweatpants did little to contain his arousal. Her body responded to the evidence of his interest, pressing into him even as he pressed against her. He reached past and flicked the lock on the door, his knuckles brushing her hip as he withdrew. A shudder rumbled over her. Raising his arms, he placed a hand on either side of her head, and leaned closer, looming over her, but his size did not threaten, it soothed her. No one would ever hurt her if he were around.

"Kissing you seemed like a good idea at the time," he growled. "And you know what?" She shook her head, unable to trust her voice anymore. "It seems like a better idea now."

His mouth took hers. He tasted of the sea—salt and fury. Was he angry at himself, at her or at what they felt despite the futility? Suddenly the why didn't matter, she had to kiss him back—to touch his skin or go mad.

Opening her mouth, she met his intensity with all the pent-up desire and need of a lifetime. She splayed her hands on his chest, fingers tangling in the hair, palms smoothing the taut muscles.

He moaned into her mouth, nipped her lip, then his hands were in her hair, yanking the pins free with a desperation that matched her own. The bun she'd so carefully constructed sprang free, and her hair spilled over his hands, over her shoulders. Grasping great handfuls, he tilted her head and plundered her mouth more deeply. This man would never do anything halfway. When he kissed he did so with all of himself.

Her hands flitted over his belly, and the muscles fluttered like butterfly wings against her fingertips. When she ran a finger inside the waistband of his sweatpants, he took a deep, rasping breath, and before she could delve inside he grabbed her hand and pressed her palm to his arousal.

A pounding on the door at her back vibrated through Jessica, causing her to freeze as if ice water had been dumped over them both. McGuire tore his mouth from hers. "Get lost," he shouted, his voice harsh and loud in the silent room. "I'm busy."

Whoever it was moved away, grumbling. Doug lowered his forehead to hers. "You make me lose my mind, Jess."

He let go of her hand, which still cupped him in her palm, and she jerked her fingers away, the loss of his heat and hardness making her ache despite the knowledge she should not be touching him that way.

What had come over her? She had thought their conduct had been irresponsible last night. How was this for crazy?

He raised his head and looked down at her. She didn't remember touching his hair, but the usually well-combed strands were rumpled, and a wayward lock drifted across his forehead. His mouth was wet from hers, the day's growth of beard and dark circles beneath his eyes giving him a haunted look she knew too well. The same look had stared back at her from the mirror that morning.

"Let me go," she whispered.

He frowned but did as she asked. Her hair swirled about her face as she bent to pick up the pins on the floor. He knelt to help and their hands brushed. They both pulled back as if scalded, and Jessica held her breath until he moved away, trying to ignore the intense flare of need his mere touch sent up her arm.

She stood and turned away, then began to repin her hair. Her trembling hands caused the task to take longer than usual. What if someone had come in and seen them? What if someone saw her now? Hair unbound, makeup kissed off her mouth, her jacket askew and her blouse completely untucked.

"So, what are we going to do about this?" he asked.

She took a deep breath and turned. "This?"

His lips tightened and his blue eyes went icy. "You know what I mean, Jess. You annoy the hell out of me."

"The feeling's mutual."

"I know. Still I don't think I'm going to be able to keep my hands off you. What are we going to do about that?"

Well, there she had it, an answer to the question that had haunted her all night. He wanted her. She wanted him. What could be simpler?

But she could see that any kind of relationship with McGuire wouldn't be simple. How could a man like him be anything but complicated? Once she took this step there would be no going back. This man could not be as easily dismissed as Dennis Wolcott. He could never be forgotten. And she had a feeling that someone was going to get hurt. That someone would probably be her.

"Jess?" he pressed.

Fear made her stiffen her spine, pick up the things she'd dropped and walk to the door. She'd been naive enough to believe they could have a casual affair, but now she knew better. She could never keep it casual—and McGuire would want nothing more. "We're not going to do anything, McGuire. Not ever again."

She left him behind and went to work.

The descent of the sun finally signaled the end of a very bad day. Jessica watched the sun go to sleep in the west then turned to stare at her living room. The sight only made her feel lonelier than she'd ever felt in her life.

As she had no court appearance scheduled that day, she'd finally relented to Liz's insistence and gone home early. A nap had taken care of her headache, but the dreams set her more on edge. She could push McGuire out of her mind while she was awake, but when she was asleep he returned to torment her.

So she decided a special "just for Jessica" night was in order. A split of champagne and a romance novel read in a tub full of bubbles. The electric lights were doused, giving way to the swaying flames of every candle in her apartment. After donning her favorite white silk lounging gown and negligee, she feasted on her last box of Godiva chocolates to the soothing sounds of a New Age CD recording of falling water and gentle winds.

She still felt lousy.

She jumped at a sudden pounding on the door. Since her building was secure, unauthorized people could not enter unless cleared and admitted by the doorman. Perhaps her father had gotten her message and come over instead of calling as she'd asked. Jessica hurried over and opened the door.

The sight of Doug McGuire lifted her depression. Why fight fate? With a resigned smile, she threw caution to the wind.

"What kept you?" she asked.

Chapter 4

His gaze wandered over her silk-clad body. Approval—and something else—lit his eyes. Jessica went hot all over.

He stepped inside, crowding her. The slam of the door as he kicked it shut behind them barely registered, because her mind went from thought to sensation when his hand snaked around her waist, yanked her against him, and his lips took hers.

The scrape of his teeth along her lip matched the scrape of his belt along her belly, his clothes coarse against skin softened and scented from the bath, sensitive from his recent touch. His hands were hard—rough at her waist—and the calluses on his palms snagged the silk, pulling so the material slid against her hips. She shivered, despite the heat in the room.

Their tongues teased, met, mated. She yanked on his jacket, wanting to touch skin and not clothes. Why did he have on a jacket in the middle of summer anyway?

As she slid her hands down his arms, her wrist scraped his service revolver. He swallowed her gasp with another openmouthed kiss, and she forgot the gun as her body exploded with sensation. Pulling her clinging fingers from his arms, he placed them at her sides with a little shake that cautioned "don't touch." Her fingertips slid on silk— his mouth along the satin of her lips.

They no longer touched anywhere but lip to lip, tongue to tongue, and that only made her wild for more.

Then he pulled away. Moaning, she leaned toward him. "Hush, baby," he muttered, his voice harsh and heavy against the flute and water medley that filled the room. "Hold on."

She opened heavy eyes to find him reaching up to place the gun and badge on top of her bookcase. He hadn't removed his hands to make her crazy, but only to take off his holster.

A man with a very big gun shouldn't excite a thoroughly modern woman like herself. But she was. When he turned to her again, she pressed him back against the door and kissed him as her fingers made short work of tie and shirt—his the flowing negligee.

Candlelight flickered across his chest turning the dark whirls of hair to gold. A sigh shuddered through them both when she began to trace the defined muscles of his chest, her fingers splaying across his skin and tangling in the hair, familiarizing herself with his body in a way she'd only dreamed of before.

He pulled his mouth from hers and buried his face in her loose hair. Drawing a deep breath, he rubbed his cheek along the length. "You smell like flowers," he whispered.

"Uh-huh," she agreed. Her lips walked a path over his shadowed jaw and neck, then traced his collarbone with her tongue. "You taste like a man."

He shuddered. "That's it." He picked her up suddenly and so high that she had no choice but to wrap her arms around his neck. He went still and closed his eyes, sucking in a breath between his teeth when her thighs slid along his belly and her legs hugged his waist. The muscles of his stomach hardened against the delicate, rarely touched flesh of her inner thighs.

Her gaze was drawn to his face. Eyes closed, jaw clenched, he looked softer somehow than she'd ever seen him. Must be the candlelight, she thought. Without meaning to she loosed one hand from behind his neck and cupped the sharp plane of his cheek.

She expected him to jerk away, or at least open those smoldering eyes. Instead he sighed, his face relaxed, and he rubbed his cheek against her palm, as he'd rubbed his face in her hair. Her heart did a funny little jig and she swallowed, hard.

Opening his eyes, he pulled her tighter against his hardened, muscled torso and moved forward. Under an exquisite shiver of anticipation she threw her head back, and his lips closed over the peak of one breast, taking silk and nipple within his fevered mouth. Shifting restlessly against him, she gasped when the hair on his stomach rasped across her throbbing center.

Then she was falling and although the sensation should have been frightening, instead it was the most exciting thing she'd ever experienced. He might be stronger than her, and bigger than her, and more dangerous than he looked, but he would never hurt her—and no one else would, either, while he was around.

Her back hit the couch, and he towered over her, staring down with dark and secretive eyes. Her breasts throbbed as his gaze wandered over them, then continued along her body. What must she look like with her hair tumbled all about her shoulders, laying there in the candlelight with her nightgown bunched at the small of her back, the skirt rucked to her waist, and the bodice wet and clinging against the nipple that his mouth had taken. She did the only thing her instincts allowed—she reached out for him.

His eyes met hers and slowly his fingers went to his

belt. For a moment she considered helping him, hurrying him. But the way his gaze seared into hers, she knew he wanted her to watch. So she lowered her seeking hands and bunched them into fists to make them behave.

The belt gaped open, followed by the button at the top of his trousers. Mesmerized, she watched the shadows that danced upon the two fingers that grasped the zipper. Strained by the bulge beneath, the teeth resisted the movement, and slowed the zipper's descent as he pulled it down until his erection was freed.

Her fingers clenched again wanting to reach inside those pants and press an itching palm to the heat and fullness. He would be smooth and hard and perfect. Fingernails dug into her palms.

Looping his thumbs in the waistband he drew his pants down, leaving his boxers in place.

Annoyance rumbled deep in her throat and his lips turned up. Kicking off his shoes and pants, he straightened and she started to rise, determined to rid him of those damned blue shorts, which kept her from seeing what she wanted to see—and touching what she wanted to touch.

"Uh-uh," he warned. "Lay back, Jess."

And because she knew that the longer she waited, the better this would be, she did, even though her body screamed to touch him, taste him, take him now.

He knelt at her side and his hand skimmed her thigh. A finger traced the surface, teasing, promising, then his thumb rubbed her center, and she arched into the sensation. The movement made her breasts strain against the revealing bodice of her nightgown, and all he needed to do was hook a free finger between them and tug. They sprang free, the slide of the silk along the sensitive peaks making her body hum onto a higher plane so that when his mouth touched them, flesh to flesh, for the first time she nearly climaxed right then.

She was on the edge—had been since that kiss in the

weight room yesterday—and his control was beginning to annoy her. Reaching between them, she cupped him in her palm, sliding her finger up his length as he'd slid his thumb along hers. When he cursed and jerked away, she smiled. *Not so in control after all.*

He caught her smile and raised a brow, then with deliberate movements, put his hand on her nightgown where it pooled beneath her breasts. His fingers curled against her stomach and the shriek of rending cloth split the air as he tore it down the front.

"One hundred twenty dollars and ninety-nine cents," she muttered.

"And worth every penny." The flames of the candles seemed dim when compared to the heat that lit his eyes as his gaze wandered over her body.

She had never lain naked and allowed a man to just look at her. She'd never realized how arousing a mere look could be. When he gently shoved the remnants of the torn gown off her shoulders the contrast of his violence, followed by such incredible gentleness, the hardness of those hands and the softness of that mouth made her mind go fuzzy again.

"Touch me," he said against her lips.

At last she removed the staid blue cotton and ran her fingers, then her mouth, all over him. Time lost meaning and, needing more room to explore each other, somehow along the way they left the couch and tumbled across the carpet. They each came nearly to the peak, and then came down, only to come nearer and nearer each time as they touched and kissed, murmured and gasped, tasted and suckled.

For a moment he left her, searching for his trousers, fumbling around a bit with an urgency that endeared him, even though the clinical rasp of the foil packet made her wince. But when he returned, slipping inside her, making her feel and not think, she only wanted to complete what they had begun in the way they had begun it—fast, hard, now.

Heat and lust and incomprehensible need overtook her and she convulsed with a suddenness that shocked her. Feeling him pulse deep inside made her own release lengthen and when the storm was over, a strange tenderness overtook her that she did not understand. The hand she smoothed over the nape of his neck shook, and she bit her lip, hoping he would not notice.

She tensed when he stirred, half-afraid he would make some sarcastic comment and ruin what for her had been a wonderful, terrifying experience.

He raised his head and stared at her for a long moment. The candles flickered in his eyes, making her wonder if she saw confusion there, too, or nothing but the dancing flames. Then he bent foreward and kissed her temple in a tender gesture that did not seem like McGuire at all.

''Hi,'' he said. She smiled. ''You want to adjourn to the bedroom?''

Silly and schoolgirlish as it was, she blushed. She was lying naked on the floor of her apartment, having just had mad passionate sex all over the room with the man who she could still feel against her; yet she blushed when he asked if she'd like to go another round on the bed.

''Uh…sure,'' she said, then gritted her teeth at her lack of social grace. Was there an etiquette to this? She hadn't a clue. Her experiences in the land of slap and tickle did not include how to get from the floor to the bed with grace and class. Probably because once you'd *done it* on the floor you'd pretty much killed any hope of being classy again.

McGuire didn't seem embarrassed though. He probably did this all the time. That thought made Jessica narrow her eyes at his back as he stood. Then he turned and reached for her, lifting her to her feet with ease, and pulling her against him for a long, mind-numbing kiss. After that, when he led her down the hall, she went, and she didn't think anymore.

At least not until she drifted toward sleep in his arms, the scent of him—of them—all around her and wondered just what in the name of common sense she had done.

The sound of a cell phone going off in the distance dragged her from a deep and satisfying sleep. Blinking she looked around the bedroom. The grayish cast revealed they'd slept the rest of the night, which hadn't been much after they'd played a repeat performance—make that a double feature—on Jessica's bed.

Doug got up cursing and walked down the hall toward the living room. She heard him thrashing around, bumping into furniture and continuing to curse, presumably trying to find his pants—and his phone. Then the ringing stopped and a few seconds later she heard the low, somehow comforting murmur of him talking on the phone.

She drifted in a pleasant half awake, half asleep state until he touched her shoulder. Jessica opened her eyes to find him fully dressed, gun and all, staring down at her with a bemused smile as the light of the rising sun tinted the window behind him an orange, yellow and pink.

"Hi." Jessica shoved her hair out of her face, grimacing as she felt the tangles a night rolling around had caused.

Doug sat down on the bed and she rolled against him, the bump of their hips making her body kick into lust overdrive. She put her hand on his thigh to steady herself, and his leg clenched.

"I have to go."

She frowned at the distance in his voice and his eyes. "I understand."

"Call you later?"

Jessica nodded. Every woman's nightmare—*I'll call.* Yeah right!

"Sure," she answered and took her hand from his leg.

He kissed her, but she could tell his mind was already somewhere else. The next time she saw Doug McGuire, it would be in a courtroom.

A night spent on the couch, and the floor, and the bed—and hadn't there been a wall in there somewhere—made Jessica fall back asleep, even when she should have gotten up as soon as the door closed behind Doug McGuire.

Instead, the phone shrilling in her ear brought her awake with a gasp to bright sunlight across the bed. Her pounding heart leaped at the sight of her clock reading 8:15 a.m.

Using some of the colorful curses she'd heard McGuire use that morning, she found the phone amidst a tower of law books on her nightstand.

"So how was your night with the real man?" Her father's voice boomed in her ear.

"What?"

For a moment she thought her father knew everything, and even though he was her best friend, and she was an adult, well, everything that had happened here last night was for no one's ears but her own. Not even Liz's this time.

"What happened with that cop who dragged you away the other night?"

"Nothing, Dad," she lied as her gaze took in the state of her room. She was certain her living room looked even worse than her bedroom. Thank God her father hadn't come over, as she had wished last night.

"Nothing! I'm disappointed. A man like that…a woman like you? In my day—"

"Dad! I'm sorry but I'm late. Where have you been anyway? All I get is your machine these days."

"Just busy, sweet cheeks. You know how it is."

The teasing lilt to his voice disappeared, and Jessica frowned. Was he working too hard? Should she push him about selling Water Street Bistro and moving on to something new? It wasn't like him to keep a place so long, to be late for dinner, or to—

"That's why I called this morning. I can't go with you to the Bar Association Ball."

—*not take your loving daughter to important dates like the Bar Association Ball,* Jessica thought, but said, instead, "What? Dad, you can't back out on me now. The blasted thing is tonight."

"I know. And I'm really, really sorry, honey, but this is unavoidable."

"What is?"

Jessica frowned when her question was followed by a long silence. Finally, she asked, "Dad?"

"Why don't you ask Detective McGuire?"

"To the ball? Oh, that would really work. I can see McGuire at a formal event for lawyers. He hates lawyers."

"I don't think so. I read a lot into his body language the other night."

"I think you need glasses."

"What's the harm in asking him? It would be worth it just to see Wolcott's face when you show up with a real man."

"Dad!"

Her father started laughing, sounding more like himself at least, and Jessica smiled. "See you Thursday," he said and hung up.

As she lowered the phone to her lap, she realized he had never explained what was so unavoidable.

Doug hung up the phone and leaned back in his chair. *Another dead end.* Ninety percent of murder investigations were spent on the telephone following up worthless leads.

Earlier that morning, he and Vic had checked Gilbert's old rooming house and the landlord had told them Gilbert hadn't even shown up to claim his belongings. They got the same story at his favorite bar. Nothing. No one. So they'd returned to the station to start making calls. He glanced over at Vic, who'd been working the phone, too, in time to see him slam it down and shake his head.

"No luck," he said.

"So what else is new?" Doug grumbled.

In most cases, the murdered victims are killed by someone they know—a family member or a friend. It appeared that LeRoy Gilbert had neither.

As if Vic had read his mind, he said, "Guess when Gilbert killed his girlfriend he knocked off the only friend he had. You have any luck?"

"Nothing. Nobody claimed they saw him."

"I'm having the same luck finding anyone connected to Cindy Fires. The girls she worked with all claim she never spoke of any family—but they're threatening to start a defense fund for whoever did whack Gilbert. What about the autopsy report?"

"Couple days, but the M.E. said there's no sign of a head contusion or any skin abrasions. And no neck bruises to indicate he was strangled."

"Well, it's for sure Gilbert didn't tie that plastic bag around his head himself."

"Maybe he wanted to keep his hair dry when he went swimming."

"This job's making you jaded, partner," Vic said.

Yawning, Doug shoved back his chair. After the last few hours spent on the phone, he had begun to feel the effects of last night's missed sleep. He walked over and refilled his cup. He sipped the hot brew as he stared out the window and thought about Jess.

Lord, what a night! In the twenty years he'd been having sex, he'd never gotten into it like he had with her. The two of them couldn't get enough of each other.

Jess. His body responded to just the thought of her name. He'd never known a woman like her. She gave as much as she took. The thought of her flooded every one of his senses: the image of that long hair of hers fanned against the pillow as she reached for him, her eyes full with passion. He could still taste her, hear her throaty groans of pleasure and feel the satin and heat of her. And he could smell that hundred-dollar perfume she wore.

Sweat tickled his palms. He wanted more of her. God, he was screwing himself up royally. He had no business messing with a woman like her—she was no one-nighter. What had he gotten himself into?

Spinning on his heel, he tossed the paper cup into the waste can. "Let's get out of here, Vic."

"You forget we're due in Judge Kirkland's court in a couple of hours?"

Doug stifled a groan. He *had* forgotten. Just what he needed—to face her in court after last night. The way things were going, he'd get hard on the witness stand. He had to stop thinking about her.

"We've got time to go back to that dive where Gilbert hung out. Someone had to have seen him the day he died."

"Yeah," Vic said, slipping on his jacket. "The killer."

Jessica saw Doug the moment he and Peterson entered the courtroom and sat down. She had to concentrate hard to keep her mind on what the assistant D.A. was saying, and fight the temptation to glance Doug's way. He was watching her; she could feel the intensity of his blue-eyed stare. She had always felt it, from the first time he'd ever entered her court, and after last night, she wondered what was going through his mind.

"Objection, Your Honor!"

The sudden outburst jolted her back to the business at hand. She had lost her concentration. Flushed with embarrassment, she said, "Excuse me. Mr. Haley, will you read back the question?"

The young court reporter, Stanley Haley, looked up surprised, as did the testifying witness, and both the prosecuting and defense attorneys. Jessica never asked for a read-back.

"Mr. Haley?" she reiterated.

"Objection sustained," she declared, after Stanley had read back the transcript. "You're leading the witness, Counselor."

The attorney continued, and Jessica leaned back with a silent sigh of relief that she hadn't made a bigger mistake. She was reacting like an awestruck Doug McGuire groupie! She dared not even glance his way now. If she saw that knowing grin of his, she'd crawl beneath her bench and die.

Finally, the witness was excused and the prosecuting attorney called the first of the arresting officers—Detective Douglas McGuire—to the stand. Now free to assess him boldly, her steady gaze never wavered from his tall figure as he took the oath and sat down. He looked as good to her now as he had last night...and the day before...and the week before that.

As usual, his testimony was methodical and concise. He always came to court with every fact clear in his mind. That was one of the first things she'd noticed about him— that and those sensuous blue eyes...the broad shoulders...the tight buns. Damn! Her mind was wandering down dangerous channels again!

The evidence of the case was clear: the weapon had been found in the suspect's house with his prints on it. The suspect had been found with powder residue on his hand and the victim's blood on his shoes. And then there was the little matter of an eyewitness.

This time McGuire and Peterson had played by the rules and followed the proper procedure to the letter of the law. This murderer was not going to evade sentencing through a technicality. Justice would be served.

As McGuire was excused, he stepped down and paused

in front of the bench. "You figure out yet how to let this perp go, Judge?" he said in a soft murmur.

The pound of her gavel reverberated throughout the courtroom. All heads turned in her direction as she bolted to her feet. "There'll be a fifteen minute recess. My chambers, Detective McGuire," she ordered curtly and stormed out of the room.

She was too angry to sit down. Folding her arms across her chest, she stared out the window until the door opened behind her and clicked shut. She turned and faced him. He was lounging against the door.

"I have no control over what you say outside the courtroom, Detective McGuire, but the next time you make a remark like that in my court, I'll hold you in contempt and fine you accordingly. Is that understood?"

"Yes, Your Honor. It was intended for your ears only."

"That's no excuse. I won't tolerate it—no matter what's between us."

"Well, are you?"

"Am I what?" she snapped.

"Going to figure out a way to let this bastard—who shot his wife in cold blood—walk?"

"Not unless the defense comes up with some illegal police misconduct by the investigating officers."

He raised his hand in the three-fingered Boy Scout salute. "On my honor, I promise to do—"

"Don't tell me you were a Boy Scout, McGuire?"

"God and country, ma'am."

Anger forgotten, Jessica laughed. The man was irresistible when he wanted to be. Maybe she should reconsider her father's advice. "Doug, do you own a tux?"

What was she thinking? She regretted the impetuous words the instant she said them. It was insanity to encourage any further relationship with him. *Darn you, Dad! Why did you put such a crazy notion into my head?*

He blinked at her sudden change of subject, then frowned. "God forbid! Why?"

"Oh, nothing."

"Why'd you ask, Jess?"

She might have known that she couldn't pass an ambiguous reply past Bulldog McGuire. He was too good a detective for that.

"It was stupid of me to ask. You wouldn't enjoy yourself anyway."

This time he didn't blink. "Doing what?"

"I need an escort tonight for the Bar Association Ball at the Pfister."

"What about the old guy?"

For a second she had to think to whom he was referring. "Oh, you mean my…ah, he's busy."

"I see. Well, since I filled in for him last night, I guess I could do it again."

"What do you mean by that crack? McGuire? You're the most irritating man I've ever met."

He grinned. "What time should I pick you up?"

"Cocktails are at seven." Lest he read too much into the invitation, she quickly added, "But I'll meet you there."

He put his hand on the doorknob. "Okay. See you there, then."

"Don't forget. Black tie."

"Right. Ah, Judge, if I have to wear black tie, let's keep it between us."

"You mean literally, Detective?"

Arching a brow at the sexual innuendo, he flashed a grin that almost knocked the legs out from under her. Then winking, he departed.

Chapter 5

Doug stood in the hallway outside the Grand Ballroom of the Pfister Hotel and watched the beautiful people mingle. What the devil had he been thinking when he agreed to come here tonight?

He hadn't been thinking, that was the problem. Or he hadn't been thinking with his brain since he showed up at Jess's door last night.

At the very least he should have picked her up at her condo and come to this charade with her. Meeting her here had been another mistake. She was late—just like a woman.

Doug frowned and shifted away from the wall he'd been holding up. She wasn't the type to be late. And despite his efforts to the contrary there was still a murderer on the loose. He doubted whoever had done Gilbert even knew Jessica Kirkland existed. So then why was he suddenly so nervous? Why did he have the urge to go storming out of this joint and find her? Where was she?

As if in answer to his question, an elevator binged, the

door slid open and a stream of tuxes and bangles poured out. Amidst the finery, she stood out and for a moment Doug just observed her, dazzled despite himself.

She'd twisted her hair into a fancy knot and secured it with a rhinestone...something. Whatever it was he could see that one little tug would have her hair tumbling over her bare, smooth shoulders. He stuffed his itching fingers into the pockets of his best suit. Black, but not a tux, and he'd worn a black tie. The tie had seemed funny when he put it on. Black tie, he'd been complying with their silly little rules. But now, for just a minute he wished he'd gone and rented a damned monkey suit.

Her dress was white satin, tight in the right places, loose about her knees. The material sparkled beneath the lights, flashy but classy. Her stockings had a sparkle to them, too, drawing his eyes to her calves, which looked even better than usual above silver stiletto heels.

The corner of his mouth lifted. She could take a guy's eye out with one of those things.

She paused, and the others flowed by her, leaving her alone, hovering between the elevator bank and the hall where everyone thronged about having their preboredom cocktails.

Though he would have liked to look at her for a while longer, he approached, stopping a few feet away and tried to think of something quick and smart to say, but she must have sensed him coming and turned. Whatever he'd been going to say stuck in his throat, and he stared like a love-struck schoolboy.

She'd done something different to her face. More color on her lips and cheeks. Shadowed her eyes, darkened her lashes. The stones at her neck and ears were not rhinestones. The clip in her hair probably wasn't, either.

Judge Jessica Kirkland was... Beautiful? Yes. Classy? Definitely. Sexy? Extremely. Out of his league? Damn straight.

"Hi, Doug." She smiled and walked toward him with a scent that was part Jess and part insanity floating before her. His mind went blank and he clenched his hands into fists inside his pockets. He would not grab her. Not here. Not now anyway. "Doug?"

"Huh?" He'd been staring at her neck, wondering if he put his lips to the pulse thudding there if he could taste cinnamon and spice on her skin.

"You look great," she said.

He grunted, and when she took his arm, he tensed. He wasn't used to prancing around in pretty clothes, making nicey-nice with a woman whose body he'd been inside only hours before. In his part of the world, women you slept with, well, you slept with them. Maybe you ate out, caught a movie once in a while to keep them happy. But not this...this...this torture of pretending you were acquaintances when you knew how she sighed your name when she came.

"Oh, hell!" he muttered.

"Is that an observation or a personal commentary?"

"Sorry." He took his hand out of his pocket, hoping she would release his arm. Instead she slid her hand into his and laced their fingers together. His heart pounded harder and he glanced around the room to see if anyone had noticed. A few people looked their way, but mostly they stared at his suit.

Jessica squeezed his hand. "Are you ready for something to drink?"

Her voice sounded worried, and he glanced down to find her face scrunched up.

"Yeah. That sounds like a good idea."

She led him to the bar. "Chardonnay," she said, and turned to him with a raised brow.

"What's on tap?" The bartender's lip curled, and Doug scowled. He wasn't at a real bar. He considered ordering a shot of Wild Turkey, but that would be juvenile. "Just give me something with malt."

The guy popped the cap off a specialty beer made with cranberries and bound in a dinky red bottle. "Glass, sir?"

"No, I like roughing it," Doug said, reaching for the bottle. He took a sip, looked around for a spittoon, then swallowed the stuff with a gurgle.

Jessica started laughing, took the bottle from his hand and put it back on the bar. "You asked for it." She turned to the smirking bartender. "Heineken," she ordered. "I know you have that."

Drinks in hand, they walked toward the ballroom, but before they could get there a lanky blond man in an immaculate tuxedo stepped into their path.

Dennis Wolcott. Doug actually thought he heard Jess growl.

"Hello, Jessica." He looked Doug up and down. "If I remember, the invitation said black tie."

"For members. Detective McGuire is my guest."

"Ah, McGuire. Yes. I couldn't quite place you."

"Funny, I knew who you were right away." Wolcott preened. "You lost the Seymour case. High media. Tough break about that DNA match and bloody sock. Gotta say, good detective work, though. Do you guys get paid even if you lose the case?"

Jessica choked, then coughed. Wolcott went red above the too-tight neck of his tux. Doug reached for Jessica's hand, lacing his fingers with hers. Wolcott's gaze latched onto their hands and his frown would have been formidable if he'd had the kind of face for that. As it was he looked like a spoiled three-year-old whose favorite toy had just been snatched by an older, stronger child.

"See you around, Wolcott." Doug led Jessica toward the ballroom. He could feel the other man's frustration and fury focused like a laser beam upon his back. If Wolcott had a gun, Doug might be worried. As it was, the man could only glare.

"The guy's still got it bad for you," he observed as they sat down at the table Jessica indicated near the front of the room.

Her shrug drew his eyes to those delectable shoulders again. He had definitely not paid enough attention to those shoulders last night. He would make amends later.

"No. He just wants what he no longer has. That's the way he is."

"Spoiled brat."

"You don't know the half of it."

"So tell me."

"About him? Let's not ruin the evening."

"So why'd you almost marry him?"

"Appearances can be deceiving Doug."

"From where I was sitting it looked like a close call."

She stared at him for a long moment. "And where were you sitting, Detective, that you could observe my personal life?"

He'd put his foot in it there. What could he say? There'd always been a spark between the two of them. Even when they were arguing in the courtroom or on TV. Now that he'd had a taste of her, he knew there'd been latent lust for a long, long time. And seeing her picture in the paper with Wolcott—a moron if there'd ever been one—had always ticked him off. Still did. Especially after watching the guy's scaly eyes slither all over Jess.

"How could I miss you two? You were all over the papers a few months back. The golden couple of law—the judge and the lawyer."

"Nauseating," she murmured. "Like the quarterback and the cheerleader."

"Well, I could see you as a cheerleader. But Wolcott as a quarterback? He'd be toast."

Jessica laughed; the sound stopped Doug's heart. She

just didn't laugh like that enough—with her whole body, her eyes lit up and her face relaxed. Seeing her like this made him realize how stressed-out she usually was. And why wouldn't she be with a job like hers?

He stopped himself right there. He wasn't actually sympathizing with Judge Jess, was he? How many of his collars had she let walk scot-free? How many murderers were on the street because of her bleeding heart justice? An image of Gilbert's bloated body flitted across his mind. One less than a few days ago anyway.

People he didn't know joined them at their table. Jess of course knew everyone. She introduced him, politely, correctly, and he made the appropriate murmurs. Still, he caught enough puzzled glances to know that everyone was wondering why the judge had brought a bodyguard.

Although the food was excellent, the meal was uncomfortable at best. He was so itchy, he wanted to scratch himself. But there seemed to be someone watching him every minute, as if waiting to see if he'd use the wrong fork or pick his teeth. When it was over, Doug reached for his beer and took several gulps, then stifled a groan when a band struck up a chord across the room. Not dancing, too! He hated to dance.

The other couples excused themselves and moved toward the dance floor. Silence stretched between him and Jess. She glanced at the dancers, at him, then away. He sighed and snagged his beer again. He could manage a dance or two. "I'm not much of a dancer, but—"

"Jessica, may I?"

Snake oil salesman, Doug thought as Wolcott's voice whispered past his ear. If this were the Wild, Wild West the weasel would be a snake oil salesman. He set his beer down and glanced over his shoulder at the salesman in question. And he'd be the sheriff who ran him out of town. Yessiree!

Doug shook his head to clear the odd vision. Too much

sex and too little sleep. He glanced at Jess and saw her looking at him with a question in her eyes. Maybe too little sleep, but definitely not too much sex.

"Doug?" she asked, her eyes entreating him for something. He just couldn't figure out what. "Do you mind?"

"Mind what?"

"Come on, Jessica, this is our song." Wolcott pulled her from the chair and Jessica went, but not without looking back over her shoulder, making a face at Doug and mouthing, "Thanks a lot!"

"My bad," he mumbled.

He still couldn't figure out women. They were a puzzle with too many missing pieces. Or maybe pieces that didn't fit. Whatever the case, he was always coming up short. Even with Jess. She was so out of his league it was damn near pitiful.

He glanced around the ballroom. Crystal chandeliers. China and silver on the tables. Tuxedos, diamonds and champagne. He hadn't even been in the Pfister Hotel before and he'd lived in Milwaukee since college. Not too much call for homicide detectives in this part of town. The rich committed their murders elsewhere—like in a nonextraditable country.

His gaze lit on Jessica and Wolcott. This was their song? What song was it? Didn't have any words. What kind of song was that? If the band switched to "As Time Goes By" he'd cut in on them for sure. Now that was a song: "Woman needs man, and man must have his mate. That no one can deny." *That* songwriter knew what he was talking about. And for damn sure, Doug McGuire would be the last man to ever deny it—if that woman was Jess. Lord, how he wanted that woman!

Wolcott was smooth on the dance floor, Doug would give him that. But Jess was the one who drew his eyes. Even in those sinfully high heels she moved with a grace that fascinated. Wolcott spun her about and her head tipped back. Doug held his breath, waiting for the foolish knot in her hair to tumble free. If Wolcott so much as sniffed her perfume, Doug planned to deck him.

The band continued into a second song. Jessica and Wolcott continued to dance. Doug stood up and decided to look for some air. He stopped to snag another beer.

Same bartender. Same smirk. "Glass, sir?"

He'd have liked to have told the jerk "Yeah, in a dirty glass," but Bob Hope had already used that line in one of those Road pictures Doug enjoyed watching.

He snatched up the bottle. "How many asses did you have to kiss to get this job, sonny?"

Doug found a large, double window at the end of a long hall, sipped his beer and gazed out at Lake Michigan in the distance. Why was she with him? She belonged here, amidst the crystal and diamonds and Chardonnay. If he had a preference, he'd be anywhere but here.

"Bored, Detective?"

His fingers clenched on the neck of the bottle, but he didn't bother to turn around. He didn't have to. "I thought you and the judge were tripping the light fantastic, Wolcott. Did you step on her toes one too many times?"

Wolcott stepped up next to him, hogging the window and crowding Doug as if he had a right to. Doug shrugged his shoulder, smacking Wolcott's in the process. When the lawyer shifted away, Doug hid a smile behind a swallow of beer. Man stuff—territorial—don't piss in my pond. This Doug understood.

"I must say I'm surprised to see you and Jessica here together after the show you put on for Sherilyn Matthews. But then Jessica has always been attracted to the rougher element. That's why she became a judge."

"Opposites do attract."

"No offense, Detective, I'm sure a man of your, uh, shall we say attributes, is a wonderful toy for a woman like Jessica. Just be sure you don't get the idea that she'd actually keep you permanently. Ultimately, she'll marry me.''

"Does she know this?"

"Deep down, where it counts. She needs her space right now. Wild oats. I don't mind. In fact, I'm confident she'll come back to me with some incredible innovations in the bedroom. Slumming does have its advantages in that regard. I thank you in advance, Detective.''

Doug didn't bother to answer. Wolcott might have a nasty mouth, but what he was saying was true. Jessica wanted him—in bed. He wanted her in the same place. There was no future for them. This night only illustrated that. And that was fine with him...wasn't it?

Yet the thought of being Judge Jessica's stud muffin didn't sit too well right now—especially coming from the mouth of this prick.

Wolcott clapped his hand on Doug's shoulder. "As long as we understand each other, there's no reason we can't be friends, ah...I don't recall your first name. What can I call you besides Detective?''

Doug took a step away so the man could no longer touch him, and turned to look the attorney right in the eye. Man stuff should be delivered face-to-face. "It's Doug. And what do they call you besides Prick?''

As Wolcott sputtered, Doug turned back toward the ballroom—only to find Jessica standing close enough to trip over. He couldn't tell by her face how much she'd heard, but she had to have heard his juvenile retort.

He walked past her, planning to leave, but she turned and accompanied him into the elevator. As the doors closed, sealing them inside together, Doug got a good look at Wolcott's face.

The man looked mad enough to kill.

Chapter 6

The silence in the elevator was oppressive. Doug didn't know what to say—a first for him. Usually he could come up with a snappy retort for any situation. But a snappy retort was what had gotten him into this mess in the first place.

He didn't even want to look at Jess and see the disappointment in her eyes. His dad had always looked at him like that whenever Doug screwed up—or didn't toe the appropriate line. Jess would have her "you are out of order, Detective" look on her face: tight lips, pale cheeks, ice princess spine. He hated that!

"Uh, Jess, I—"

She snorted. Snorted!…Jess! Slowly, Doug turned his head and looked at her. Laughing hysterically, she collapsed against the back wall of the elevator.

"Wh-what d-do they c-call you besides Prick?" She put her hand to her stomach. "I can't stand it!"

Her eyes were watering, and Doug just continued to

stare at her, trying to comprehend what he saw. She wasn't angry; she was laughing.

"Did you see his face?"

Doug's lips twitched. "Yeah."

She drew in a deep breath, which caught in the middle and sounded like a sob. "No one's ever called him that to his face before."

"No? I'm surprised."

She choked and dissolved into laughter again.

The elevator doors swished open and several well-dressed stiffs waited for him and Jess to exit so they could get on. The sight of Judge Kirkland clinging to the wall and laughing uncontrollably had them narrowing suspicious eyes as if he'd flashed her or something.

He grabbed Jess by the elbow and helped her out of the elevator. Her body still shook with laughter, the silken flesh of her arm rubbing against his palm.

"It's not that funny," he muttered, annoyed with his body's continued response to everything about her.

"I'm sorry." She took another deep breath, fighting for control. "But I've wanted to call him that for so long. It's just…"

"Crude, rude and socially unacceptable?"

"No. Well, yes. But perfect."

Doug nodded a thank-you to the doorman as they walked from the hotel and stepped onto the sidewalk. "Something a woman like you would never do."

She paused and turned to face him. The movement removed her arm from his grasp. He tried not to miss the warmth of her skin against his, but he couldn't help it.

"I suppose not. But that doesn't mean I don't admire someone who has the guts to do it."

"You mean the lack of the social graces needed to know any better."

She tilted her head to look into his face, and he was struck again by the grace in her every movement. The sparkle of diamonds in her dark red hair reminded him of the stars that had begun to pop out in the night sky above.

"I mean what I said, Doug." Her brow creased. "Why are you so touchy? Did someone say something…ah… unpleasant to you?"

"Unpleasant?" This time he snorted. She sure had a way with words. But he wasn't about to tell her what Wolcott had said, and that some of it had struck home.

All evening he'd felt like Judge Jess's boy toy, and he didn't like it, which made no sense. If he wanted her for the sex and nothing else, what difference did it make if she wanted him for the same reason?

The situation was a single man's dream come true. Jess was a gorgeous, sexy, willing woman. He'd wanted her since the first time she looked down her nose at him from way up on the high bench. Now he had her, and when the fire burned out they would shake hands and retreat to their respective corners—or their respective sides of the tracks. No harm, no foul.

So why did the thought that she was slumming make him so mad? He needed to think about this about them. And the need to think about it was so surprising that he needed to think about that, too.

"Doug?"

Concern etched her features. He was acting nuts, not at all like the glib, practiced guy she knew. But right now he didn't feel like that guy at all.

He stuffed his hands into his pockets to keep from touching her. "I'll take you home."

"I have my car."

"Oh, yeah." What was wrong with him? "Where's your car?"

She nodded directly across the street and he followed her there, reminded of the first time he'd walked her to her car, the first time he'd given in to the irresistible urge to kiss her.

She hesitated with her hand on the door, obviously remembering, too, and waiting for him to kiss her again. But he knew where kissing Jess would lead. Right back to her bedroom, and tonight he just needed to go home.

So he stepped out of reach, away from temptation. "Good night, Jess."

She frowned, opened her mouth, and then snapped it shut. She was too classy to ask him to come over, or to beg him to kiss her.

Touch me. The sound of his own words whispered through his head, mocking him. She hadn't begged last night, he had.

Doug spun on his heel and stalked toward his car. Her voice drifted after on the warm night wind. "Thank you for coming, Doug."

He flinched at the connotation his mind put on the words. She meant the dinner, not last night. God, he was pathetic. This had to stop. Right now. Before he did something really stupid.

Like falling in love with her.

Confused, and more than a little hurt, Jessica watched Doug walk away. She'd made a mistake asking him to come tonight. It was clear he'd felt out of place, and no doubt Dennis had honed in on that, then needled and wheedled until Doug struck back. Dennis was good at that. That's why he was such a good defense lawyer.

She climbed inside and pulled away from the curb. Doug's car immediately pulled in behind hers and continued to follow her all the way to Lake Drive. He was following her home. She felt a quick rise of hope—perhaps he'd changed his mind and… No, he was just seeing her home safely.

He was such a gentleman—even when he was acting like a caveman. He held doors, took her elbow when they walked and followed her home when she was alone—old-world gestures nearly lost in the new-world order. She enjoyed his manners. She enjoyed him, not just in bed, but everywhere—except in court. Then he was a pain in the behind. She was sure he thought the same about her.

Reaching her condo, she pulled into the underground parking lot, and the automatic garage door slid shut behind her, blocking out McGuire's car idling on the street.

Several moments later she let herself inside her apartment, then crossed to the window without turning on any lights. Below, on the street, McGuire's car still waited. When she reached over and flicked on the light, the car inched away from the curb and pulled into traffic. A few blocks down it disappeared around a corner, making the circle back toward the freeway.

As she turned away from the window, she looked down at her gown. All dressed up and no place to go. She'd had lovely fantasies while getting dressed earlier. Images of Doug pulling the zipper down her back and discovering that beneath the white satin there was only Jessica and perfume. Now she would have to get out of the ridiculously tight dress herself. Not half the fun.

Stepping into the living room, she pulled the clip from her hair and tossed it on an end table. She'd worn her hair like this for him, too, knowing a single tug would allow the entire contraption to fall free. So much for that fairy tale—not even close to midnight and the ball had fizzled out for poor Cinderella! Back to the real world of pumpkins and mice—of crimes and punishments.

Shaking out her hair, the tresses slid along her bare shoulders. Suddenly she stopped dead in the center of the room. Frowning she turned slowly to look back at the end table. The picture of her and Karen was gone. Her heart began to thud—half concerned that something so important was missing, half fearful as to *why* it was missing. She looked around the room, and immediately saw the picture perched on the opposite end table. Odd. She always put the cherished photo on the table closest to where she usually sat.

The frame must have gotten knocked over last night, and Doug had put it back in the wrong place. That was the only explanation.

Thoughts of last night made Jess remember Doug's odd behavior tonight. She wouldn't be surprised if she'd seen the last of Detective McGuire—unless she counted courtroom appearances.

She had no one to blame but herself. Why had she asked him to the Bar Association Ball? As if she attended nonsense like that every day. The ball was a once-a-year occurrence—requisite torture.

Perhaps she should explain that to him, then thought the better of it. She wasn't explaining anything. They'd had a one-night stand. Just because she'd never had one before didn't mean she couldn't figure out the etiquette. She'd screwed up by inviting him to the ball. And he hadn't known how to tell her no, so he'd gone along. Pity date.

Jessica winced. Things would be embarrassing for a while, at least for her. She'd get over it. Or at least pretend to.

Obviously one night had been enough for McGuire to get her out of his system. Too bad it hadn't been nearly enough to get him out of hers.

After a sleepless night of anguishing over her ecstatic—but brief—relationship with the complex Detective Douglas I. McGuire... What did his middle initial stand for anyway? Ill-tempered? Indomitable? Irreverent? Irritating? Most likely all of the above with an *irrevocable* thrown in.

Darn it, she was doing it again! Blaming him for her mistakes. This kind of situation happened all the time between men and women. She was just new to the game.

And he's a master at it, Little Grasshopper.

* * *

"What did she say?" Vic asked.

"She said she meant it," Doug murmured to himself. "But I think she was stroking me."

"What?"

Doug looked up startled. Dammit, all morning his mind kept straying back to Jess—and what a jerk he'd made of himself last night. Why had he called that stuffed shirt a prick? They'd been among her friends and associates. Why couldn't he have kept his mouth shut for once? But no, he always had to have the last word.

"She was stroking you? What in hell are you talking about? You must have really got lucky last night. I sure wanna hear about it, but I was referring to the medical examiner. The autopsy, partner? The one they worked all night to get to us."

"Ah…" Doug shuffled through the papers on his desk. He didn't plan on seeing Jess again. That much he'd figured out on his own. He was only asking for trouble if he continued on the way he was. And since he had no intention of seeing her again, he had no intention of even breathing her name to Vic.

He found the report and leaned back in his chair, only to find Vic studying him with a smirk on his lips and a frown in his eyes.

"I talked to the M.E.," he blurted, to stave off the inevitable questions. "She said Gilbert died of asphyxiation, most likely induced by the plastic bag over his head. No water in his lungs, so he wasn't breathing when he went into the river."

Vic grabbed the report and scanned it himself. "No blow to the head, no bruises on the neck or torso." He glanced at Doug. "How in hell do you overpower a guy the size of Gilbert, tie a bag around his head and dump him in the river without him putting up a fight?"

"There was insulin in his blood, so the M.E. checked

further and found a puncture on his arm. I guess he had very hairy arms which is why she missed it the first time.''

"So the gorilla was diabetic." Vic shrugged.

"But he wasn't diabetic. That's the point."

"I don't get it."

"She said an overdose of insulin in a nondiabetic can induce an instant coma. Usually not enough to kill, but it will incapacitate. Pharmacies keep records of insulin users, don't they?''

Vic pursed his lips in a long, low whistle. "So all we've got to do is check out a connection between Gilbert and one of the thousands of diabetics in the city—or possibly the whole country. Piece of cake. You start with New York, I'll take California."

"Meet you in St. Louis," Doug answered, grinning when Vic growled. "What did Forensics say?''

"No DNA. Probably washed away in the river if there had been.''

"And the rope and plastic bag?''

"Both were common and ordinary. The bag can be purchased at any grocery store, and the rope at any hardware store. No prints on, either.''

Doug slipped his arms into his still wet trench coat. "Might as well get started in Gilbert's old neighborhood in the Third Ward. We'll check out the pharmacies, grocers and hardware stores. Maybe we'll get lucky with a name that connects to Gilbert.''

Another morning of rain had added to Doug's ornery mood, so he'd worked off some of his tension in the weight room. Yesterday's canvassing of the stores in Gilbert's neighborhood resulted in nothing but he and Vic getting soaked. Today he'd made up his mind that he wasn't going to budge from his desk. He began going over the local pharmacy printouts of insulin users.

When it was time to knock off, Doug declined Vic's

dinner offer again and went home to his three-room apartment.

After changing into shorts, he checked the refrigerator; he had a choice between a frozen chicken potpie or bacon and eggs. It was an easy decision. Popping a can of beer, he went to the phone and ordered a pizza, then sat down on the couch and channel surfed until it arrived.

As he ate the pizza, he popped another can of Miller, chased it down with a shot of Seagrams, and stuck an old movie in the VCR. For at least the twenty-fifth time in his thirty-six years, he watched *Casablanca,* killed another Miller and Seagrams, and managed not to think of Jess for intervals of ten and fifteen minutes at a time.

"Good morning." Liz looked up from her computer with a welcoming smile.

"Good morning. Thank goodness the rain's over. Any calls?"

Liz handed her several pink telephone messages, and Jessica read through them quickly. None were from Doug. Of course not—why would there be? Telephone calls, roses, thank-you notes would not be Doug McGuire's modus operandi. The past two days without a sign of him had seemed like two years. Well, as they say, one had to face these things one day at a time.

She went into her chambers and was quickly joined by Liz, with a cup of coffee.

"You look like you need this."

Unable to sleep, Jessica had already drunk three cups of coffee that morning. Another cup would probably have her flying into the courtroom, rather than walking. Nevertheless, she took the proffered mug.

"Liz, have you ever had a one-night stand?"

Arching a brow, Liz eyed her warily. "What brought this on?"

"I was just wondering how you handle it."

Blowing on the coffee, Jessica leaned back in her chair. "Did you know I was a virgin when I met Dennis Wolcott?" She shook her head. "Yep, all through school I kept myself squeaky clean—saved myself for Mr. Right."

"Do I denote a tone of regret?"

"I guess, but only because he turned out to be such a..." Jessica smiled as the image of Doug flashed through her mind. "...prick."

"This wouldn't have anything to do with Doug McGuire, would it?" Liz asked, in a voice weighted with concern. "I know I've teased you about him, but—"

"What makes you think that?" Jessica jerked up, almost spilling the coffee. She put the cup down on her desk.

"Honey, the truth's written all over that pretty face of yours. You want to talk about it?"

The phone rang. "Rotten timing." Liz gave her an apologetic look, and then hurried back to her desk to answer it.

At the moment Jessica wasn't ready to tell Liz about her bungled affair with Doug, but knowing her secretary, Liz would be relentless until she got the whole story. Disgusted with herself, Jessica sat back. She'd bungled again. She just wasn't sophisticated enough to participate in boy and girl games.

When the morning session ended, rather than join Liz in the cafeteria, Jess asked her to bring a salad back when she finished her lunch. She knew if they went to lunch together, Liz would start pumping her about Doug.

Of course, the sensible thing to do would be to spill it all out and get it over with. In fact, with Liz's curiosity, no doubt she'd be back in minutes, a salad in hand for both of them.

Jess had just picked up a law book to look up a ruling when the chamber door opened.

''That was fast, Liz. I figured, you couldn't stay away too long.'' Laughing, Jess looked up.

Detective Douglas—*I* for *irresistible*—McGuire stood in the doorway.

He didn't look happy.

Chapter 7

Jessica's stomach began doing flip-flops, but she didn't even blink, waging a silent struggle to quash the exhilarating current that charged through her at his mere presence. Her voice even sounded normal to her ears—which now must be flushed to pink—when she asked, "Detective McGuire, what's your middle name?"

"Ian." He stepped into the room. "Why?"

"Curious, that's all. Do you have a problem, Detective?"

"Yeah, I've got a big problem."

"Legal or personal?"

"Personal." He closed the door. "Very personal."

Jessica became aware she was holding her breath, waiting for him to tell her he didn't want to see her anymore. As if she wouldn't have figured that out for herself.

"I want to apologize, Jess—"

Finding her breath, she interrupted him. "Apologies aren't necessary." No longer able to sit calmly and look him in the eyes, she bolted to her feet. "I understand per-

fectly. We're both adults—we knew what we were doing."
She forced a game smile. "It was great while it lasted."
Her brave smile faded to poignancy. "And I don't regret
a minute of it, Doug, except for subjecting you to that
insufferable ball the other night."

"Yeah, I was pretty bad. I'm sorry I embarrassed you."

"You didn't embarrass me, Doug. It's I who owe you
the apology for putting you through it."

"You sound like you mean that," he said, surprised.

"Of course I do. You were a good sport for tolerating
it."

He stepped closer. "It wasn't all that difficult. Matter
of fact, that white satin dress you had on helped make it
real tolerable." His sudden, shy grin, appealing in its boy-
ishness—and uncharacteristic for this walking testosterone
advertisement—rocked her back on her heels.

Her hand fluttered to her chest in a feminine gesture so
maidenly it embarrassed her. "I didn't think you'd noticed."

"Oh, I noticed. I definitely noticed. That's the problem—that's what I came to talk about."

He stepped closer, invading her space, his nearness so
male, so encompassing, she could feel the heat he gener-
ated. Her heart began pounding erratically.

"Well," she managed to get the word past the lump in
her throat. "I'm glad to see we both understand that this,
ah…kind of attraction happens. Fortunately, we're both
mature enough to recognize it can often be a mistake."

"Yeah, a mistake. We'd be better off forgetting it ever
happened, right?"

"Definitely."

"And we don't fit in each other's worlds, right?"

"That's right."

"Yeah, that's what I've been telling myself for the past
couple days." He put his hands on her shoulders. "And

it'd be another big mistake if I were to kiss you right now. Wouldn't it, Judge Jess?'' He lowered his head.

The touch of his lips topped off the effect his nearness had set in motion. Reason or argument were eclipsed by the electrifying excitement of his kiss. And when it ended, she knew neither of them were ready—or able—to bring an end to their relationship.

''A big mistake, Detective. Doug, we're crazy, you know that?'' she murmured, when he slid his mouth along her neck.

''Yeah, I know.'' That didn't stop him from working the buttons of her blouse. He slid in his hand and his warm palm found her flesh. The bra strap snapped when he forced his hand inside and cupped her breast.

An erotic shiver rippled her spine. She shuddered and he raised his head and stared into her eyes.

''Feeling the way we do, we'd be even crazier to give up each other.'' His head dipped and he took her nipple.

Sensation blackened her brain as he toyed and did tantalizing things with his tongue and mouth until every nerve in her body cried out for more. His mouth reclaimed hers as she groped for him wildly, desperate in her need to feel him inside her. Yanking up her skirt, he slid his hand between her legs, shoving aside the wispy crotch of her panties. Driven by urgency, her hands reached for his fly, and with trembling fingers she worked the zipper. His breathing turned ragged when she reached past the elastic of his boxers. He felt hard and hot, and she began to massage him, her own breath coming in gasps as his fingers probed inside of her.

''Judge Kirkland.''

Even in the throes of passion, she recognized that it wasn't Doug calling her name. He heard it, too, because he froze in motion, and they stared in shock and disbelief at one another.

A rap sounded on the door, and her name was repeated.

Now she recognized the caller's voice. Horrified, she remembered she'd asked the court reporter to bring her a copy of a transcript. If he thought she wasn't there, he'd open the door and put it on her desk.

"The bathroom," she whispered to Doug. They just made it, when Stanley Haley walked into her office and over to her desk.

"What in hell is he waiting for?" Doug whispered, when the clerk lingered at the desk.

Jessica buttoned her blouse and adjusted her skirt. Opening the bathroom door, she walked out.

"Oh, Stanley..."

"I'm sorry to disturb you, Judge Kirkland. I brought the transcript you asked for."

"Thank you, Stanley." She sat down at her desk and picked it up.

He started to back out. "Is there anything else you need, Judge Kirkland?"

She looked up and smiled kindly. Short and slightly built, what the young court reporter lacked in stature he counterbalanced with thoughtfulness toward everyone and a willingness to be helpful. From the time he'd been hired, Stanley had attached himself to Liz. On the other hand, Liz doted on him like a mother.

"No, this is fine. Thank you again, Stanley." After all, it wasn't his fault he'd picked the worst possible moment to deliver the transcript to her. On the other hand, she'd been conducting herself more like a sex-starved nympho than the dignified judge Stanley considered her to be.

As soon as he was gone, Doug came out of the bathroom, his clothing properly adjusted. "Close call."

"You bet it was. I don't know what got into me."

"Almost got into you," he corrected. "I'm still aching as proof."

She wasn't amused. "Well, I've learned a lesson."

"I hope so. The police have been advocating it for years—lock your doors."

"It's not funny, Doug."

"Worried about besmirching your reputation, Judge?" An undertone of irritation had crept into his voice. "The judge caught slumming with a cop?"

"That's not it at all. Must you always be so defensive, Doug? I just don't believe we should play bedroom games in my chambers."

"Then I'll get out of here. I'll pick you up at six o'clock. And strictly no black tie—wear jeans or shorts."

"Jeans or shorts? Is this another one of your exotic dinner invitations?"

"No, my softball game. If you're hungry, we can grab a sandwich afterwards."

"Softball!" She grinned wickedly. "I figured you as strictly a hardball player, McGuire."

He shook his head. "Shame on you, Judge Jess. Keep up those kind of remarks and you'll find your hands full of more than you can handle."

"In your dreams, McGuire."

He left the door open. Smiling, Jessica watched him walk as far as Liz's desk. Jessica saw that Liz had returned, and apparently chosen not to interrupt them. Doug paused long enough to say hello, then disappeared through the door of the outer office.

Liz spun around in her chair, and their gazes met. Picking up the plastic container of salad, she came into Jessica's chamber.

"Okay, honey, we need to talk."

Doug didn't even need to flash his badge at the guard in Jessica's building; the man buzzed him through as soon as Doug walked in the door.

Instead of heading for the elevator, Doug leaned on the

counter. "You let just anyone go up to the judge's door whenever they want to?"

The man turned his attention from the television that played a closed circuit camera view of the underground parking garage. Several other monitors showed the hallways on various floors as well as a bird's-eye view of the front entrance.

"No, Detective. Judge Kirkland just called and asked me to send you straight up when you got here." His gaze flicked over Doug's white baseball pants, blue T-shirt with the precinct logo and regulation baseball cap. "Hot date?"

Doug hesitated, glanced back at the door through which a hot, sunny evening still shined. Maybe he should just go this alone.

"Chicken, Detective?"

Doug frowned and turned back to the guard. "What was that?"

"Just looked to me like you were going to turn tail and run. I'd be disappointed."

"Oh really? And why's that?"

"Judge Kirkland's a nice lady. Smart and pretty and plain good people."

"So?"

"So she deserves some happiness."

"And I would come into this where?"

"You make her happy."

"You figure?"

The guard waved at the bank of televisions. "I see a lot."

Doug narrowed his eyes, remembering what time he'd left Jessica's apartment a few mornings ago. If this guy was planning to mention it, Doug planned to rearrange his face.

"Relax," the guard said. "I watch people leave for work and come back home every day. I get to know when they're happy, when they're sad. You can tell just by how a person walks.''

"Uh-huh.''

"And the judge was really happy tonight.''

The uneasiness that had been plaguing Doug since he'd asked Jess to come to the game suddenly drained away. She was happy tonight. So was he. Couldn't they just leave it at that? At least for a little while.

Doug grinned at the guard. "Thanks, pal.''

"Any time.''

Jessica opened the door almost as soon as he rapped. Her smile was tentative. "Hi.''

She wore jeans and a Milwaukee Brewers jersey emblazoned with the number nineteen. Doug's eyebrows rose at that. Robin Yount. And the thing looked real—white with blue stripes, a home team jersey from the glory days of the '80s. Hell, with the people she knew, the jersey had probably come right off Yount's back. But no one had bothered to mention to her that you don't wear sports memorabilia, you hang it in a case.

"You think I could talk you out of that shirt?'' he asked.

"Already?'' Her brow creased. "Won't we be late?''

She thought he meant... The image that followed the heels of that thought made Doug grin. He wanted to kiss her. With her hair in a ponytail and her lips without color, she looked like a girl going on a date. That's what she was—and he was just the guy to take her.

"Never mind,'' he said. "Ready?''

"Batter up.''

As they walked down the hallway to the elevator, her hand brushed his. Accident or design? He didn't care. Clasping her hand, he linked his fingers with hers and swung their arms. Out of the corner of his eye, he caught her confused, sideways glance. He was acting like a kid, but he didn't give a damn. He kept walking, swinging their hands like two teenagers browsing at the mall. As they passed beneath the security camera Doug looked directly into the lens and winked.

When they arrived at the ballpark Jessica waited on the sidewalk while Doug locked the doors. He joined her and took her hand. The gesture seemed so right, she barely noticed—barely.

"Ever been to a city league game?" he asked when they reached the diamonds.

"No."

"Well, it's different than a Brewer's game."

"How?"

"You'll see." He nodded and waved as a member of his team hailed him. "I have to go warm up." He pointed to a stack of bleachers. "This is our side. Sit up high so you can see. Some of the wives and girlfriends…"

His voice drifted off and she glanced at him to discover he stared at her with a frown.

"Girlfriends?" she asked. "Anyone I should know about? Am I going to have to fight for you, McGuire?"

He didn't smile at her teasing tone. "Would you?"

Something in his face caused her smile to fade. He had that lost little boy look that just dug a hole in her heart. She reached up and ran a finger down his nose, touched the tip to his mouth.

"Sure," she said, meaning to be flippant. The word came out anything but. Her voice, just above a whisper and hoarse for no reason at all, made the single, silly word sound like a promise, or a vow.

His gaze kissed her. He clasped her hand and squeezed it; and her breath caught as it always did whenever he touched her in any way. Their eyes held for another long moment—then someone called his name, impatiently. He took a step back and the moment was gone.

"Do you want a beer?"

"I can manage. You better go."

He turned away mumbling. "A beer, like she'd drink a beer."

Jessica frowned. He seemed to think she was some kind of priss. She had no one to blame but herself after the disastrous Bar Association Ball. Well, she'd show him. She could fit into his world.

Jessica straightened her back and marched up to the concession stand. A huge, burly guy who filled out a Harley T-shirt quite nicely was behind a bar filling plastic cups from twin spigots. He seemed to sense her presence because he continued doing so without even glancing her way. "What'll ya have?"

"A Miller."

"Lite or G.D.?"

"G.D.?" she asked.

He took a longer look at her. His eyes lit on her Yount jersey, and his heavy black brows shot up like startled twin caterpillars. What was it about this shirt that caused such a reaction? It wasn't like she filled it out half as well as the Harley guy did his.

"Genuine Draft, sweet thing, or Lite?"

Sweet thing? Now there was one name she didn't get called much. She should probably be offended, but she sensed it wasn't an insult.

"You look like a Lite kind of girl to me."

"I do? Why's that?"

"If you don't know what G.D. is, then you haven't been around beer enough to drink one."

Now *that* sounded like an insult. She jabbed a finger at the other spigot. "What's that?"

He grinned. "Red Dog."

"Let me guess—it'll put hair on my chest."

His gaze dropped to her chest, clung to the number nineteen, then came back to hers. "Want one?"

"Fill her up."

"Anything you say, sweet thing."

Beer in hand, Jessica carefully climbed to the top of the bleachers and sat down just in time to see Doug look her way. She lifted her beer in a "here's to you" gesture. He grinned.

"On deck—Doug McGuire."

Some of the players were monstrous. She hadn't seen thighs the size of the second baseman since…come to think of it, she'd never seen thighs that size. Not even on television. Jessica bit her lip. If Doug ran into that guy, he was toast.

Crack! The sound of a bat connecting jerked her to attention. Doug was already running with incredible speed to first as the ball continued its arc toward the outfield. The center fielder backed up to the fence and the ball sailed over his head into home-run land.

"Yes!" Jessica shouted, jumping to her feet, and sloshed beer all over the bench. She set the plastic cup down, then clapped and stomped as Doug ran around the bases. All his teammates met him at home plate and high-fived him one by one. Their exuberance was really sort of sweet. She'd never imagined that the tough cops and detectives she met in her courtroom spent their evenings playing games, but if anyone needed a little levity in their lives, it was these men and women.

Right before Doug went back to the bench, he stopped and gave her a thumbs-up sign, which she returned. When she sat down she found the coffee klatch of women had all turned around to stare at her.

"Hi, I'm Jessica," she said.

A couple of the women gave her weak smiles, but did not bother to introduce themselves. Then they all turned around, and she was left staring at their backs again. A few minutes later they resumed talking, but in hushed whispers. Still, Jessica wasn't deaf, and she heard most of what they said. She felt like she was in high school again—the too-smart, geeky kid left out of the prom queen's clique.

"Isn't that—?"

"Shh! Yes."

"What's she doing here with Doug?"

"Probably what you'd be doing with him, if you could," one taunted. The remark set up a round of laughter among them.

"Did you see them on TV?"

"I thought he was going to throttle her."

"Maybe he did later."

"Kinky, Deb. Kinky."

"Hey, when I look at McGuire, I think kinky."

Jessica wanted to press her hands to her ears. It seemed like the people in their respective worlds resented her and Doug's relationship. She turned her attention back to the game, and found that if she concentrated, she could forget that only a few feet away she was being diced and roasted.

Well, she'd come here with Doug, for Doug, and she was going to watch Doug—which was really no hardship.

He was right—this was nothing like the Brewers. The hits were all flyouts or long, hard line drives. The throws came down to the wire. The slides proved physical and dangerous. A lot of shoving, swearing and manly swaggering went on. The recent rains had soaked the field just enough to make the dirt beneath the dust the consistency of mud paste.

Doug came to the plate again, hit a double and went plowing into the colossus on second. The second baseman went flying. Doug headed for home on the next hit, slid face first into the catcher, and when he stood up his face was one big mud ball, but his teeth flashed through the ooze, and his eyes laughed.

Jessica hated to admit it, but she was hooked.

Bottom of the ninth and Doug's team was winning by a solitary run. Jessica went to get another Red Dog. It was kind of an acquired taste. Before she could get back to her seat the inning started, and she remained behind the dugout rather than climb past the wives again.

The thought gave her pause. Did she want to become a cop wife? She remembered back to the first time she'd eaten dinner with McGuire—the waitress who'd lost her cop husband and now cared for her injured cop son. Could Jessica bear such fear every day of her life? She'd lived with the remnants of violent death for a long time, and she still wasn't over it. She'd never be over Karen's death. But how would it feel to love a man, live with him, hold him, bear his children and lose him to a violent death?

Jessica winced and took a huge gulp of beer. Better not to go there. With McGuire the question would never come up, so why worry? Enjoy while the enjoying was good— that was going to be her motto for the duration of this relationship—if that's what you wanted to call whatever she and McGuire had.

"Geez, Jessica, let it go!" she ordered. Luckily, the crack of a bat and a cheer from the bench drew her attention away from hopeless speculation and back into the real world.

Jessica didn't see Doug—not in the field, and not on the bench. Then the catcher stood and threw the ball to the pitcher. She'd know that butt anywhere. The next batter up was that colossus second baseman.

"Two out," the umpire called, holding up one hand for the guys in the field.

Colossus didn't even wait to see what the pitcher was throwing; he swung at the first pitch and hit a long fly ball to deep center.

"Catch it, catch it, catch it," Jess chanted, moving forward until her nose was pressed to the chain-link fence behind home plate.

The center fielder missed the catch, but swooped up the ball and immediately hitched his arm back to throw for home. At first Jessica didn't understand what was happening. Not until she saw Doug yank his mask off and put his body in front of the plate.

Her gaze shot to third. The runner had already rounded third and was barreling for home—and McGuire.

Jessica groaned. The collision would send Doug into the stratosphere.

Seconds before the colossus hit him, Doug caught the ball, and put his glove down for the tag. Colossus's shoulder caught Doug in the chest, and he flew all the way past home plate.

He hit with a thud, a grunt and a puff of dust. Then he lay still. The crowd went quiet.

"Did he hold on to the ball?" someone shouted.

Doug's arm shot up, the softball clutched in the heart of his glove. His teammates erupted into cheers. He stood up, his gaze went to the stands, then he frowned.

But Jessica had already slipped past the fence. She launched herself into his arms before she realized she still held the Red Dog. Beer showered them, mixing with the dirt. She started laughing, then he kissed her, and she stopped long enough to kiss him back.

He lifted his head and looked down at her. "What did you think?"

"Yogi Bera couldn't have done it better."

"Yeah, he was good, too."

Then he grinned—dirt, and sweat, and beer, and man.

It wasn't until they walked down the hallway of her condo that she noticed him limping. "Hey, what's the matter, hero?"

He shrugged. "I'm getting too old for this."

"Didn't look like it to me."

"Well, it feels like it to me." He unlocked her door. "You want to go eat as soon as I wash off this mud?"

She raised her eyebrows at him. "We can order a pizza.

The way you look, you'd be considered a health hazard right now.''

''Me?'' He smirked. ''What's the matter?''

''Nothing that my whirlpool tub won't fix. You can wash off and work out the kinks.''

He shook his head. ''Tub! I don't sit in my own dirt.''

''You do have a way with words, McGuire. The tub is for your aches and pains. I'm just trying to be helpful.''

''I've got an ache you can help.''

She gave him a saucy smile. ''Sounds like time for a plea bargain. Water, soap, pizza—in that order...and then—''

''Water and soap—to hell with the pizza,'' he said, heading for the bathroom.

The sound of a shower pinging merrily told her Doug had not taken her advice about the whirlpool. Scooping up his dirty clothes, she tossed them into the washing machine, then stripped and tossed hers in as well.

He really should soak his knee, she thought. Perhaps there was another way to persuade him of the merits of warm swirling water.

A smile was all she wore as she let herself into the steaming bathroom. It took her five minutes to fill the whirlpool and slip beneath the bubbles.

Stepping out of the shower, Doug had the surprise of his life. Submerged in bubbles up to her neck, Jess lazed in the bathtub, her eyes closed and her auburn hair pinned up on the top of her head. The fragrance of the scented bath caressed his libido like fingers stroking his spine. Drying himself off, he wrapped the towel around his waist and walked over to the tub.

''You look very sexy in that tub, lady.''

She opened her eyes. ''You look very sexy in that towel, mister. Why don't you climb in and test the waters?''

"I'd rather smell you than smell like you. How long are you planning on staying in there?"

"Why do you ask?"

"I figure I'm good for about thirty seconds more." And he wasn't joking. Lord how that woman turned him on! As exciting as that was, it scared the hell out of him. No woman had ever made him feel this vulnerable. He needed sex like any guy, but there'd never been a woman before that he *had* to have—until Jess.

She looked up with a smile that cut his estimate time down to fifteen, then she stood up. Water and bubbles raced down the length of her, hugging the curves with the same tenacity of an Olympic luge racing the clock—the same as he was at that moment. He grabbed a bath towel and spread it open. She stepped into it, and his mouth was on hers before he finished wrapping the towel around her.

The kiss was wet and hot. Their tongues mated in the seconds it took to swoop her up in his arms. The few yards from the bathroom to the bed looked the length of a football field, but he made it. Then she was under him, and the sweet smell of her filled his nostrils—the soft flesh of her, his hands.

She was as ready as he—every inch of that luscious body flushed, satiny—and throbbing. For sure, neither of them needed any more foreplay. As if thinking about this moment in the past days apart hadn't been enough, the unfinished session in her office today had escalated their hunger.

He entered her, and she cried out his name in ecstasy. Then his mind and body merged, sinking deeper and deeper into the remembered rapture of Jess.

Chapter 8

After sex Doug had never been a cuddler. No way would he ever lie basking in the afterglow. He'd always fallen asleep, or gotten out of bed and left.

Now as he lay with Jess asleep in the curve of his arm, her head resting in the cradle of his shoulder, and the soft flutter of her warm breath on his flesh, he figured it would take a SWAT team to blast him out of the bed.

He felt good. Jess felt better. He nudged her closer. He loved touching her. He stroked his hand along the satin surface of her arm, which was flung across his chest, and wove his fingers into the silky mass of her hair. The fragrance from her scented bath was all over her, over him— the way she'd been all over him, the way he'd been over her.

Neither of them held back anything when they had sex. That's what made it so good. They met on a level playing field, and the different worlds they traveled in became non-existent.

His arm tightened around her. Yeah, it would take a

SWAT team to get him out of the bed, all right—or his damn cell phone. He cursed silently as the persistent buzz of it impugned the quietness.

Easing his arm out from under her, he got off the bed. The phone was on the dresser where he'd left it, along with his gun and badge. He checked the caller ID. Same old, same old. After a grumbled conversation with the duty sergeant, he hung up the phone and began to look for his clothes.

Suddenly a flood of light from a bedside lamp illuminated part of the room. ''What are you looking for, Doug?'' Jess asked. She sat up in bed, sleepy-eyed, disheveled and looking sexy as sin.

He felt like a fool stumbling around in the dark. A naked fool. ''I have to go. Where are my clothes?''

''Still in the dryer. I'll get them.''

''No. Stay in bed. I'll find them and get out of here.''

He dressed hurriedly. Thank goodness he'd brought jeans and shoes to change into after the game, but he'd forgotten a shirt.

Doug returned to the bedroom. Jess had turned off the lamp. Grabbing his belongings from the dresser, he went over to the bed. ''I'll call you.'' He gave her a quick kiss and got out of there fast.

Yellow tape roped off the crime area at the river. There were a couple of patrol cars on the scene with the officers standing around fending off spectators. A fellow from the crime lab had just finished taking photographs and another was bagging the body. Doug halted him long enough to kneel down and take a look at the victim. He recognized the dead man immediately: Sam Bellemy, one of his and Vic's old collars. The man had raped and murdered an eight-year-old girl, and beat the rap on a technicality. One of the touchy issues between him and Jess.

Vic came over and took a long look at the team baseball

shirt and cap Doug had on. "Looks like the game went into extra innings."

"So fill me in," Doug said, ignoring the gibe.

"Same M.O. as Gilbert. A floater. Hands tied, plastic bag over his head." Vic nodded when Doug arched a brow. "Yeah, you've got it, partner. Looks like we've got a serial killer on our hands."

"Or a crusader," Doug murmured.

They questioned the spectators and the young couple who discovered the body. Nobody was able to offer any other information.

"Let's check out his place," Vic said.

"Give me a few minutes to change my clothes."

Vic nodded. "Take a couple more to take a shower. Your perfume is turning me on, McGuire. I'll meet you at the station."

Vic was waiting in the Crown Victoria when Doug drove into the police lot. He parked his car and climbed in beside Vic.

"So you've finally nailed Judge Jessica, huh, Wolf Man?" Vic said as they headed out.

"Who said I was with the judge?"

"It's the talk of the precinct. I can't believe you took her to the softball game?"

"So what? Does that mean I'm sleeping with her?"

"Partner, either you slept with her tonight or changed your shaving lotion."

"Gee, Officer, we're both over eighteen."

"Hope you know what you're doing, McGuire. You and the judge don't exactly travel in the same circles."

"I don't need you to tell me that."

"I just don't want to see you screw yourself up, partner."

Vic was his best friend. Doug knew eventually Vic would get the whole story out of him, but right now he wasn't ready to talk about Jess to anybody. He didn't understand his relationship with her himself, so he couldn't try to explain it to Vic. Fortunately, they'd been partners for so long that Vic knew how far he could push Doug's buttons. That was the beauty of their partnership.

Vic pulled up in front of a cheap hotel on the lower East Side. The desk clerk recognized the detectives from their previous investigation of Bellemy, shoved a passkey at them and then went back to sleep.

A search of Bellemy's one-room apartment produced nothing more than a half dozen porno pictures of children.

Incensed, Vic tore them down. "God, what a perverted bastard!"

"I think most of this filth is computer-generated now," Doug said. "But the city still ought to pin a medal on the guy who whacked this pervert."

"Who said it has to be a man? A woman could stick a needle into him to immobilize him, tie up his hands and then put a plastic bag over his head."

Doug doubted that. "She'd have to be damn strong to get his body into the river."

"I figure a gal in good condition could do it easily," Vic pressed.

"I don't doubt that there's a long line of women who'd like to try."

"The judge for one. Of course she's in the clear. She was in bed with a detective."

"What are you getting at, Vic? Why would the judge be a suspect?"

"She had to throw Gilbert's and Bellemy's cases out of court, didn't she? Good reason to take the law into her own hands."

"If that's your argument, they were our cases, too, so either one of us could be the killer. And don't rule out the Tate girl's mother or dad."

"I can see the Tate kid's parents knocking off Bellemy, but not Gilbert," Vic said.

"We don't even know for certain what time Bellemy was killed."

"The M.E. said there was no rigor mortis and there was still blood pooled on a couple of scrapes on his arms, so without an examination he figured it couldn't have been much more than an hour."

Doug chuckled. "Then that leaves you and the Tates our only suspects, Vic, 'cause Jess and I have an alibi."

"Jess?" Vic snorted. "Sounds like the two of you are getting real tight, partner. Let's get out of here. This joint stinks."

Night had slipped into daylight by the time they returned to the precinct. While Vic wrote up a report, Doug pulled Kellie Tate's file. Although every detail was still clear in his mind, he read it again. His stomach knotted when he looked at the photographs of the lifeless body of the adorable eight-year-old. He and Vic had worked their butts off tracking down her killer. And even though Sam Bellemy had confessed to the sadistic rape and murder of the child, he later denied it and walked on a technicality.

Doug closed the file and reached for Cindy Fire's. Her slaying at the hands of LeRoy Gilbert had been just as brutal. These two cases, above all others, had really gotten to him. No matter what he'd said to the contrary, he'd felt guilt for being indirectly responsible that the two killers had gone free. And it was little consolation to know both of them had finally paid for their crimes.

Frustrated, he shoved the files aside. He'd had it. He was sick of dealing with the dregs of society: pedophiles molesting children, junkies robbing and killing to support their drug habits, spouses killing one another in domestic disputes. Gang wars. Hate crimes. Murderous rages. Perversion. Revenge. Hatred. Greed. How many ways—and reasons—could people find to kill each other? Lately it was getting harder and harder to look into the pained faces of the loved ones of the murdered victims. It was time he gave it up. There sure as hell had to be something better in life than this. Putting pieces of the puzzles together wasn't doing it for him anymore. He reached for the files again.

From what he could tell at this point, the only link between the two victims was that he and Vic had been the arresting officers on both cases. What if Crusader Rabbit decided that he and Vic deserved the same fate for fouling up the arrests. "Yeah, well come and get me, you damn scumball."

Vic glanced up. "What?"

"I was thinking aloud, Vic. What if whoever's out there playing 'I, the Jury' gets the bright idea to blame us for these guys getting off and decides to try and whack us?"

"He can try."

Doug was suddenly struck with another damning thought. Jess! "Or the judge who let them walk?"

Vic sighed deeply. "McGuire, did you ever think of spending your nights sleeping instead of screwing your brains out?"

Doug wasn't giving up on the idea. He decided to bounce it off Jess. He reached for the telephone, and slammed it down when all he got was the steady drone of a busy signal. It gave him an excuse to see her. Doug bolted to his feet. "I'll be right back."

He made it to the high rise in seven minutes flat. Charlie, the security guard, shook his head when Doug entered.

"You just missed her, Detective. The Judge drove off a couple minutes ago."

Dammit! "Thanks." He went back to his car. He'd give her a few minutes and then call her. Besides, Vic was right. He was grasping at straws. He had nothing to go on except a hunch, so why alarm her?

* * *

Jess was late. She'd overslept and Liz's call had detained her more. She could see it now. With Liz home sick today, the office would be in turmoil. Liz always kept things running as smoothly as a well-oiled machine.

As usual she thought of Doug. These days he was all she thought about. She'd discovered that there was a lot more to Doug McGuire than great sex. He had an incredible sensitivity under that tough shell he wore like a suit of armor. She'd witnessed it the night he'd told her about Kate Harrington and her son Danny; she'd felt it in the way he made love—as much of a desire to satisfy as to be satisfied.

Jess pulled into her reserved spot in the parking garage and turned off the ignition. Deep in thought, she sat with her arms slumped over the steering wheel.

Doug McGuire was an enigma, all right. And every time they were together she found herself more and more aware of how vulnerable this tough detective really was. Was he afraid of being hurt? What in his life had caused this distrust? Clearly he was far from admitting that what was between them was developing quickly into a feeling much deeper than sex. The question was would he ever admit it to himself—much less to her?

Getting emotionally involved with him was the very thing she had hoped to avoid. A seven year relationship with Dennis Wolcott had foolishly led her to the naive belief that she was sophisticated enough to play these bedroom games. But Doug McGuire was no Dennis Wolcott.

"Judge Kirkland, are you okay?" The rapping on the car window startled her out of her musing. Stanley Haley was peering worriedly into the window. "Are you okay, Judge Kirkland?"

She opened the car door. "Oh, good morning, Stanley. I'm fine. I'm just wondering how I'll get through the day without Liz."

"Did something happen to Ms. Alexander?" the young man asked as they walked to the elevator.

"She's not feeling well, so she won't be in today."

"Is there anything I can do to help?"

"What's your workload, Stanley?"

"I'm scheduled for your court," he said.

"That would work out perfectly. Stanley, I've got a lot of paperwork to clear off my desk today. Would you consider covering Liz's desk when we're not in court?"

Stanley grinned widely. "I'd love to, Judge Kirkland."

The morning was passing swiftly. In between her two court sessions, Jessica tried unsuccessfully to read a previous transcript of the case next on her docket but her mind constantly drifted to thoughts of Doug. She finally gave up trying.

Shoving the transcript aside, she picked up the telephone and dialed Liz to find out if she needed anything. All Jess got was an answering machine and a promise of a call back. She then tried her father to unload her woes on him, and struck out at both the restaurant and his house. She went back to trying to concentrate on the transcript.

Jessica struggled through the afternoon session, thanked Stanley for his help and sent him on his way. Deciding to leave, she tried to reach Liz and ended up talking to the answering machine again. Frustrated, she reached for the stack of telephone messages Stanley had put in front of her and discovered four of them were from Doug. No call back number. She telephoned his precinct, only to be told Detective McGuire was out of the office.

Since it definitely wasn't her day, Jessica decided to leave. She pondered whether to check on Liz. If she was too sick to answer the telephone, she might need medical attention. They had exchanged keys years ago in case of emergencies, and kept them in Liz's desk. To Jess's surprise there must have been a tagged key for half of the people who worked in the courthouse in the lower drawer of Liz's desk. She finally found Liz's housekey among them.

There was no sign of Liz at home and the answering machine was blinking. Jessica's anxiety increased. Curious, she played the messages; they were the same two she had left, which meant that Liz had never played them back. This was cause for alarm. If Liz had ended up in the hospital, surely someone would have notified her by now. Jessica tried unsuccessfully to reach Doug again. Then she called her father and finally reached him at the restaurant.

When she told him of her concern, he sounded remarkably calm, and tried to reassure her that there was nothing to be concerned about. He convinced her into coming to the restaurant. As soon as she drove up, he came out to meet her. Seeing her distressed expression, he put his arms around her.

"I'm so worried, Dad. What could have happened to Liz?"

"Sweetheart, I'm sure it's nothing serious. She probably just stepped out for a while."

"But she hasn't even listened to her incoming calls."

"Knowing Liz, she probably just didn't want to talk to anybody. Haven't you ever felt that way?"

As a matter of fact that was exactly what she'd done all day. For a long moment she remained in his arms, drawing on his strength and the conviction of his words.

"Come on inside and have dinner with me. You can call Liz again."

"Tomorrow is our dinner night."

"So is there a law against a father and daughter having dinner together two nights in a row, Your Honor?"

Jessica smiled and slipped her arm around his waist. "There probably is somewhere, but let's live dangerously."

* * *

Doug and Vic finished canvassing the neighborhood for anyone who might have seen Bellemy last night and returned to their car. Just as he was about to drive off, Doug saw Jess pull into the parking lot of the Water Street Bistro. When the old guy rushed out and took her in his arms, Doug clenched the steering wheel so tightly that his knuckles turned white.

So what's it to you, McGuire? You gonna deck the old guy? He belongs in her day world—you're just good for her nights.

Hell, wasn't that what their relationship was all about from the beginning? Great sex was all they owed each other. When it burned out they'd go their separate ways with a thanks for the memories.

Vic was right. He should never have taken her to that softball game. She and the old guy were probably having a good laugh right now about it. Or maybe she kept Detective Doug McGuire—her boy toy extraordinaire—a secret from the poor sucker.

"It ain't getting any earlier, McGuire," Vic groused, beside him.

Doug turned on the ignition and pulled out. He glanced in the side-view mirror and saw Jess slip her arm around the guy's waist. He had nothing to say on the way back to the precinct.

After parking the car, he signed out, stopped at a drive-through for a burger and fries and topped them off with a can of beer when he got home. He switched on the tube, listened to Sherilyn Matthews for all of sixty seconds, then turned it off and headed for the bedroom and a shower.

He let the hot spray of water hit him in the face for about twenty minutes. A waste of time and water—it didn't help. What were she and the old guy doing right now? Sitting in that fancy restaurant sipping glasses of hundred-dollar wine, or had they moved on to her apartment and were… He turned off the water and grabbed a towel.

He tried another beer and the television again. Neither worked. His three-room apartment had suddenly shrunk to one room with the walls closing in fast, and he had to get out of there. He headed for The Precinct, figuring he'd sit in on the Sheepshead game. As he drove past the Water Street Bistro, he saw Jess's Park Avenue was still in the parking lot.

Without conscious intention, he ended up at Jess's highrise. It was time they spelled out the game rules. He nodded to the security guard and took the elevator up to her floor. He'd been a cop too long not to know how to trip a lock.

Doug checked out the bedroom first to make sure he wasn't interrupting anything. He'd be making a real ass of himself if he'd walked in on them.

He could feel her aura in the pale green and cream serenity of the room, smell the faintest hint of her perfume. He shifted his gaze to the bed. His loins knotted as he recalled the last time he was in it with her. He left the room hurriedly, went into the den and turned on a lamp. Then he sank down on a couch that conjured up a very torrid memory and reached for the television remote.

"Doug, wake up." He opened his eyes and sat up. Jess was standing in the room's doorway. "Doug, what are you doing here?"

Glancing at his watch, he discovered he'd been asleep for the past two hours. "I guess I dozed off."

"That doesn't answer my question." Her body language said it all when she walked over, picked up the remote and zapped the picture on the tube. "How did you get in here?"

She was ticked off all right. And he felt like a damn

fool. Of all the dumb moves he'd made in his life, this one was right up there with the dumbest.

"I thought we needed to talk."

"I want to know how you got in here."

He tried to lighten her mood with a grin. "Trade secret." *Dumb and dumber. She wasn't amused.*

"Who do you think you are? Get out of here, Doug. I won't stand for you entering my apartment uninvited."

She didn't give a damn what he wanted to talk about, and was making it clear she was the piper, and he had to waltz to her tune. Well he wasn't buying it. When he was on the dance floor, he did the leading.

"I don't think the issue is who I think I am, but more *what* you think I am. What happened, Your Honor, didn't things go your way tonight? Can't the old guy get it up on a full stomach?"

Jess turned white. She was too much of a lady to smack him in the face, but he could tell she sure as hell wanted to. Anger? Fury? Shock? Whatever she was feeling, anyone who was as idiot as he'd been to make such a crack was too stupid to figure it out anyway.

She squared those classy shoulders of hers and raised her head with that intrinsic dignity she possessed. "That *old guy* happens to be my father, Detective. Now please get out of here or I'll call security and have you thrown out."

Her father? The old guy was her father! This time he'd really blown it! He was a loudmouth smart-ass. He knew it, and now she knew it, too. He raised a hand to reach out to her, but she turned away, walked to the door and opened it.

Doug had no choice but to follow, and then paused on his way out.

"Jess, I'm—"

She closed the door.

Chapter 9

Doug had lost count of how often he'd glanced at the clock. He still had a couple of hours before it was time to get up. It was a mistake to lie in bed waiting. It gave your thoughts the chance to really screw you up—like they'd been doing all night.

He got out of bed and put on his sweats and sneakers. He'd try jogging. He'd always been good for about four miles. Maybe that would be enough to run it off. Like hell it would. It'd take a damn sight more than a four-mile jog to get over Jess.

Once outside he headed east toward Lake Michigan. By some quirk after a couple of miles he ended up smack in front of Jess's high-rise on Lake Drive.

The security guard buzzed him in and Doug stopped at his desk.

"Don't you have a home, Charlie? Seems like you're always here."

"I live here," Charlie said.

"Really. Pay must be pretty good, pal."

"Oh, I don't have one of them fancy apartments like the judge. Three rooms downstairs. It's real comfortable and the price is right. Comes with the job."

"So you're happy in your work."

"Yeah, can't complain. Pay's decent, and I get along good with most of the occupants. And at Christmastime it's a real bonanza. Couple of them have their noses in the air, but take the judge, for instance, she ain't got a snooty bone in her body."

Damn straight.

"I figure you for an ex-cop, Charlie. Am I right?"

"Yeah, put in my twenty years and took retirement."

"You married, Charlie?" Small talk. Stalling. Gathering enough nerve to face her.

"Naw. I've got a easy life. Better than when I pounded a beat. Why spoil it? You jog every morning?"

"If I get the chance. That or I work out when time allows."

"I oughta start doing that. This sitting around all day ain't doing me no good."

"You've got that right, pal," Doug said, and pushed the elevator button.

He knocked and braced himself for the worst. *Sorry's not enough.* But he'd have to try and get it out before she could slam the door.

Jess looked surprised when she opened the door and saw him. Since she had plenty of time to close it in the awkward moment they just stared at each other, he figured he had a shot at the apology. "Hi."

"What do you want, Doug?"

"May I come in?"

"What for?"

"I'd like to talk to you."

"This is a bad time. I have to get dressed, and—"

"It won't take long, Jess."

She walked away, but didn't close the door, so he took

it as a yes. He stepped in, then quietly shut the door behind him, and leaned back against it until he heard the lock click. Jess had her back to him and was staring out the window, her arms folded across her chest.

"I'm sorry, Jess. You've got the right to be mad." He fought to concentrate on what he'd come to say, but the robe she had on was a white satiny thing and he could tell by the way it clung to the curve of her hips that there was nothing but Jess beneath it. He swallowed to try and slip the words past the lump that had suddenly formed in his throat. "I...kind of freaked when I saw you with the old... Dammit, Jess, why didn't you tell me sooner that he was your father?"

She turned her head and glared at him. "You're supposed to be the detective." She resumed staring out the window.

"You're right. I screwed up royally last night. It was a stupid assumption. You're too classy to string an old guy along and sleep with a younger one."

"Thank you, Doug. I'm afraid it's getting late and I have the shower running."

"Yeah, I understand." He reached behind him for the doorknob. "I just wanted you to know how sorry I am. And for what it's worth, Jess, I think you're one grand woman. It was great while it lasted." He turned to leave.

"Are you calling it off, Detective?" His hand froze on the knob and he turned his head and looked at her. She was staring at him with the same smile he figured Eve wore when she handed Adam the apple. "You look like you could use a shower yourself."

She unzipped the robe and started to slip it off her shoulders. His hormones shifted into overdrive and propelled him across the room before her robe hit the floor. His sweats and sneakers met the same fate, then he swooped her up into his arms. They broke the kiss when the pelting spray of the shower forced them to breathe or drown.

Breath was too precious to waste on words, need too great to delay. Their foreplay had been in the wait, the wanting, the unspoken word—and in the contrition and forgiveness of their spoken ones.

They now breathed as one, their hearts beat as one, and in those exquisite moments when their bodies molded, fused and then climaxed, their souls combined and became one. Then and only then did they find time to kiss, to caress and to taste.

As soon as they dressed, Jess offered to drive him home on her way to the courthouse, but his pride opted him to get back the way he had come. Another dumb move, but he was a victim of his own male chauvinism. He kissed her goodbye and said he'd call her later.

Jogging back gave him a good chance to think. Jess was no more ready to give up on him than he was on her, and he had to face the reality that his need for her was quickly becoming much more than just a physical one. The thought scared the hell out of him.

Liz was on the job and hard at work when Jess arrived. After a quick greeting, she resumed typing.

"You gave me a real scare yesterday when I went to your house and you weren't there."

Liz didn't look up. "I'm sorry. I should have called you. I felt better so I went out."

She was acting unnatural, and had been for several days. They were too close for Jess to ignore it any longer. "Liz, what's going on?"

Startled, Liz glanced up at her. "What do you mean?"

"Liz, you haven't been yourself for days. Do you have a problem?"

"No, of course not."

"I'd believe that if I wasn't looking at you when you said it. Are you sure you're feeling okay?"

"I'm fine, Jess. Truly, I am."

"Okay, but if there's any way I can help let me know."

Jess went into her chambers and sat down at her desk. She knew Liz was holding back something.

This must be the season for it? After his apology, she and Doug hadn't said another word about last night's quarrel, either. She understood why he was jealous. Jess smiled despite the seriousness of the incident. His enigmatic nature again. The man wasn't the least bit intimidated by her seven-year relationship with Dennis, but seeing her twice with Dad had sent him ballistic.

Doug McGuire was the last man on earth who would admit to being jealous, but he didn't have to. She knew enough about men to at least recognize jealousy.

What had upset her was his entering her apartment. She had nothing to hide, but she was uncomfortable with the idea. As intimate as they were physically—and the Lord knew how intimate that was—there was also a kind of standoff reserve in their relationship. He liked old movies and Sinatra, that *a babe in Sheboygan got a gold watch out of me once*, and his father was the police chief of a small town in Northern Illinois was about all he had ever volunteered about his personal life. And he didn't seem too curious about hers, either. Was it his way of keeping their relationship confined to the bedroom only?

She wouldn't be much of a judge if she didn't try to weigh both sides of the scales. She was just as guilty. It took a quarrel between them for her to even identify her father to him. And just as bad, she'd never told him about Karen's murder, even though he was a homicide detective. Maybe it was time they both came out of the bedroom.

Jess reached for the telephone.

"McGuire, Line 2. Some broad waiting to talk to you," Novack shouted across the room.

"So what else is new," Vic commented, and returned his attention to the file he was reading.

Hoping it was a lead in response to his calls, Doug hung up the routine call he'd been on and punched the blinking light on his phone. "Detective McGuire."

"Hello, Detective McGuire."

Jess's voice stroked him like a velvet glove. "Hi." He glanced across at Vic, then swiveled his chair so his back was to his partner. "What can I do for you?" He got hard just thinking about what he could do for her.

"I think you've figured that out a long time ago."

"I should warn you, lady, if this is an obscene call I might be forced to cuff you and pull you in."

"Mmm, sounds kinky. Pull me into what? Tell me, Detective McGuire, since I'm kind of new at this, are we having phone sex right now?"

"I don't know about you, but I am."

Her light laugh turned him on as much as the thought of her cuffed to his bedpost.

"Seriously, Doug, I was wondering if you'd join me and my father for dinner tonight?"

"Thought you had dinner with him last night?"

"That was unexpected. I'd been worried about Liz because she didn't come to work yesterday, and she wasn't at home, either. I tried you first with no luck, so I called Dad. We ended up having dinner."

"Did you track her down?" Small talk, just to keep her talking. He liked listening to her voice.

"Finally, from the restaurant."

"So where had she been?"

"Come to think of it, she didn't say. Only that she felt better and had gone out. So are we on for tonight or not?" Jess asked.

"Wish I could, Jess, but we're tied up here on this case. And unless we get a break, it looks like we will be for a couple of nights." Thank God, he didn't have to lie to her, because he wasn't ready to meet dear old Dad. He visualized the old guy's look of disapproval when Jess told her father she was dating him.

"You really want me to crawl, don't you, McGuire? How about Saturday night?"

That got a chuckle out of him. "I thought you'd never ask."

"Good. I've got symphony tickets."

"Symphony tickets! Not fair. You bushwhacked me, lady."

"I promise to make it up to you."

"You've got that right."

"I've got to run, Doug. I'm due in court. Bye."

Doug hung up the phone and swiveled around to his desk. He picked up the Bellemy file in front of him. Something Jess had said replayed in his mind—Liz's strange behavior the day after Bellemy's murder. He had brushed off Vic's theory that a woman as well as a man could have committed Gilbert's and Bellemy's murders. Maybe the possibility had some merit after all. He recalled Liz once telling him that being single and living alone she worked out vigorously ever day—pumped iron and the whole nine yards. But murder? Murders were committed by the real sleaze and screwups of the world. Liz Alexander always struck him as having a pretty level head on her shoulders. But he had nothing to lose by checking her out. He began rooting through the records piled high on his desk.

"Vic, where's that insulin users' printout?"

"What's up?" Vic asked, tossing it over to him.

"I'm not sure."

Doug perused it quickly, but there was no Elizabeth Alexander listed among the eighty-some names listed in Milwaukee and the adjoining counties. But that didn't mean one of them couldn't have been a relative, which could mean Liz might have access to the medicine.

Telephone time again. The phone company should start paying half his salary.

* * *

Fortunately her workload had kept Jess busy for the past two days; even so tonight had been on her mind. She thought it would never come.

When the intercom buzzed three times, Jess recognized the signal and slid quickly into her shoes, which were nothing more than wide straps across the front and stiletto heels attached to soles. She'd told Charlie to warn her when Doug was on his way up and wanted to be ready when she met him at the door, or there was no doubt in her mind that they'd end up in the bedroom and not the Performing Arts Center. *Lead us not into temptation.*

Jess hurried to the mirror. As she spun around for a final inspection she felt as excited as a schoolgirl going to her first date.

She'd never paid so much attention to dressing as she had tonight. She'd even bought a new dress for the occasion. She wanted to look especially nice for Doug.

The top of the black crepe dress draped her breasts and dropped in a flattering flare to her knees. Her shoulders were bare except for the two narrow spaghetti straps that crisscrossed attached at the small of her back. She smiled wickedly. Doug would love it. All he'd have to do is lower the straps off her shoulders and the dress would drop to the floor. She wore nothing under it except for a pair of wispy chiffon bikinis.

Her gaze shifted to her bare legs. After shaving them, she had creamed them until they felt as smooth as satin, and a deep summer tan prevented the need for hose.

Doug told her she had great legs. Dennis had never commented on her legs one way or the other. He seemed to have taken the whole package for granted. Doug, on the contrary, was just the opposite—he didn't take anything about her for granted. Her hair, her eyes, her breasts, her legs fell under his scrutiny and homage when he made love to her.

She'd always felt her looks were adequate, and that they paled in comparison to Karen's breathtaking, ethereal blond beauty. But Doug—Doug made her feel beautiful.

She grabbed the shawl and clutch bag off the bed and hurried to answer the knock at her door.

"Wow!" they said in unison when she opened it.

He was wearing his black suit, a white shirt and a black and gold striped tie. He looked so gorgeous it took her breath away.

Admiration gleamed in his eyes. "Great dress."

"Great tie," she responded.

"Christmas gift from my mom. Sure you want to go to that symphony?" He started to reach for her. "Why don't we—"

"Don't even think it, McGuire." She shoved him gently back, stepped out in the hallway and closed the door before she could change her mind.

I love your apartment, Jess. It's silly, but I feel your presence as if you were with me. And it makes me laugh how easily I dodge the security cameras getting up here. I'd like to tell you as much, but then you'd know I'd been here, and that would end it.

As much fun as this is, it can't compare to how much I enjoyed killing Gilbert and Bellemy. Gilbert was the easiest. We had a few drinks together and then I invited him to come home with me to shoot up on heroin. Boy, he was stupid. Thought he was getting a free fix. That's how I immobilized him. Bellemy was harder. At the last minute he decided not to shoot up, so I pretended I was. When he turned his back, I stuck the needle into his leg. We struggled for a few minutes, but it was too late.

The most brilliant part was the wheelchair to get them to my car. Just in case anyone might see me with the body, it would look like he was handicapped. But no one saw me. I'm too smart for that.

And putting the bodies in the river was a nice touch, don't you think, Jess? I liked the idea of them floating down the river. "Rollin', rollin', rollin' on the river." Love that song. Kind of sends a message, too, don't you think?

This picture of Karen and you is so beautiful, Jess. I never tire of looking at it. My heart aches knowing how you still grieve for her. I wish I could find her killer for you. It would finally give you peace.

Chapter 10

"Well, this is a first," Jess said the next morning as Doug leaned over and kissed her goodbye. "You actually got through the whole night without your darn cell phone going off."

Doug chuckled. "Yes, Virginia, there is a Santa Claus. Just the same, I better recharge the battery." He gave her another quick kiss. "I'll be back about noon."

Jess got out of bed and wandered listlessly into the living room. Her dress was flung across the back of a chair where Doug must have picked it up on his way out this morning. She'd been right about the dress. He'd had her out of it in a single, fluid motion. She found her shoes and on the way back to the bedroom, she picked up her earrings from the end table.

Jess couldn't help smiling. She'd taken them off and tossed them there when Doug said making love to a woman wearing *real* diamonds dangling from her ears made him feel like a gigolo. He was such a lovable contradiction—a self-deprecating, macho male.

Jess's smile dissipated when she saw Karen's picture was missing again. She glanced immediately at the opposite end table and there it sat.

"Darn you, Doug. Will you quit rearranging my decor," she mumbled good-naturedly. Returning the picture to its rightful spot, she went back to the bedroom.

When Doug returned several hours later he was wearing jeans and a muscle shirt. He looked so darn sexy that she had to fight to keep her hands off him. Since it was hotter than Hades, Jess dressed in a halter-top, shorts and flat sandals.

Doug gave her a long, appreciative once over. "Great legs," he said.

"Thank you. You have mentioned that before."

"So I have." His shifted his gaze to her breasts. "Well then, great—"

She raised a hand to halt what he was about to say. "I believe you've touched on that subject a time or two, also. Or should I say you've done considerably more than just touched."

"And how sweet they were. Guess then, that just leaves your trim little—"

"If you say it, I'm not stepping one foot out of this door," she threatened.

He flashed his irresistible grin that always succeeded in melting her feeble efforts to resist him. "I was just going to comment on what trim little toes you have, Grandma."

"The better to kick you in those tight little buns of yours, my dear." She gave him a shove. "Shall we go?"

Jess was on edge on the ride to the Precinct. Ski was celebrating the bar's first anniversary, and Vic and his wife would be there. She'd been around detectives enough to know how close partners can become and the importance of their spouses or sweethearts getting along.

She might have guessed Doug would notice her nervousness, and wasn't surprised when he finally popped the question.

"So what's bothering you, Jess?"

"I'm a little nervous about meeting Vic's wife."

"Bev's a jewel."

"Easy for you to say. I'm still shivering from the cold shoulder I got from the wives at the baseball game."

"Hey, Bev isn't like that, Jess. She's one hundred percent. You'll like her."

There was friendly curiosity in Bev Peterson's eyes when Doug introduced Jess to Vic's dark-haired wife. Jess liked Bev on sight and within the hour had forgotten her earlier trepidation. The two women had no trouble chatting away and agreed that Doug and Vic had the best partner either one could have ever hoped for. By the time it came to leave, they'd planned to talk the fellows into taking them to a movie.

"We'll find a good comedy," Bev said. "These murders have gotten Vic a little uptight. At least that Sam Bellemy won't be able to molest any other eight-year-olds."

"Sam Bellemy? It was LeRoy Gilbert who was murdered."

"Yeah, sure. And then Bellemy."

"I didn't know about Bellemy."

Bev looked surprised. "Where have you been, Jess? They found Bellemy's body last Tuesday or Wednesday. Good heavens, it's been on television and in the newspaper."

"I've stopped reading the newspaper, and I haven't turned my television on for a week."

It must have been the night of the baseball game, Jess reflected. That must have been why Doug had been called away. Why hadn't he even mentioned it to her? They'd even argued over Bellemy in the past.

As much as Jess enjoyed Bev's company, she couldn't

wait to leave. The news of Bellemy's murder had shaken her up, and she was uncertain why it was so disturbing to her.

She had to think it out clearly before she brought it up with Doug. He'd probably clam up more if he thought she was challenging him. Although, since he hadn't even mentioned it to her, he could hardly say less than he'd done already.

As soon as they got inside her apartment, rather than reach for her, as she had expected him to do, Doug sat down in a chair.

"Okay. So what's the problem now? I had the impression you were enjoying yourself or I would have brought you home sooner."

Darn that sixth sense of his. How did he do it? "I didn't say there was a problem, Doug."

He ignored her denial. "Vic say something you didn't like?"

"Not at all. He couldn't have been nicer, and Bev is everything you led me to believe."

"Guess that narrows it down to me. What did I do?"

"Let's discuss it tomorrow. Right now I feel grimy. I'm going to take a shower. Are you staying or leaving?"

He gave her a reflective look. "Sounds like you'd prefer I leave."

"I didn't mean for it to sound like that. Of course you're welcome to stay."

"*I'm welcome to stay!* Excuse me, I'm not too bright. What does that mean? I'm welcome to stay for a drink or for breakfast?"

This was exactly what she'd been afraid would happen. Once again they were quarreling indirectly over Sam Bellemy.

"Doug, why didn't you tell me Sam Bellemy had been murdered?"

He looked at her as if she'd just sprouted fangs and horns. "Is *that* what this is all about?"

"Why must you always answer a question with a question, Detective?"

"Sorry, *Your Honor.* Why would I tell you any more about my cases then you'd tell me about yours?"

"What do you think?"

"Now who's answering a question with a question?"

"Doug, please. Just tell me why you never mentioned it."

"I thought we had agreed that we don't talk shop when we're together."

"This is different. Bellemy was both our cases," she declared.

"Gilbert's and Bellemy's murders have been the lead stories on television since Wednesday morning, and the newspapers are still carrying the stories on the front page. Why would I have to mention it to you?"

She slumped in defeat. His point was too logical to argue. She just hadn't stayed abreast of the local news. "You're right. I'm sorry. Why are we arguing over Sam Bellemy again?"

"You brought it up, Jess."

"I guess I'm just tired." She smiled contritely. "And I need that shower. But that breakfast invitation still stands, Doug. So how about joining me in that shower?" It was obvious in the inflexible look in his eyes that they weren't connecting.

"I have a better idea. Let's have sex right here and now, while we're both grimy and sweaty. Forget the shower and those immaculate silk sheets on your bed. How about it, Jess? Come down to my level and roll in the mud for a change."

"I wouldn't hesitate if I believed that's what you really mean, but you're talking figuratively, aren't you? You believe you're not good enough for me. Oh, Doug…" Unable to control the urge to touch him, she went over to him and sat down on his lap. "Why do you do this to yourself? To us?" Jess tenderly traced the line of his stubborn jaw with her fingertips. "You have this fixation that I'm slumming. Don't you know me better than that by now? Our relationship's not a game to me. I enjoy your company."

"Especially the sex."

She didn't appreciate that comment, but she knew it was the basis for all his doubts. "I enjoy that, too. But sex aside, I enjoy just being with you, Doug. Why can't you believe that?"

Jess tried to smile, but it was hard while looking into the suspicion and doubt she saw in his eyes. "Aren't you supposed to be an astute detective? You may know my body better than any man—and for the record, Doug, there's only been one other man—but you don't know my mind, or you wouldn't have these doubts."

He cupped her buttocks in his hands and as she looked beseechingly into those mesmerizing blue eyes of his, Jess came to the revelation that in the short course of their relationship she had fallen in love with Doug McGuire. The how and why was confusing to her, but the reality was that it had happened.

And the incredible exhilaration of that reality struggled with the hopelessness of it.

"Dammit, I'm a sucker for that look." His hands moved up her back, drawing her closer. "I've never known a woman like you, Jess," Doug said in that husky tone of wonderment that often materialized in tender moments between them. "You scare the hell out of me, honey. There's so much about our being together that I don't understand. That scares me, too."

"You're shattering my trust in you, Detective," Jess said lightly, to try and push back the tears that threatened to slide out. *Please, God, don't let me break down like a sentimental fool.* "I didn't think anything could scare you."

"You do. You move effortlessly between our two worlds, Jess. You can fit into mine, but I don't belong in yours."

"My world? If Dennis Wolcott is an example of *my* world, Doug, maybe neither of us belongs there."

"It's not just Wolcott. That hundred-dollar perfume you wear scares me, real diamonds instead of rhinestones dangling from your ears scare me and those damn silk sheets scare the hell out of me."

"Silk sheets? Oh, come on now, Doug," she scoffed.

"Yeah, I'm afraid of dirtying the damn things."

"Doug," she groaned. He was so incredibly vulnerable for a tough guy.

She pressed her mouth against his neck and closed her eyes when she felt the strength of his arms tighten around her. Dare she tell him she loved him, or would that scare him even more? She no longer had any doubts about her feelings for him. She loved this man completely. Body and mind. Heart and soul. She loved him.

Raising her head, she looked him squarely in the eyes. "Enough talk. It's time for action. So what's it going to be?" she asked, slipping her arms around his neck. "Down and dirty right here, or a shower and those silk sheets? It's your call, McGuire."

Doug chuckled. "All right, lady, we'll go for the silk sheets. I guess with a little practice I could get used to them."

"Take all the practice you need, Detective McGuire." She grinned seductively. "I'm told practice makes perfect." She kissed him in a long, slow, deliciously arousing kiss that left them needing more. Much more.

Jess clung to him as he bolted to his feet. "I think we better hurry, Judge Jess, or it's gonna be too late for practice."

* * *

Doug had just begun to doze off when he thought he heard a door close in the living room. He opened his eyes. Jess was asleep beside him. He sat up and listened, but there was no further sound.

Just the same, he decided to check it out. There had been a series of robberies in the area lately, and even though the building was secure, he wasn't taking any chances. Besides, he knew the sound of a door closing when he heard it. He got out of bed, pulled on his jeans and grabbed his gun.

The center of the living room glowed in moonlight, but the corners were shrouded in darkness. Thick carpeting padded his footsteps as he slipped into the room. There was no sound except for the faint whir of the air conditioner. The sudden chime of a clock caused him to swing, gun in hand, in that direction.

After several more seconds he tripped the wall switch and several lamps illuminated the room. He shut the bedroom door and thoroughly checked the living room. The door was firmly closed with the deadbolt in place, but the chain was dangling. He opened the door. The hallway was empty, not that he'd expected an intruder to be hanging around.

The living room closet was empty except for a couple of winter coats, so he moved on into the dining room and then the kitchen and laundry room. After checking the broom closet, he did the same to the two closets in the den. Nothing appeared disturbed. The same was true of the guest bedroom and bathroom. He even looked under the bed.

Satisfied, he returned to the living room and pressed the intercom. Charlie answered sleepily.

"Charlie, this is McGuire. Anyone come in the last fifteen or twenty minutes?"

"Not through the front. A couple on the second floor drove in about fifteen minutes ago."

"Anything unusual about them?"

"Whatta ya mean?"

"Were they alone? Did they act normal?"

"Sure. I followed them on camera to their door. Nothing unusual. What's wrong?"

"Nothing, I guess. Thought I heard something earlier. You didn't doze off, did you?"

"Hell no!"

Yeah, right. "I guess I must have been dreaming. Go back to sleep, pal." Doug hung up.

It was time for him to leave anyway, but for his own peace of mind he checked out every nook and cranny in the apartment again, including Jess's bedroom this time. Then he finished dressing and woke her.

"I'm leaving, Angel Face."

"Don't tell me you've been called away again."

"No. I just think it's better if I go. Seeing my car parked in front two nights in a row might start your neighbors talking."

"Hang the neighbors," she said.

"When I leave, I want you to put the chain on the door."

"Why?"

"As long as you've got one, use it. There's been some robberies in this neighborhood." He didn't tell her about the noise or the fact he was edgy about her welfare since the murders.

"This building's secure, Doug."

"Honey, no building is secure if someone wants to get in badly enough."

"Thanks for those comforting words, Detective."

Despite her protests, he took her hand and pulled her out of bed. He gave her a long, hard kiss that was tempting enough to make him change his mind about leaving, but stepped out in the hallway and closed the door. Then he waited until he heard her slide the deadbolt and chain in place.

Doug stopped at Charlie's desk.

"I'm going downstairs and check out the garage before I leave."

"What in hell's going on, McGuire?"

"I heard a sound I didn't like. When that couple came home you said you followed them on camera. That means you weren't watching any of the other cameras, right?"

"Yeah, I guess so."

"Then someone on foot could have snuck in behind their car," Doug said. "Keep your eyes open, pal." He pressed the down button.

The elevator opened below into a small lobby. It had an exterior exit door, a stairway, a door opening into the garage and another locked door that Doug assumed was Charlie's living quarters.

There was no sign of a forced entry on the exit door, so Doug pulled his Glock and entered the garage. It was well lit. Jess's Park Avenue looked commonplace among the shiny Porsches, Cadillacs, Lincoln Continentals and Beamers parked there. He couldn't help grinning. His five-year-old Chevy Camero would look right at home. He tried the door handle on her car. It was locked and he moved on, keeping his gun pointed to the floor as he walked among the couple dozen parked cars. They all were locked and nothing seemed out of the ordinary.

What appeared to be a storage closet was secured with a padlock, and the overhead door and access door were firmly secured. He went back to the lobby and left the building by the exit door. It opened into a garden and backyard lawn. He waved to the security camera and went out the door, walked around the building and climbed into his car. Then he glanced back at the building. Dammit! Something just didn't feel right to him.

"To hell with what the neighbors think."

He climbed out of his car and Charlie buzzed him in. "Back so soon?"

"Just making sure my car wasn't stolen, pal."

"Who'd want it, McGuire?" Charlie called out as the elevator door closed.

Once upstairs, Doug rapped on Jessica's apartment. Within seconds she opened the door.

"Do you always open the door in the middle of the night?"

"Only to detectives who want to have sex with me," she said.

"Then we both just got lucky." He stepped inside. "All kidding aside, Jess, I wish you'd be more careful about whom you open your door to."

"Doug, I looked through the peephole and there you were—the man of my dreams. How come you came back? Did you forget something?"

"Talked to Charlie for a few minutes, and decided to stay. Would you rather I leave?"

"Yeah right," she said, in an imitation of him. She took his hand and led him into the bedroom. "Let's go to bed."

You came close to catching me, Detective. It was very careless of me to go to her apartment tonight, but I felt so lonely that I just wanted to see her. She always looks so peaceful when she's asleep. You're there too much. You're going to besmirch her reputation. At first I thought you were good for her, but now I see you're as harmful as the others who have hurt her.

You just care about the sex—using her for your own gratification.

I can't let you do that, Detective. Tonight was a close call. It won't be long before you figure it all out. I can't let you catch me. It would spoil everything.

Jess was a morning person and usually woke in good spirits. This morning was no exception. As soon as Doug left, she washed their coffee cups, and then dressed for work.

When her car failed to start, she took the setback in stride, called her favorite garage, and left the car key with Charlie. Then she telephoned Liz, and her secretary picked her up.

By the time Jess finished her morning cases, the mechanic had called and left word that they had to tow her car into the garage and rattled off several problems which were all Greek to Jess. The bottom line was that she'd be without transportation for a couple of days.

Jess's good spirits plunged until Doug called. Just hearing his voice was beginning to have that effect on her. Upon hearing the news about her car, he said he'd pick her up at five and drive her home.

Chapter 11

Promptly at five o'clock Jess stepped outside into blazing hot sunshine just as Doug drove up. The man was always punctual. He leaned across the car seat and opened the door.

"Hey, Judge, can I offer you a ride?"

"Is that your best offer, Detective?" she asked, climbing in.

"No, that's for the benefit of the press in case Ms. Matthews is lurking in the shadows with a zoom lens." He gave her a quick kiss and pulled out into traffic.

After a long day in court, Doug looked so good to her. He'd taken off his suit jacket, loosened his tie, and rolled up the sleeves of his white shirt. Of course he still wore the holster attached to his belt. Would she ever get used to seeing that gun strapped at his side?

"How about going to my place?" he asked.

"I thought you'd never ask, McGuire," Jess said, pleased. So the time had come to beard the lion in his den.

Doug guarded his privacy tenaciously, so the invitation

could not have been easy for him to make. All things being equal, the invitation to go home with him equated to inviting her home to meet his mother. And despite his appeal to women, she doubted he had exposed this privacy to many of his previous girlfriends.

Like it or not, Doug McGuire, we're becoming committed.

Jess smiled at the thought. She'd been independent for so long she'd forgotten how comforting it felt to have someone take over, make the decisions. And Doug was a takeover kind of guy, no matter how much he tried to please her. And strangely enough that contradiction pleased her, too.

Jess settled back and relaxed, enjoying the soothing intimacy of the car: the nearness of Doug, the mellow strains of a jazz saxophone from the tape player and the comforting feel of cool air on the scorching hot day.

Her gaze shifted to his hands on the wheel. He had great hands with long, tanned fingers. The touch of them comforted even as they excited. She followed the line of his bronzed forearms dusted with dark hair to where it disappeared under rolled shirtsleeves.

As if reading her thoughts, he reached over and wove his fingers through hers. "How come so quiet?"

"Enjoying the moment," she said.

Doug turned right on Wisconsin Avenue, passed Marquette University, and several blocks later pulled into the parking lot of a four-story, red-brick apartment building. The lobby was clean and well tended with mailboxes on each side. Doug paused to retrieve his mail consisting of several pieces of advertising that he immediately tossed into a trash can set in the corner.

They climbed the stairs to the second floor. Three apartment doors lined each side of the hallway. Doug's apartment was at the rear on the right.

There was no denying it was a bachelor's apartment,

and the kindest thing she could think of was at least it was clean. An air conditioner in the living room window kept the three-room apartment adequately cooled. The decor bordered on monastic. Several strategically placed end tables and lamps, several shelves of books, and a mammoth entertainment unit that monopolized one wall were the only luxuries. The color scheme was monochromatic: beige carpeting, beige drapes, a beige couch and chair set and a beige-colored leather chair.

Jess followed Doug into the kitchen. She wasn't surprised by what she saw. The kitchen held a small round table and two chairs. A Mr. Coffee machine and a microwave oven sat on the beige countertop.

"What would you like to drink?" he asked.

"A glass of wine if you have it."

"Sorry. Seagrams or a Miller?"

"I'll have the Miller. Just a glass, though."

He poured her a glass of beer, and then gave her a quick kiss on the cheek. "Make yourself comfortable while I change."

"That's supposed to be the woman's line, McGuire." She followed him into the bedroom.

"I need a quick shower. I was in some real sleazy dumps today," he said.

He stripped off his tie and shirt. "Feel free to do the same," he said, and sat down on the edge of the bed.

Mesmerized, Jess watched the ripple of his shoulder muscles as he removed his shoes and socks. It was turning her on. Her hands itched to trace her fingertips along the wide breadth of those powerful shoulders. Or was it just being in a bedroom with him? *His* bedroom. *His* bed. That was even a greater turn-on.

They needed some time to cool off and wind down before even thinking about having sex. *So why are you thinking about having sex?*

Jess took a gulp of the beer and turned away. She focused her thoughts on a blue and gold Marquette Warriors pennant on the wall.

"Marquette Warriors? I thought they're the Golden Eagles."

"They are now, but fifteen years ago when I graduated, we were called Marquette Warriors."

"So Marquette University is your alma mater."

"Yeah."

"Were you into athletics?"

"I warmed the basketball bench," he said, stripping down to his shorts. "My roommate was the real jock. That pennant's his. He left it behind."

"So the two of you roomed together after you graduated."

"Not after. We lived here while we went to school."

"You mean literally? In this very apartment?"

"Yep. Since I didn't intend to return to Illinois, I figured this apartment was as good of a place as any."

Jess almost choked on the beer she was sipping. "Doug, are you saying you've lived in this same apartment for almost twenty years?"

"Yeah. What's wrong with that?"

She glanced around at the furnishings. The room was as austere as the other room. "When are you planning to unpack?"

"What kind of crack is that?"

Doug McGuire with hands on hips would be quite a formidable challenge to any red-blooded, thirty-four-year-old woman such as herself, but facing her with hands on hips, dressed in boxer shorts, and his long powerful legs parted in an intimidating stance made concentration near to impossible. Jess swallowed hard. How could one man be so darn sexy!

"The place could use some dressing up, Doug. Other than your suits in the closet, there's nothing much here that says Doug McGuire lives here. Everything is so stark.

Don't you sometimes have the urge to look at something pretty?''

His grin was irresistible. "When I do, I look at you."

Damn him, he was the most reticent man she'd ever known, but when he wanted to be charming, he was lethal.

"I have everything I need. Why hold on to something useless?"

"You're right, McGuire. No one can ever accuse you of being a pack rat."

"Material things don't mean anything to me, Jess. I have a car and a Harley. What else does a man need?"

She would like to suggest a wife, children and a home in the country, but that wouldn't make them any more desirable to him.

"What are you saving your money for? I understand you homicide detectives make big bucks because of all the overtime you have to put in. You know you can't take it with you, Doug."

"I haven't thought about it. Retirement, I guess. If I don't make it to retirement, I've made the Peterson kids the beneficiaries of my savings account and life insurance. It'll come in handy for college."

He grabbed a clean pair of shorts out of a bureau drawer. "This won't take long."

Jess kicked off her pumps and tossed her purse and jacket on the bed, then she walked over to check out her appearance in a mirror that hung above the bureau. Shoved into one side of the mirror frame was a newspaper clipping. She gasped in surprise when she recognized it at once. It originally had been of her and Dennis taken two years earlier when they had announced their engagement, only Dennis's face had been carefully cut out of the picture so that only hers remained.

She tried unsuccessfully to conjure up a vision of Detective Doug McGuire clipping the picture out of the newspaper, unless at the time he intended to throw darts at it.

Or could it be he'd been as attracted to her back then as much as she'd been to him. That thought pleased her considerably more.

Jess strolled back into the living room and studied the book titles on the shelf. Most of them were reference books relating to crime solving, forensic science or analyzing the criminal mind. His taste in fiction ran to Clancy, Grisham, James Patterson and William Diehl. She glanced at his video selections. He hadn't exaggerated about liking old movies. There must have been over a hundred videos. John Wayne, Randolph Scott and Humphrey Bogart made up the majority of them. There wasn't a *Star Wars* or *Jurassic Park* among the lot. At least he wasn't a Walter Mitty dreamer.

Jess continued to sip the beer while she moved on and studied two framed pictures—the only decoration on either of the four walls.

One was Doug in a cap and gown standing between what clearly appeared to be his parents. His mother had dark hair and blue eyes. She looked diminutive beside the two tall men. Father and son were similar in height and features. The same trio was on the other picture, with the exception that this time his mother was dwarfed between Doug and his father, who was wearing a police chief's uniform.

"That was taken when my father was promoted to Chief," Doug said, suddenly behind her. He slipped his arms around her waist and pulled her back against him. He smelled wonderful—the seductive combination of bay and man.

"They're a very handsome couple. You and your father are real look-alikes."

"Yeah." He nuzzled her neck, planted a provocative kiss in its hollow that sent a shock up her spine, bounced off her brain and sped directly to the source of her sex. Then he went into the kitchen and popped a can of beer.

Was he toying with her, or just playing house? Either one, she liked it.

"So what about dinner?" he asked, returning to the room. "In or out?"

"How about in?"

"You've got it." He picked up the telephone. "Pizza or Chinese?"

"I meant I'd cook it."

He replaced the phone on the hook. "You cook?"

"Wipe that skeptical look off your face, McGuire. Of course I cook. My father owns a restaurant, doesn't he?" Like her dad had ever let her even boil water in it.

"Does he?"

"Oh, didn't I mention that?"

"No. Where is it?"

"The Water Street Bistro."

He looked at her astounded. "Your father owns that fancy place? No, Jessica, you didn't mention it."

"What's in the fridge?" she asked, quickly changing the subject before he could say more.

Jess opened the refrigerator door. Other than cans of Miller Beer, there were a half dozen eggs, an unopened package of bacon, an opened jar of pickles and another jar containing a single hot pepper floating in the brine. There was also a hunk of mold-covered cheese wrapped in waxed paper. What there wasn't was a single piece of fresh fruit or vegetable. Bacon and eggs would have to do.

Jess pulled out the egg carton. "Doug, when was the last time you ate one of these eggs?"

He was leaning against the doorjamb with his arms folded across his chest. "I can't remember. Seems like a while ago."

"I hope so, because they expired three months ago." She dumped the eggs down the garbage disposal, and tossed the carton into the trashcan. A closer inspection of the unopened package of bacon revealed that mold had started to form on the bacon strips. The package met the same fate as the egg carton. So much for bacon and eggs.

"Pizza or Chinese?" he repeated, with a cocky smile.

Jess gave him a disgusted look, and checked out the freezer. "Aha!" she exclaimed, at the sight of several frozen dinners. She handed him the trashcan. "Get rid of this before it starts smelling up the kitchen, then sit down and watch television, or whatever you do. Dinner will be ready shortly." She shoved him out of the kitchen.

As soon as the oven preheated, Jess popped in two chicken potpies and set the timer. While she waited for them to bake, she checked out the cupboards. She couldn't find a tablecloth, but much to her amazement there were two candles and holders in the back of one of the kitchen drawers. At least they would add a feminine touch.

Surprisingly enough she found a set of china in one of the cabinets, and in another she found a box of Wheaties. What value they were to him, since there was no milk, was a mystery to her.

The cabinet also contained a can of coffee, packages of microwave popcorn, several cans of Campbell's tomato soup, and a box of Triscuits. Every little bit helped.

By the time she had finished setting the table, heating a can of tomato soup and letting Mr. Coffee do its thing, the potpies were almost through baking and Doug had not returned from taking out the garbage.

Just as the timer went off, he came in and handed her a paper bag. "This is the best I could do at the neighborhood store." The bag contained a bottle of wine and a box of Oreo cookies.

"This is wonderful!" she exclaimed. He raised the arm he'd been holding behind him and handed her a small bunch of violets.

"I picked them from Mrs. Murphy's garden."

"Oh, Doug, how sweet. Thank you." It was too good an opportunity to let pass; she gave him a long, drugging kiss that came close to canceling out the dinner plans. Breathless, she broke it off.

"You open the wine while I put dinner on."

Jess put the flowers in a water glass and set it in the center of the table. She lit the candles, and as soon as Doug opened the wine and filled their glasses they sat down and ate their meal of canned tomato soup served with Triscuits, frozen chicken potpies and a dessert of Oreo cookies served with cups of black coffee.

It was the most romantic meal she had ever eaten.

Later as he dried the dishes beside her, Jess's curiosity got the better of her. "Who gave you the candles? I know you didn't buy them because they're white, not beige."

"A couple of years ago I was laid up and my mom came and nursed me for a week. Mom bought the candles and some plants to dress up the place."

"What ever happened to the plants?"

"They died a couple weeks after she left. I guess they missed her talking to them."

"I suspect it was more likely from lack of watering."

"You've got that right." He chuckled. "You've really got my number, don't you, Judge Jess?"

Laughing, she looked at him. "And *you've* got that right, Detective."

Gee, it felt good to be in love.

Chapter 12

After dinner, Jess rejected Doug's idea that they go out to a movie, and suggested instead that they stay there and watch one of his.

"Fine with me," he said. "Any one in particular?"

"No, just as long as it's not cowboys and Indians." She was in too mellow a mood for a lot of shooting and yelping.

"How about *Casablanca?* That's my favorite."

Jess hadn't seen it in years, so she agreed. Halfway through the movie, Doug put a package of popcorn in the microwave, and they munched popcorn and finished the bottle of wine as they watched the rest of the video.

"So that's one of your favorite movies," she said when it was over.

Doug nodded. "All-time favorite."

"I'm surprised."

"Why does that surprise you?" He stretched out on the couch and put his head in her lap.

"Because it's a romantic movie," she said, and began

to gently brush his hair with her fingers. "I would have thought you'd prefer something more action-filled."

"Romantic? How do you figure? Bogart doesn't even get Bergman in the end. The movie's about how war affects people's lives. Different characters with different agendas are all brought together in Rick's Café."

"So what's your favorite scene?"

"The one in Rick's Café when he tells Sam to play his and Ilsa's favorite song. And as he's slugging down straight shots, he mumbles that classic line, 'Of all the gin joints in all the towns in all the world, she walks into mine.' There was a man in real torment. No one could have played that scene like Bogie."

"'As Time Goes By,'" Jess said. "That's the name of the song that Sam sang."

"Yeah, I know. Great song. My favorite."

"I suppose you're going to try and tell me the song isn't romantic, either."

He sat up. "Just because the song's romantic, doesn't mean the movie is." He quickly shifted gears. "So what scene do you like the most? I bet it's the one at the airport when Rick says, 'Here's looking at you, kid,'" Doug quoted in a Bogie imitation.

"Wrong, McGuire. I admit I always get goose bumps in the scene where all the French people stand up and sing 'La Marseillaise' in order to drown out the Germans singing their own national anthem, but my favorite part in the movie is the very end scene when Bogart and the French Prefect of Police—"

"Claude Rains," he interjected.

"When Bogart and Claude Rains walk off together and Rick comments to Louie that he thinks it's the beginning of a beautiful friendship. You get the feeling that despite all the trouble they're in, and all the obstacles they'll have to overcome, the two of them will make it." She nibbled at his ear. "So it's your favorite, huh?"

"Yeah. All-time favorite movie."

"I meant the song." She started to croon softly in his ear, "You must remember this, a kiss is just a kiss—"

His mouth cut off her words as he eased her gently back until she was stretched out on the couch. Then he proceeded to demonstrate how a kiss is not just *any* kiss.

Sensation spiraled to every nerve in her body, and she responded with all the fervor of her own passion when she felt the excitement of arousal surge through her.

He broke the kiss reluctantly. "Dammit!" He started to get up. "I'll be right back. I need a con—"

She grabbed his arm. "I went back on the pill, Doug."

"But what about—"

"Dennis was the only man I was ever with, and we always used protection. Just the same, I had myself tested after our breakup. What about you?"

"Same with me. I know I'm clean."

"Then why—"

"Oh, God, Jess." His hands were warm and caressing as he cupped her cheeks between them. "I've never known a woman like you, Jess." He kissed her with a devouring intensity until breathlessness forced them apart.

For the first time in their relationship, worship gleamed in his eyes as he gazed down at her. Her heart felt near to bursting, she was so filled with love for him.

The moment was so emotional that she knew she had to keep it light or burst into tears. She slipped her arms around his neck and wove her fingers into his hair.

His mouth claimed her again and the kiss deepened, their tongues teased. Slipping her hands under his shirt, she sought the divine feel of his chest at her fingertips. She stroked it, savoring the sensation.

A shiver of anticipation rippled her spine when his fingers worked the buttons on her blouse. Then parting it, he released the front closure of her brassiere and shoved the blouse and bra off her shoulders. They bunched beneath her when he lowered her back down. Sliding his hands under her, he gently nudged her hips up and slid her skirt and panties off her.

She'd been waiting—wanting—this moment from the instant they stepped into his apartment. Now, consumed by her love and desire for him, her body trembled for more of his touch.

The nipples of her breasts hardened to peaks under the sweep of his sensuous gaze, and then he lowered his head and his mouth and tongue played havoc with hers as his hands caressed the length of her and settled against the throbbing core of her sex.

And then he began the sweet massage.

Her body flooded in a tide of sensation, drowning her in the exquisite mindlessness of an arousal that scaled the point of no return. She swirled in an eddy of wanton lust, crying out his name and begging him not to stop.

"'Woman needs man, and man must have his mate,' don't they, Jess?" he murmured.

He stood up and stripped off his clothes, and then the sublime warmth of his body was on hers, his flesh bared to her hands and mouth. Now she could touch him, kiss him, palm the throbbing evidence of his need for her—her need for him.

As always their mutual passions exploded in an uninhibited exploration of each other that the limited space permitted, until their minds and bodies combined in that erotic dance of lovers to the music of the rhythm of their pounding hearts and the words of their gasps of pleasure and groans of ecstasy that ended in the divine rapture of release.

And for the first time in her life, Jess felt fulfillment as a woman when the man she loved filled her with the hot nectar of their union.

For a long moment she lay cocooned in the dormant

power of Doug's arms and body. The pure male scent of him filled her nostrils, his ragged breaths her ears.

When finally her own breath was restored enough to speak, she asked, "Am I, Doug?"

He raised his head. "Are you what?" His eyes still burned with the passion of their lovemaking.

"Your mate."

"That's what the song says, doesn't it?"

"Forget the song. I'm asking what Doug says."

For the longest moment he stared at her with a tenderness she had never seen in his eyes before. Her heart did flip-flops waiting for him to speak, hoping he'd say the words she longed to hear from him.

Then he stood up, pulled on his clothes, and walked over and shut off the television. When he turned around to face her, the enigmatic expression had returned to his eyes.

"Doug says it's time he takes you home."

Jess sat up and started to dress. "Sounds like you're anxious to get rid of me."

"You know better than that."

"Then what's the hurry? It's not *that* late."

"You know as well as I that if you stay we'll end up in bed."

"Does that bother you?"

"It does."

He went into the bedroom and came back with her purse, shoes and jacket. He handed them to her and then went to the door and opened it. "Ready?"

Would she ever understand this man? They had just spent an intimate evening together that had ended with incredible sex, and now he was dismissing her like she was a whore he'd rented for the evening. She felt cheap, unclean—and confused. Was this how he really viewed her?

Jess stood up and brushed past him on her way out. They didn't speak again until he pulled into the parking lot of her apartment. Then he shut off the motor and shifted in the seat to face her.

"So you're angry."

She regretted he couldn't see her glare in the darkened car. "Confused," she replied.

"About what?"

"I guess I was naive enough to believe there was a little more between us than just sex."

"Of course there is. I think you're an incredible woman, Jess—in or out of bed."

"Then why treat me like I'm a hooker."

"Is this a joke?"

"Do you see me laughing?" she snapped.

"Dammit, Jess, I wanted you to leave because I feel you're too classy to have to sneak out of my place at dawn."

"Isn't that what *you* do when you come to mine?"

"Wrong. I don't have to sneak. Charlie and I have an unspoken understanding. He keeps his mouth shut, and I don't rearrange his face."

"Damn you, Doug!" she cried, unable to hold back her anger. "Are you really as tough as you'd like me to believe?"

His tone was intense. "Tip of the iceberg. Don't fool yourself into believing otherwise, Judge Jess."

It was senseless to continue. She was getting nowhere with him, and the conversation was developing quickly into an all-out argument.

"Perhaps so. I'd like to believe otherwise. Good night, Doug." Jess reached for the door handle.

His hand closed on her shoulder and pulled her back. He kissed her before she could utter a protest.

"Whether you believe it or not, I want to go upstairs with you, Jess."

"All right, I believe you."

His cell phone went off, and for the length of their

drawn sighs of frustration, he stared at her. Then he reached for it. She knew what that meant.

Jess got out of the car and as she entered the building she glanced back. He was still parked. She stopped and said a few words to Charlie and moved on.

She had no sooner entered her apartment then the telephone rang. She wondered who would be calling at this time of night, and hoped it wasn't Liz phoning to tell her she wouldn't be in the office tomorrow.

"Did you put the chain on the door?"

"Doug! Where are you?"

"Still in the parking lot. That call was from the precinct. I have to go in."

"I never doubted that for a moment."

"Well, did you put on the chain?"

Jess glanced over at the dangling chain. "Ah…"

"Jess, go over and chain the door," he said in a firm tone. "I'll wait."

She went to the door and slid the chain in place, then returned to the telephone. "All right, it's done. How did I ever get along without you, McGuire?"

"When I figure that out, you'll be the first to know. I'll pick you up at eight-thirty in the morning. Until then, be good."

"I try to be."

"Oh, you are, Angel Face. You are so-o-o good. Good night."

"Good night." The phone clicked in her ear.

Smiling, she replaced the phone on the cradle. *You care. You're such a fraud, McGuire. No matter how much you pretend to the contrary, you care about me.*

"Just be patient, Jessica. All you need is a little patience, gal," she assured herself later as she luxuriated in a bubble bath.

Jess was still smiling when she climbed into bed.

* * *

The next morning the smile reappeared when Doug drove up promptly at eight-thirty.

"Good morning, Doug. I'm sorry to be such a bother to you," she said, climbing into the car.

"You are that, Angel Face. You've bothered me since the first time I saw you. Fasten your seat belt."

"You look tired. Did you get any sleep last night?"

"Don't ask." He looked askance at her. "You must have. Do you always look this good in the mornings?"

"If you'd ever manage to hang around long enough in the morning, you could judge for yourself."

She sat back and relaxed as he wove through the morning traffic with his usual competence. Was there anything he didn't do well—that is other than ignoring the letter of the law in the execution of his duties? Of course, come to think of it, he *did* do that well.

"What are you grinning about?"

"Oh, am I grinning? I didn't realize it." She looked out the window and began to hum "As Time Goes By."

"If I can get away, how about taking in Summerfest? Tonight's the opening night."

"Do you know I've never been to Summerfest? I've seen the fireworks from my apartment, but I've actually never attended."

He drew back in surprise. "Hmmm, that sounds like a felony, Your Honor, or at least a misdemeanor. After all, Milwaukee's Summerfest is the largest music festival in these United States."

"So I've heard. Are you moonlighting as a hawker for it, McGuire?"

"Shucks, ma'am. No one can pull anything over on you." He grinned. "Actually, Neil Diamond's performing at the Amphitheater tonight. It's sold out, but one of the guys had tickets for tonight, and his wife delivered prematurely this morning, so he offered them to me. So what about it?"

"Wonderful. I love Neil Diamond."

"Good." He pulled up in front of the courthouse. "Barring anything unexpected, I'll pick you up right here at five, get you home so you can change and we'll get an early start. There's a lot to see for anyone who's never been there before."

Doug waited and watched as she climbed the stairs and entered the building, then he pulled out and headed for the precinct.

After he'd left her last night, he'd done a lot of thinking about Jess—in between chasing false leads in the middle of the night with Vic. He and Jess had been seeing each other now for almost two weeks. When it began, he'd figured that after a couple of tumbles in the sack the affair would burn out. But that hadn't happened. They had either talked on the phone or been together every day since then.

The funny thing was that he really liked her. He'd be plumb crazy to give her up. He liked the way she could laugh at herself, the way that laughter carried to her eyes, the scent of that hundred-dollar perfume she wore. He liked waking up and seeing her sleeping beside him, or sitting across a table eating frozen dinners even if she insisted upon candlelight for a feminine touch.

He even liked driving her to work and taking her home at night as if they were…*as if they were a married couple.*

But what was there not to like about Jess except maybe that "letter of the law" attitude of hers—but having gotten to know her, he now understood she was doing what she believed was proper.

He'd never felt this way about any other woman. Last night that realization had hit him hard. He hadn't wanted Jess to leave his place—to go back to that fancy palace she lived in. He'd wanted her to stay with him. Sleep in his bed.

The hardest thing he'd ever done was making her leave

knowing how much she wanted to stay. But he had to prove something to himself—he could do it if he had to.

Because—sure as God made little green apples—that day would come when he would have to.

Chapter 13

When Doug returned to the squad room Vic was on the telephone. He went over to his desk, sat down and glanced desolately at the stacked pile of printouts. He and Vic were no closer to solving these murders than when they had started.

Vic hung up. ''Well, so much for that lead. Let's get out of here and ring some more doorbells. Maybe we'll get lucky.''

After lunch Doug and Vic were due in court to testify in an earlier case, but this time it wasn't in Jess's court. In the course of a robbery of a service station, Roger Bolton, the station attendant, had been shot to death. Doug and Vic had been the homicide detectives called to the scene. After some extensive investigation, they had found the culprit.

Dennis Wolcott was the defense attorney and was trying to get his client a lighter charge of involuntary manslaughter instead of intentional homicide. During the examination he came at Vic like Perry Mason in an effort to convince the jury that the defendant's only intention had been to rob the service station, not kill the attendant.

Doug remained unflappable when it was his turn to testify, calmly repeating the time the detectives arrived on the scene, the condition of the victim and his own observations of the crime scene. Wolcott attacked him in an effort to cross him up.

"Isn't it true, Detective McGuire, that according to the medical examiner's report the bullet that *actually* killed Roger Bolton ricocheted off the cash register and then struck him in the head, killing him instantly."

"That's what I've been told."

"Then speaking from your professional experience as a homicide detective you would have to concur, Detective McGuire, that Mr. Bolton's death was accidental."

"The victim was shot four times. You may call it accidental, Mr. Wolcott...I call it overkill."

Flushed with anger, Wolcott turned to the bench. "Your Honor, I request that last statement be stricken from the record."

Later as Doug picked up Jess, Wolcott came up to the car. "You're looking lovely, Jessica."

"Thank you, Dennis."

"Apparently slumming agrees with you. I'm surprised to see that the two of you are still playing footsie. I'd have thought the novelty would have worn off by now." He looked at Doug. "You were quite impressive in court today, McGuire."

"Sorry I can't return the compliment, Wolcott."

Doug turned on the ignition and drove away. "How could you get mixed up with that prick, Jess?"

"I really don't know. Naive, I guess. I was young—had never been in a serious relationship with a man before. My career had monopolized all my time and interests for years.

I met Dennis when I was working as an assistant D.A. He was charming and persuasive. He kind of swept me off my feet. Overwhelmed me, you might say.''

"For seven years?"

"Habit, I guess. Or maybe I used him as a safety net to keep me from getting entangled with any other man.''

"Such as?"

"Sexy detectives who came into my court.''

"Didn't work, did it, Angel Face?" They grinned at each other, and then he squeezed her hand.

Doug had had the foresight to take a change of clothing to the precinct and had already changed into jeans, T-shirt and sneakers. He chatted with Charlie while Jess went upstairs and put on a pair of jeans and her Robin Yount shirt.

By the time they arrived—the gates of Summerfest had been opened since before noon—the after-work crowd had begun to pour in for the Big Bang, the opening day fireworks display scheduled for later that evening.

The festival offered everything from a twenty-ride amusement park for children to an amphitheater that seated twenty-four thousand.

They rode the Sky View that gave her a bird's-eye view of the whole layout, then hand in hand they strolled along from venue to venue where famous musical entertainers from the past and present performed daily on over a dozen open stages, offering everything from jazz to rock and roll.

Doug was drawn to a stage where several popular athletes from the Milwaukee Bucks, the Brewers and the Green Bay Packers were giving sports demonstrations to youngsters.

They decided to eat in courses, but Jess was at a loss what to select first. It was an ethnic delight with over forty of the city's most popular restaurants offering everything from Thai fried squid to American hot dogs, Greek gyros to Tuscany bread, Italian prepared pasta to delectable French desserts.

They sat down and while they listened to the sound of jazz coming from a nearby stage, Jess ate a fresh fruit salad, and Doug settled for a beer. When they finished, once again, he reached for her hand and they moved on into one of the marketplaces.

Jess couldn't resist stopping at a vendor selling paste-on tattoos. She picked out chains of hearts and pasted them around the biceps of Doug's arms. In return, he had a rose painted on her cheek.

They halted their strolling and ate the next course. Doug bought barbecue ribs for himself, while Jess opted for Viennese chicken. This time they were entertained by Ringo Starr and his All Star Band.

In the next marketplace while Doug studied a large poster of a Harley Davidson motorcycle, Jess bought him a Harley bandanna. She tied the bandanna around his neck and stepped back to admire it. "You look marvelous," she said, pleased with the result. "George Clooney, you're toast."

They finally capped off their meal with dessert. Deciding to split their choices, Jess fed him some of her chocolate-covered strawberries, and he gave her bites of his cheesecake.

By this time, Jess was exhausted and as she sat enjoying a glass of iced cappuccino, Doug excused himself and came back shortly and handed her a small bag.

"I love surprises! What is it?" Jess asked.

"Open it and find out."

She grinned at him and opened the bag. Inside was a Mickey Mouse watch. "Oh, Doug, I love it."

Jess quickly removed the expensive Gucci watch she had on, and showed it into the pocket of her jeans.

"Hey, what are you doing?" he asked. "You might lose that."

"So what?" Her gaze held his and she said softly, "If a babe cares enough about the guy who gave her a Mickey

Mouse watch, it's more valuable to her than any Gucci watch.''

She could tell by his expression that he knew she was referring to the story he'd told her about the diamond earrings. For a long moment their gazes were locked. She yearned to tell him she loved him, and prayed he'd say it to her first.

"You're no babe, Jess. You couldn't be if you tried. Right now, I want to kiss you so badly I ache."

"Then what's stopping you?" she asked.

"I'm afraid if I started, I wouldn't be able to stop."

"Well, if this isn't a cozy sight."

Startled, they both looked up to discover Sherilyn Matthews and her ever-present microphone and cameraman. "Bernie, look what I've found—Law and Order Doing Summerfest," she said. "What a great lead-in for tonight's late news." She nodded to the cameraman and he turned on the camera, spotlighting them in blinding light.

"Tell us, Judge Kirkland, what is your impression of the festival?"

"It's truly remarkable. As usual the Summerfest directors have done Milwaukee proud."

"And your impression, Detective McGuire?" Sherilyn asked, shifting the microphone in his direction.

"Ditto," Doug replied.

"Not to change the subject, Detective McGuire, but since you and your partner are the investigating detectives on the 'Rollin' On the River' murders, could you tell the viewing audience if you're near to solving the crimes."

"I'd like to, Ms. Matthews, but then I'd be telling the killer, too, wouldn't I?"

For the barest of seconds anger flashed in her eyes, then she smiled into the camera. "Just two of the many thousands of people who are enjoying this opening night of Summerfest. Thank you," she said. Then Sherilyn Matthews, her microphone and cameraman moved on.

Jess glanced at Doug. He didn't say anything, but his enigmatic expression followed the reporter.

"Well, according to my brand-new Mickey Mouse watch, Detective, if we intend to see that show, we'd better get moving."

Jess thoroughly enjoyed the Neil Diamond concert. She had the biggest surprise of her life when they left the amphitheater and she saw that thousands more people had arrived while they were attending the concert.

The grass was completely covered with shoulder-to-shoulder spectators waiting for the fireworks to start. Doug found space for them to sit down in a spot as far from the crowd as possible.

"Tired?" Doug asked when Jess yawned.

She nodded. "It's been a long day. How do you keep going? You've been up all night."

"Lean back against me." He spread his legs apart and drew her between them. She leaned back against him, and his arms closed around her.

"I'm really having a good time tonight, Doug."

"I am, too."

"I enjoy being with you."

His arms tightened. "Same goes for me."

"You know we still have time to get back to my apartment before the Big Bang begins."

He nuzzled her ear. "I love it when you talk dirty, Judge Jess."

"I was referring to the fireworks exhibition, McGuire. We can watch it perfectly in comfortable chairs on my terrace."

"Yeah, but you'd miss the crowd's ohs and ahs."

"Trust me, Doug. I wouldn't *miss* them."

He lifted up her wrist to read her watch. "Well, if we're going to do it, we better get moving."

He stood up and just as he reached out a hand to pull

her to her feet, two young boys ran up to the couple sitting next to them.

"Daddy, Mom, we saw a dead man in the water."

Doug dropped his hand and looked at the boys. "What did you say?"

"My brother and I saw a dead man in the water, mister," the eldest one said.

"I'm with the police department. Will you show me where you saw him?"

"Sure."

"Jess, you stay here." Doug hurried away with the two boys.

Jess had intended to do what he said until the couple followed them, so she did, too. By the time they reached the spot where the boys were pointing, Doug had started to climb down on the water-slick rocks. The area was in darkness but she was able to make out a dark outline at the water's edge.

Shortly after, he climbed back up. "It's a body all right. I'm going to need some help in getting him out of the water." He asked the boys' father to get a couple of security people.

While they waited, Doug called Vic on the cell phone, gave him the details, and told him to contact the necessary departments, then get over there as soon as possible.

By the time he hung up, the man had returned with two security guards. Doug came over to Jess and handed her his wallet, badge, gun and cell phone. She felt numb and she clutched the items against her and watched Doug and the other two men climb back down the treacherous rocks. Between the three of them, they managed to get the dead man out of the water and haul him up the rocks. They laid the body on the ground and Doug came over and retrieved his belongings from her.

By now, the scene had attracted the attention of the nearby crowd. Many began to come over. Several more security men arrived and started to push back the swarming crowd.

"Keep those people back," Doug ordered, returning to the corpse. "I don't want this site contaminated any more than it has been already."

At that instant the night reverberated with the whistle of roman candles streaking skyward and bursting with deafening boom into a myriad of color.

"What happened?" a multitude of voices inquired around Jess.

"Someone got hurt, I guess," others replied.

Jess covered her ears to muffle these sounds from the curious who crowded in around her. The pyrotechnic display in the sky overhead cast the ground below in an ever-changing kaleidoscope of color. The heat from the pressing crowd became suffocating. The sound overhead shattering. The smell of sulfur from the exploding fireworks stung her nostrils.

She felt as if she were in the midst of a surreal nightmare as she stared, horrified, at the body lying on the ground.

The dead man's hands were tied behind his back, his head and face swathed in plastic.

Chapter 14

More security guards arrived along with some M.P.D. Doug ordered them to get the crowd back and string up some crime scene tape. And as they did so, in a bizarre contrast, thousands of other people continued to cheer the fireworks overhead, unaware of the drama being enacted just a short distance away.

Doug came over to Jess and put his arm around her shoulders. "Jess, in a few minutes this spot's going to be crawling with activity. I'll be tied up here for awhile."

"I don't mind waiting, Doug."

"No. You can take my car. One of the police officers will escort you to it." He handed her his car keys. "Park it at your place and leave the keys in the glove compartment. I have a spare key in my wallet." He looked at her longingly. "I'm sorry, Jess. This sure isn't how I planned to end the evening. I'll call you in the morning."

He nodded to a nearby uniform policeman and the officer came over. "Ready, ma'am?" Jess nodded.

For a moment Doug watched as the patrolman led her

away. She was the most incredible woman he'd ever known. The whole evening had been magical. That's exactly what it had been—an enchanting illusion. He should have known it couldn't last.

He turned and went back to the real world of Doug McGuire.

He was in the process of getting the names and addresses of the two young boys who discovered the body when Vic and the crime scene investigators arrived. The situation was made considerably more workable when the fireworks ended and the police routed the exiting crowd away from the crime scene. The Summerfest crew had rigged up floodlights to aid the investigation by the time the CSI crew removed the plastic from the victim's head.

"Recognize him?" Doug asked when he and Vic hunched down and studied the face of the corpse.

"No. I've never seen him before. At least he wasn't one of our cases."

"He is now," Doug said grimly. "So what can you tell us?" he asked the woman from the medical examiner's office.

"Victim's a male Caucasian. Looks about mid-forties. No bleeding or entry wounds. Ligature marks around neck and petechial hemorrhaging on eyelids would indicate death by strangulation."

She looked up and smirked. "He's stiffer than a board, so it's either rigor mortis or he's frozen. There's no body decomposition, but the water temperature is only forty-five degrees so that would delay it. Death could have occurred anywhere from four hours to four days ago. My guess is he's been in the water for a couple days, but I'll know more—"

"When you get him in the lab," Doug said. "Yeah, we know the drill."

"What do you guys expect? You want me to find the perp for you?"

While one guy from CSI was taking pictures, another one came over and took prints and hair samples of Doug and the two security guards who helped pull the victim out of the water.

"You guys aren't supposed to touch the victim until we do our thing," he grumbled, yanking at several of Doug's hairs, folding them up in paper, and squeezing them into a pill box. "Now the hair and prints of you guys are probably all over the victim."

"We'll be glad to shove him back into the water, if you feel like a swim," Doug declared.

Vic put on gloves and riffled gingerly through the contents of the victim's wallet. "Name's Marcus Sands according to his driver's license. Lives in a pretty fair neighborhood, and he's got a couple hundred dollars in his wallet." Doug wrote down the address and Vic handed the wallet over to CSI.

"Let's split, partner," Doug said. "Nothing more we can do here…unless we collar the two kids as suspects," he added, cynically. "As soon as they run his prints, we'll see if he's got a record."

On the way back to the precinct Vic dropped Doug off at Jess's condominium to pick up his car. Before pulling out, Doug dialed Jess on his cell phone. Just the sound of her "hello" was a pick-me-up for him.

"Just calling to say good night."

"I'm glad you did, Doug." He could visualize her smile, and the way it would light up her eyes. "How are things going?"

"We're all finished at the lake."

"Where are you now?"

"Downstairs in my car."

"Are you coming up?" Her voice held a velvet huskiness that made him want to forget all about dead bodies floating in rivers and lakes. Oh, God, how he wanted to just curl around her and never let go.

"Can't. I'm on my way back to the precinct. I've got to get going."

"I understand. Good night, Doug. And try and get some sleep."

"Yeah, right. Good night, Angel Face."

He hung up and pulled out of the parking lot.

As soon as Doug drove away, a figure moved stealthily out of the bushes.

So they finally found our friend, Mr. Sands. He's been dead for the past two days. I was afraid that maybe his body had drifted out of the breakwater and sank. That would have spoiled the fun.

As it was, it worked out well after all. A real send-off for Summerfest, wouldn't you say? And McGuire right there when the body was discovered. What a treat. I couldn't have planned it better if I'd tried.

I watched you a lot tonight. You and McGuire were really having a good time together. I can see how much you love him, Jessica, and for your sake I hope I don't have to kill him. But my hands are tied—or maybe I should say his will be—if he doesn't leave me alone.

I'll be going back to using the river. Besides, I like the term the "Rollin' On the River Murders." Sherilyn Matthews coined the phrase using the words from the chorus of that old "Proud Mary" song. You remember it, don't you, Jessica? I know you don't like Miss Matthews, but you have to admit it's kind of funny.

The figure sashayed away singing " "Rollin', rollin', rollin' on the river. Rollin', rollin', rollin' on the river." " Then broke into laughter.

By the time Doug walked into the precinct, Vic had already run a search on Marcus Sands.

"No rap sheet. *Nada.* Nil. Zilch. We'll have to wait for the prints. Maybe we can get a match."

"Sands is probably an alias," Doug said. "Up to now Crusader Rabbit's only hit murderers who've walked. I figure Sands must be a member of that fraternity."

"Well, if he is, he didn't look familiar to me."

"Pretty hard to get a good look at him in the dark. Let's check out his place and see what we can dig up."

"If he didn't live alone we'll need a warrant, partner," Vic said. "You wouldn't want to upset your girlfriend."

"So we'll break the news to whoever lives with him, and get invited in." Doug replied, and headed for the parking lot.

Marcus Sands lived in an apartment building near the campus of Milwaukee's University of Wisconsin. The superintendent's name was Attwater, and he didn't appreciate being awakened at such a late hour.

They flashed their badges, and then Vic said, "Mr. Attwater, we understand you have a tenant named Marcus Sands."

"That's right. Apartment 108 at the rear. Did something happen to him?"

"Why do you ask?" Doug said.

"Ain't seen him around for a couple of days, and his newspapers are piling up in front of his door. Ain't like him to let that happen."

"So I gather Mr. Sands lives alone," Vic said.

"Yep."

Doug decided he'd let Vic do all the questioning. Vic had the patience for it.

"Any girlfriend or anyone come to visit him on a regular basis?"

"How would I know? I've got forty-eight apartments here. I don't pry into the personal business of any one of my tenants."

"How long has Sands lived here?"

"About five years," Attwater said.

"Has he had any previous trouble with the police?"

"Ain't you the police? You ought to know better than me. He's a good tenant. Don't cause no trouble, minds his own business, pays his rent on time and he don't bring in women at night. You gonna tell me why you're asking all these questions?"

"Mr. Sands's body was found floating in Lake Michigan tonight."

Attwater's eyes almost popped out of his head. "You mean he drowned?"

"We don't have the coroner's report yet," Vic said. "Do you know the name of his closest relative, or someone to contact in the event of an emergency?"

"Ain't got a clue." Attwater's eyes gleamed with curiosity. "Does it look like he was bumped off like one of them 'Rollin' On the River' murders?"

"Why do you ask? Did you see him talking to anyone suspicious lately?" Doug asked, impatiently.

"No. I told you he stayed to himself. Didn't talk to nobody. It was foul play, wasn't it?"

"Where did he work?" Vic asked, patiently continuing on with routine questioning.

"I don't think he had a job."

"Then how did he support himself?"

"I told you, I don't pry into—"

"Cut that crap, Attwater," Doug burst in, unable to restrain himself. "You probably know what every one of these tenants eats for breakfast and how many times a day they take a leak. Now quit trying to jerk us around, and start giving us some straight answers."

"He gets some kind of a check each month. Trust fund or something like that."

"Who from?"

"I don't know." His glance swung to Doug. "I swear. I don't know."

"Does he own a vehicle?"

"If he does, he don't park it here."

"All right," Vic said. "We want to take a look in his apartment now."

"You got a search warrant?"

"We don't need a warrant as long as Mr. Sands lived alone," Vic explained.

"Are you sure about that?"

"Open the damn door!" Doug declared, exasperated. He strode down the hallway.

Attwater grabbed a chain of keys hanging from his wall. "I was only trying to cover my butt. What's he so all fired up about?"

"Hemorrhoids," Vic said aside, in a confidential tone.

Attwater nodded. "Oh, yeah. That'll do it every time. Especially in this heat."

Sands's apartment was as tidy as a model house. There wasn't a book out of place or a spot of dust on the furniture. His suits and shirts were hung neatly together by color: blues, grays, browns. The white shirts were on their own. Corresponding shoes sat on the floor beneath each grouping.

The bureau drawers were the same. All his underclothes were in neat little piles. One of the drawers was even partitioned for socks and marked with paste-on tags to identify what color belonged in them. The same grouping and tags applied to the bathroom towels and bed sheets in the linen closet.

There were a few routine over-the-counter drugs in the medicine cabinet, but no prescription drugs.

"This guy was a freak!" Drug grumbled, after moving on to a search of the desk drawers. There wasn't a piece of paper or pencil out of place.

Vic came out of the kitchen. "You won't believe this

guy, McGuire, all the food on the pantry shelves is arranged alphabetically.''

"By product or producer?'' Doug asked. He continued on with the search of the desk. He found the name and address of a New York fiduciary handling a trust account payable to Sands, some rent and utility bills and monthly statements for the rental of a storage locker. All had been paid by cash.

Doug was puzzled by the fact that Sands had no telephone or answering machine, so he either communicated by cell phone or public telephone—if he communicated with anyone at all. But there were no receipts to indicate he used a cell phone.

He shook his head. The guy had to have one. How in hell could he order a pizza?

On their way out Doug paused in the doorway and looked back. Something caught his attention. "Hold it, Vic."

He went over and hunched down to study some faint smudge marks on the floor. "What do you make of this?" he asked, when Vic joined him.

"It looks like a muddy tire tread," Vic said. "Bicycle maybe."

"It's narrow enough for a bike, but I don't think so." Doug pointed to a parallel tread. "This looks like a double track. And look over there." He scrambled across the floor to a faint similar track near the door. "Here's another one. Same double tread. A wagon maybe, or a cart of some kind."

Doug jerked up his head, hit by a new possibility. "A wheelchair! Maybe this Sands guy was handicapped."

"You'd never guess by the condition of his living habits. This place is spotless," Doug said.

"That's right, so Mr. Clean would never have tolerated muddy tire marks on the floor."

"Are you thinking what I'm thinking?" Vic asked.

"That's right, partner. If it's tracks from a wheelchair and Sands didn't use one, that may be how the killer was able to move the bodies. Let's wake up that super again."

When they got back to the precinct, Doug found a lab photo of Sands on his desk. He tossed it over to Vic. "Seems like I've seen him before. Do you recognize him in this close-up?"

Vic studied it and handed it back. "Yeah, he does look a little familiar, but I know it's not from any case I was ever on."

One of the women from Central Records came up and handed Doug a file. "We put your floater's fingerprints on the National wire. AFIS came up with a positive hit to those of a Mark Sanderson."

A short time later Doug was able to compare Sanderson's mug shot to Sands's autopsy photo. Another match. He glanced at the photos of the nineteen-year-old victim who had been raped and murdered by Sanderson, read the file and then passed it over to Vic.

"Read it and weep. According to the file our Mr. Sands, aka Mark Sanderson, was indicted for the rape and murder of a young woman right here in Milwaukee. It appears the D.A.'s office wouldn't cut a deal and due to the brutality of the crime asked for a charge of Murder One and life imprisonment. Since the evidence was circumstantial, the jury didn't agree, so Mr. Sanderson got a free Get Out of Jail card."

"Yeah, I remember that case now. Bronowski and Evans made the collar."

Doug nodded. "Eleven or twelve years ago. I hadn't made detective yet. Well, like Ski always said whenever one of these rapists got a free walk, 'he who rapes and gets away is sure to rape another day.'"

"You're too cynical, McGuire. Maybe the guy was innocent."

"I doubt it. Our perp may be a loony tune, but he's hell-bent to wipe up the sleaze that slips through the cracks."

"At least this knocks out one theory," Vic said. "The victims aren't only from our cases."

"Knocks out another," Doug replied. "They're not Jess's, either. According to this file, Judge Richard Thorton was the presiding judge on this case."

"I guess that means we can quit worrying we're next on the list," Vic said.

"Yeah, right. Like you were worried."

While Doug waited until it was late enough to start working the phone, the medical examiner's office finished the superficial examination on Sands. There were no surprises. The cause of the victim's death was identical to the two other victims.

Finally, after a long-distance call, the New York fiduciary of Sand's trust fund faxed them a copy of the trust. Marcus Sands was his real name, and upon the death of his parents when Marcus was thirteen, his paternal grandparents had established the fund. There was still two hundred thousand dollars remaining in the trust, and with no beneficiary, the balance would revert to an orphanage in upstate New York.

By noon Doug and Vic had traced all the information they could on Sands. The Wisconsin Department of Taxation confirmed that according to Sands's filed taxes his only income was from the trust, the telephone company reported he had no record of a cell phone and a check with the Motor Vehicle Department established that he had no driver's license or a licensed vehicle in his name. None of this information changed Doug's opinion: he was still convinced that Marcus Sands raped and murdered a nineteen-year-old girl.

The only remaining thing left for them to do was check out Sands's rental locker.

Vic shoved back his chair. "We've been at this all night

and half the day. I'm sorry, partner, but I can hardly keep my eyes open. I'm signing out and going home to bed.''

"Yeah, go home, old man, and get some sleep. I'll see you in the morning. I figure I'm good for a couple more hours, so I'll drive out and see what Sands has in that locker."

"Before I leave, I've gotta ask, McGuire, are those hearts engraved with I love you?'' Vic asked.

"What are you talking about?"

Vic pointed to the chain of hearts circling Doug's biceps. He'd forgotten all about the fake tattoos Jess had pasted on his arm. He went to the john, got rid of them, and then splashed some cold water on his face.

By the time he returned, Vic had left, and Doug sat down and dialed Jess while he waited for the warrant authorizing him to open the locker.

Hearing her voice was as good as grabbing eight hours of shut-eye. Well, maybe a couple hours anyway. He told her that he wouldn't be seeing her that night and they talked for another twenty minutes—part sex, part small talk—until the assistant D.A. showed up with the warrant.

Stepping outside was like walking into a blast furnace. The heat, humidity and lack of sleep were physically debilitating, and he was on the verge of calling it quits for the day. The grumbling in his stomach reminded him he hadn't eaten, so he stopped at a restaurant, ate a breakfast instead of a lunch and then got on the expressway and headed north.

The rental lockers were on the far northside of town. It was a twenty-minute ride and took another fifteen minutes waiting for the guy who ran the place to show up and open up the locker for him.

There was nothing more than a couple of four-drawer filing cabinets containing old income tax records and paid receipts for the past twenty years. Sands had rented the locker for the past fifteen.

One thing he could say about Sands, the man was consistent—true to form, each year had been color coordinated. If his prints and picture hadn't matched a rapist-killer, Doug would have taken an oath that Marcus Sands was squeaky clean.

He was too tired to go through the hundreds of records and figured he'd come back if he had to. After all, Sands was a victim, not a suspect, and the only mystery about him now was why the killer had chosen him as a victim.

Doug found a metal strongbox in the bottom drawer of one of the cabinets. Since it was locked, and he had no tool to open it, Doug decided to take it with him and check it out tomorrow at the precinct.

The custodian made him sign a receipt for the box and a half an hour later Doug stripped off his clothes and plopped into bed. He was asleep before his head hit the pillow.

Doug woke up at seven o'clock the next morning, showered and dressed, and then headed to the precinct. He waited until Vic showed up, and then they put on gloves and forced open the metal strongbox.

Vic whistled and picked up a thick wad of bills. "There must be fifteen or twenty thousand dollars here. Let's run the serial numbers and see if we turn up anything."

"All right," Doug said, "but I don't think the money's hot. Sands was a rapist and murderer. Apparently he didn't trust banks."

Vic snorted. "Maybe because he robbed them."

"He had a pretty healthy income from that trust his grandparents set up. No banks. No paper trail. Remember, he only dealt with cash. I think he stashed his excess cash in that storage locker."

"Excess cash? Tell me what that is, McGuire? Some kind of bonus you single guys get for keeping the female population satisfied?"

"You got that right, partner. For service far beyond the call of duty."

The only other items in the box were four unmatched earrings. "What do you make of these, Vic?"

"Maybe they were his mother's, and he had to sell them over the years."

"Wouldn't you sell both of a set?" Doug reasoned. "I'm no expert but none of these look valuable except this one." He picked up a gold earring shaped in a figure eight with a tiny pearl in each circle. "I think I'll have them photoed and checked for prints."

As soon as they checked in the box as evidence, before starting out to ring doorbells and canvas the residents in Sands's neighborhood, Doug put in a call to Jess. He caught her just before she was due in court. He nodded, when Vic motioned he'd be outside.

Before hanging up, Jess had agreed to meet him at The Precinct for dinner.

He couldn't wait. He hadn't seen her since Summerfest, and that seemed like ages ago. They'd have a quick sandwich, and then go back to her place, put on that CD of hers with the flutes and falling water, and spend the rest of the evening making love. He glanced at his watch. It was 8:30 a.m. If all went well they'd be in bed in ten and a half more hours.

He could last until then if he had to.

Chapter 15

There were about six of the guys in the place when Doug arrived and sat down at the end of the bar where he could keep his eye on the door.

Ski came over to him. "Whiskey, Doug?"

"Just a beer."

"How's the case going?" Ski asked, filling a pilsner.

"It sucks." The cold brew felt good going down and he savored the comfort. "We don't even have a hair of a clue. And I mean that literally. The water washed off whatever DNA might have been on the victim's clothing."

"Bummer," Ski said, refilling Doug's glass.

"At least as long as the perp keeps knocking off these guys, it keeps the trail hot."

The door opened and there she was. His heart started pounding like Desi on the bongos—and pumping blood straight to his loins. Damn, he had it bad for her.

And what a sight to his hungry gaze. She filled in the sleeveless white top she had on perfectly, and her slimness and long legs did more for a pair of jeans than any of those flat-chested, no-ass, walking-dead models ever did.

Doug stood up to go over to her and froze when he recognized the guy who followed her in. What in hell was her father doing with her?

Smiling, Jess came over to him. "Hi. I've missed you, Doug." She had a way of saying his name that made him forgive her for anything—even for bringing her dad with her. "I forgot this was Thursday and I have a standing dinner date with my father. I hope you don't mind that I invited him to join us. It's about time the two of you meet, anyway."

"No problem."

Like hell it wasn't. They'd been together for only two weeks and he wasn't ready for the Dinner With Dad bit.

"Doug, my father Ben Kirkland, and, Dad, Doug McGuire."

"My pleasure, sir," Doug said.

"Just call me Ben," he replied as they shook hands.

Doug could see the old guy was as thrilled with the arrangement as he was. At least they had that in common. He couldn't blame Kirkland. He'd be upset, too, if he had a classy daughter like Jess messing around with some bum cop like him.

They moved over to the same corner table where he and Jess had sat the first time he'd brought her there. Recalling that night, and how he'd barged in on them at the Water Street Bistro, that alone would be enough to make Kirkland dislike him.

"What would you like to drink?" Doug asked when they were seated. *No hundred-dollar bottle of wine in this joint.*

"Whatever you're having," Jess said.

Ben nodded. "Same here. Jess tells me you're one of the investigating officers on these recent murders. How's the investigation going?"

Doug could tell Kirkland didn't give diddly-squat how the investigation was going. More likely he wanted to ask: Who in hell do you think you are to be banging my daughter?

Jess was trying her best to ease the tension between him and her father, and after Kate came over and took their order she finally declared, "Will the two of you lighten up, please. I'm having dinner with my two favorite men, and I want to enjoy it."

Ben Kirkland broke the tension with a grin. "She's right, Doug. I apologize. I admit my nose was out of joint. Jess has spoiled me these past years, and I've taken our Thursday dinners together for granted. It's quite selfish of me. Actually, I've looked forward to meeting you ever since Jess told me the two of you were seeing each other."

So it's not disapproval. Kirkland's just being territorial. Could be, but I don't think so. Mrs. McGuire didn't raise her son to be stupid, Doug thought.

Ben chuckled. "I have to admit though, Doug…"

Yeah, here comes the zinger. It's put on the gloves time. I figured it wouldn't take too long for him to say what he came to say.

"…I did enjoy watching the television bouts between the two of you," Ben said.

So maybe I overreacted. Doug relaxed. The guy didn't sound like he was out for blood. "You and most of Milwaukee, sir."

"Ben," he corrected.

Doug nodded. "Right, Ben."

"Guess I should take the blame. I encouraged Jess to be independent."

Doug's gaze sought hers. "I'd say that's to your credit, Ben."

"I'm not the meal's appetizer," Jess declared. "So will the two of you mind changing the subject."

Ben chuckled. "Actually, I'm a big fan of yours, Doug.

I've followed your career for years. Ever since that bank robbery when you went in alone and took out the two gunmen after they'd shot the security guard.''

"That was a long time ago. I was still a patrol officer. Since then I've learned to be less impetuous in the line of duty.''

"If I recall correctly, you were shot up pretty badly at the time.''

"Nothing that didn't heal.''

"So that's how you got those scars on your...'' Jess trailed off with a blush of embarrassment. She glanced at her father. "Ah, Doug and I agreed to never discuss our jobs with each other. It's our way of avoiding any arguments. Right, Doug?''

Jess knew he hated discussions about himself. She now had that little girl "trying to please'' look in her eyes that always made him want to sit her on his lap and hold her. He had to touch her, so he reached under the table, clasped her hand and squeezed it.

The conversation flowed smoothly after the ice was broken, and by the time Kate brought the sandwiches Doug and Ben had settled into a comfortable relationship that had him thinking that maybe he *could* get along in Jess's world.

As time passed the Sheepshead game had begun at the usual table and as much as he enjoyed Ben's company Doug wanted to be alone with Jess. Those flutes and gentle winds had begun calling him again. He wished they could get out of there.

He settled for the next best thing and went over to the jukebox, put a quarter in the slot and punched the button for Patsy Cline's "Crazy.'' Grabbing Jess's hand, he pulled her over to the dance floor. Their bodies found a fit and they began to move to the music. She felt good, she smelled good and he was really getting turned on.

"You're a great dancer, Doug. Why did you say you weren't much of a dancer?"

"I didn't mean I couldn't dance. I meant I don't dance much. When can we get out of here?"

"Don't you like my father?"

"Yeah, he's a great guy, but that's not the point."

"I know. I can feel what the point is."

"Not as badly as I do."

They were outside saying goodbye to Ben when a local television van drove up and Sherilyn Matthews popped out of it. She made a beeline for them—complete with camera and microphone.

"What a surprise! Mr. Law and Ms. Order, Milwaukee's most popular couple. Sherilyn turned the microphone to Ben. "And your name, sir?"

"Ben Kirkland—the judge's father."

"Of course. I thought you looked familiar," she said. "May I ask what you were doing here at the time?"

"Having dinner," Ben said.

"Dinner? But aren't you the owner of the Water Street Bistro, Mr. Kirkland?"

"Just checking out the competition, my dear," Ben said with a friendly smile.

Doug had gradually nudged Jess out of the picture and they started to leave.

"One more question," Sherilyn shouted. The hungry piranha came after them with swinging microphone and scrambling cameraman.

"The viewing public is following the relationship with interest between the two of you. Considering you're investigating these recent murders, Detective McGuire, isn't this a conflict of interest?"

"Why? Judge Kirkland is not involved with this case."

"But isn't there the possibility the case could come before her when you apprehend the murderer?" Sherilyn asked. "That is *if* you apprehend the murderer," she added with a snide smile.

"There is no doubt this killer will be apprehended, Ms. Matthews," Jess spoke up sharply. "In the event I draw the case, I would simply recuse myself. Justice is always served, Ms. Matthews." They walked away.

"Oh, how I dislike that woman!" Jess mumbled. "I've never wanted to get into a hair-pulling, down-in-the-mud catfight so badly in my life."

"Hey, I thought if you're going to roll in the mud, I'd have first crack at it," Doug said.

They looked at each other momentarily—read each other's thoughts—then he clasped her hand and they ran to the car.

Doug could get used to this. He lay stretched out on the bed. He couldn't remember a time he'd ever felt so at peace. Euphoric. Weightless. Floating on the gentle winds of that New Age CD being piped into the bedroom. The seductive scent of Jess swirled around his head, as soothing as the cool air caressing his naked flesh. Mind and body sated—at peace with the world.

They'd been making love for hours. He'd climaxed at least three times that he could remember. Now he couldn't even move a muscle. If the fire alarm went off, he'd have to lie there and perish—but at least he'd go out smiling.

Where hadn't they made love? The living room. The dining room table. The shower. The terrace after showering.

From the instant they'd crossed the threshold their hands and bodies—mouths and tongues—were all over each other. He couldn't get enough of her—she of him. And whenever she'd wrap her arms around him and he'd sink into her, it was like finding a refuge in the midst of a chaotic world plunging out of control.

That's what Jess was to him—a haven to his mind and body.

"I love you, Doug," she whispered softly, her voice blending in with the music that carried to his ears.

Tonight she had said it repeatedly throughout their love-making. What in hell did he know about love? Was that what he felt for her, too? Was that why he liked just being with her? Why he enjoyed just looking at her? Was that why sex was always better with her?

He believed that love was emotional; sex was physical. What did one have to do with the other? So why try and relate them? This was a new puzzle to him. And he needed to solve it soon.

Her lips pressed a light kiss on his, her hair brushing against his chest when she lowered her head. He picked up a few of the strands and rolled them in his fingers. They felt like silk.

She began to work his body—gently, leisurely. A light kiss here, the smooth caress of her fingertips there. A nibble. A moist stroke of tongue.

She was kicking a dead horse.

"I'm sorry, honey, shop's closed for the night."

"Doug McGuire crying 'uncle'? I don't think so. Besides, I'm happy in my work." She emphasized her point by lightly trailing a fingernail up his inner thigh.

So what if his muscle jerked in response? A natural thing to happen. He might be down for the count, but he wasn't dead.

He chuckled. "You're wasting your time, Angel Face. I'm afraid I've hoisted myself on my own petard."

He could feel her smile against his flesh, and her warm breath brushed his loins as she spoke. "Forget the Shakespeare, McGuire. This bed's not big enough for all three of us."

"Just wanted you to know I learned something at college besides how to chuckalug a can of beer." He tucked his hands under his head, and closed his eyes. "But have it your way, Judge Jess. Just don't get mad if I fall asleep."

Doug lay contentedly and had to admit it felt good just feeling her touch. Knowing it was Jess. It felt like the gentle brush of a butterfly or that kind of ticklish tingle he'd felt when he used to let a caterpillar creep along his arm. Slow. Tingling. Unthreatening.

It wasn't long before he became aware that the unthreatening tingle had gradually developed into an aching draw in his loins; the gentle fluttering butterfly had multiplied into hundreds of the little devils beating their wings to get out. His loins grew hotter and he felt himself getting bigger and harder as his whole being flooded with passion.

With a groan of concession, he rolled over and crushed her to him. "You're gonna be the death of me, lady," he murmured and captured her mouth with his own.

Doug had just dozed off when his cell phone rang. Dammit, he was going to throw the freaking thing away. He glanced at the clock. It was just past midnight.

"What?" he snarled, into the phone.

"McGuire, this is Sergeant O'Riley."

"Oh really, O'Riley! Like I didn't know. This better be important."

"We got an urgent call from some guy who claims he's being stalked by whoever killed Sam Bellemy."

"Sure he is. Must have a guilty conscience. How does he know this alleged stalker killed Bellemy?"

"Said the guy already tried to kill him."

"Yeah right. Sounds like a kook."

"He wants to see you and Peterson right away. Peterson's on his way in now."

"Okay. I'll be there in about fifteen minutes."

Doug dressed and bent over the bed to say goodbye to Jess. "You're leaving?" she mumbled, half-asleep.

"Yeah. Thanks for the hospitality, Judge." He kissed her and told her to go back to sleep.

Vic and Doug arrived at the precinct at the same time. "This is crap," Doug grumbled. "Getting us up in the middle of the night to appease some paranoid. Why couldn't O'Riley send a patrol car over to hold the guy's hand?"

"He told me this Rhodes asked for us specifically."

"So he read our names in the newspaper. Big deal!"

Once inside O'Riley handed them a piece of paper with a name and address on it. "Did you run his name to see if this is how the guy gets his jollies?" Doug asked.

"Yeah." O'Reilly tossed them a file.

Doug perused it quickly. "I see there's been a couple of complaints filed against him for hanging around playgrounds."

Vic yawned. "Well, let's roll, partner. If we're lucky we might get back in time to catch a couple more hours of shut-eye."

Despite the cooling effect from the lake, the temperature was still in the eighties. Doug was feeling the heat already, which only added to his irritability.

"This address sounds familiar," Vic said as Doug pulled the Crown Victoria out of the parking lot.

"Yeah, didn't Bellemy's rape victim, Kellie Tate, live somewhere around that area?"

"I think you're right. Say, my family caught yours and Jess's act on the tube earlier, and saw that her old man was with you. Looks serious, McGuire. Set the wedding date yet?"

Doug snorted. "Yeah, right. You'll be the first to know, partner."

"Bev figures it's coming up fast. So does Andrea. She ran to her room in tears."

"Cut the crap, Vic. I'm not hearing wedding bells. I

can't even figure out what in hell it means to love a woman enough to want to spend the rest of your life with her.''

"Ask your mother. Maybe she can help you out with the answer. Just the same, that Matthews dame wasn't too far wrong.''

Doug felt a rise of skepticism. "About what?''

"Conflict of interest in this case.''

"Your point being?''

"You might be letting your personal feelings cloud your thinking.''

"What in hell are you talking about? Are you still thinking Jess could be a suspect?''

"I haven't ruled out anyone, partner, and neither should you.''

"Dammit, Vic, I told you Jess was with me when Bellemy was murdered. And she wasn't the presiding judge, either, at Sands's trial. So get off my back.''

"Are you forgetting what that snitch Paulie told us? The word on the street was that someone was putting out a contract for a hit. Maybe the hit didn't stop with Gilbert.''

"And you think Jess might be picking up the tab. Sands's killing rules out that theory, partner. What's her motive?''

"So maybe Sands's death was a copycat. After all, he ended up in the lake, not the river.''

"Now you're grasping at straws.''

"Could be, but at least my brain's not between my legs.''

Doug's hands tightened on the wheel as his anger turned to fury. "Then check out her bank account, Sam Spade.''

"I already did.''

That blow was below the belt. They'd been partners for ten years, and he couldn't believe Vic would go behind his back with a stunt like that.

The conversation was over as far as Doug was concerned. He didn't ask what Vic had found out; Vic didn't offer the answer.

They rode in silence the rest of the way.

Harry Rhodes lived in a small apartment building near a West side mall. He was waiting for them and opened the door before they even knocked.

"He's out there right now. I saw him through the window," Rhodes declared in a quivering voice.

"Can you describe him?" Vic asked.

"He's about my height. Dark hair, and he's wearing gray sweats. I saw him just a couple minutes ago. He's still out there, detectives. You gotta find him. He's gonna try and kill me again."

"Okay, we'll look around outside," Vic said. "Keep the door locked. We'll be back."

"If there was anyone out here, he would have taken off by now," Doug said when they went outside.

Vic nodded. "It's too dark to see anything. There's a flashlight in the car. I'll go get it."

Doug drew his weapon and began to circle the building, checking out the shrubbery where the stalker could conceal himself.

Meanwhile, reaching the car, Vic paused when he noticed a gray Toyota parked a couple houses down on the opposite side of the street. He didn't remember seeing the car parked there before, and decided to check it out as soon as he got the flashlight. He opened the car door, leaned over and began to rummage through the glove compartment.

A figure stepped out of the concealment of the nearby bushes and approached stealthily, a hypodermic needle poised like a weapon in his hand.

Vic didn't see or hear the assailant, but felt the sudden stab of the needle. He groped helplessly to remove it, but his arms and hands had become numb. He tried to shout for help, but his throat muscles were constricted, so he slammed his arm down on the horn, and then slumped over onto the steering wheel.

Doug had just reached the rear of the building when the sound of chirping crickets was silenced by a steady blast of a car horn. As he raced around to the front he heard the squeal of tires and reached the street in time to see the brake lights of a car disappear around the next corner.

The door of the Crown Victoria was open, the overhead light revealing a slumped figure over the steering wheel. His heart pounded in his chest as he ran to the car. With sickening dread he saw the needle protruding from Vic's arm. He yanked it out, and then straightened Vic out on the car seat. Vic's eyes were open, but were glazed over; his body was as stiff as a board. He could tell Vic was trying to speak, but he couldn't move his lips.

Doug reached for the radio. ''10-17. 10-17. Officer down. I need an ambulance here fast. A half block east of 76th on Cherry Blossom Lane. Repeat. 10-17. Officer down. Send ambulance. Half block east of 76th on Cherry Blossom Lane.'' He dropped the radio and it dangled out the open door.

Doug managed to get Vic out of the car and stretched out on the grass. Then he sat down and cradled Vic's head in his lap.

''Hang in there, partner. Help's on the way.''

Vic's eyeballs rolled to the top of the sockets and he lost consciousness. Doug pressed his head to Vic's chest. He could feel a faint heartbeat. Vic was still breathing, but he was losing him. In desperation, he grabbed the dangling phone.

''Repeat. 10-17. Officer down. For God's sake, where's that ambulance?''

Clutching Vic in his arms, he began to rock him back and forth. ''Hang in there, partner. Help's on the way,'' he murmured, over and over in a woeful litany to the sound of approaching sirens in the distance.

* * *

Two patrol cars raced up and squealed to a stop. With drawn weapons, the officers vaulted from the cars and rushed over to them. Doug didn't know any of them.

"I'm McGuire, from the First Precinct. This is my partner, Vic Peterson."

"Is he still alive?" one asked.

"Barely," Vic said.

With revolving light and siren blasting the ambulance arrived. "Please step aside, Detective," a serious young attendant said. Doug relinquished Vic to them.

By now, attracted by the sirens and flashing lights, the curious had come out of their houses and the patrolmen were engaged in stringing crime tape to restrain the crowd.

Unable to stand by uselessly, Doug retrieved the needle from the car, bagged it and locked the doors. "I'll ride along," he said to the ambulance attendants who were adjusting an oxygen mask on Vic. "Will he make it?"

The attendant shrugged. "Vital signs aren't good."

As he waited for the gurney to be loaded into the ambulance, Doug's gaze swept the crowd. That's when he saw him—dark hair, gray sweats. Standing among the gawkers. He recognized him at once—Ron Tate, the father of the child Sam Bellemy had raped and murdered.

He exploded in rage and leaped over the tape. Grasping a fistful of Tate's shirt, he yanked him out of the crowd.

"You sonofabitch, I'm going to kill you."

He threw a punch and Tate hit the ground. Doug was on him at once, but before he could deliver another blow, two of the police officers wrestled him off.

"That's the bastard who did it," Doug shouted. "Don't let him get away."

Another of the officers yanked Tate to his feet and proceeded to cuff him. "I don't know what he's talking about. I didn't do anything," Tate denied.

"Listen, buddy," one of the attendants said to Doug,

"it's up to you if you want to stay and wipe up the street with that guy, but we've got to get your partner to a hospital fast. Climb in if you're coming with us."

I didn't want to hurt Peterson, but I had no choice. He saw my car and I knew he would take down the license number. He and McGuire are always underfoot. All I'm trying to do is help. So why can't they leave me do what I have to? What you asked me to do, Jessica.

Too bad it wasn't McGuire who came back to their car…

Chapter 16

Jess woke and stretched, then sighed, lay back and thought of Doug. For the past two weeks every morning she woke, her first thought was of Doug. If it was an obsession, so be it. She was crazy mad in love with him—wanted to be with him all the time.

Oh she sensed there was something that he held back from her, but it would come out eventually. If he'd only tell her, it would help her to know how to approach whatever the problem might be; but she'd learned not to press issues with Doug. It just made him clam up.

Last night she finally admitted to him that she loved him—at least he didn't run. Now, if only he would do the same... *One step at a time, Jessica.*

She would love to discuss it with Liz, but she knew her friend would only say that Doug was in it for sex only. Liz would probably even accuse her of the same thing. And that wasn't true. Not anymore, anyway.

Jess got out of bed and switched on the radio. Since the

Bellemy incident with Doug, she'd made a point of listening to the local morning news.

Doug. Doug. Doug. Her life now seemed dedicated to
pleasing him. The thought made her smile, because the
beauty of it was that she enjoyed pleasing Detective Douglas I. McGuire.

Jess hummed "As Time Goes By" as she made the bed,
and then took a shower. When she came out of the bathroom, she picked up on the voice of the newscaster on the
radio reporting some breaking news. She paused to listen.

"Mr. Tate was taken into custody early this morning
and is suspected of being the man responsible for these
three murders. One of the men he allegedly murdered had
been a suspect in the brutal slaying of Tate's eight-year-
old daughter Kellie a year ago, but had avoided prosecu-
tion on a technicality. It's believed this could be a revenge
killing on the part of the suspect. The wounded detective
was rushed to the hospital and is reported to be in critical
condition. Stay tuned for any further updates."

For several seconds Jess was too stunned to move. Doug
and Vic had to be the detectives involved. That must have
been why Doug was called out last night. Her anxiety
raced off in a dozen directions. What hospital do they take
a wounded policeman to? Maybe Doug wasn't even involved. Maybe it had been some other detectives and he
was just called into the precinct because of the incident?
Who would know? Bev Peterson, of course.

She found her telephone book, and her hand shook as
she ran a finger along the column until she located their
number. Jess dialed it quickly and slammed up the phone
in frustration when she got a recorded greeting. Her next
hope was the precinct. That number was on her Rolodex
in her chambers. Once again she reached for the telephone
book. The 9-1-1 number was blazoned in big letters, but
she needed the individual precinct number. More precious
seconds was lost as she searched and finally dialed it.

"First Precinct, Sergeant O'Riley."

"I'd like to speak to Detective McGuire," Jessica said.

"Sorry, ma'am. Detective McGuire is not here at the moment. Would you care to speak to a different detective?"

"Is Detective Peterson there?" she asked.

"No, ma'am."

"Could you tell me if either of them was the detective wounded this morning in the Tate arrest?"

"Are you related to one of these officers, ma'am?" he asked.

"No, but I'm a close friend of Detective McGuire."

"I'm sorry, ma'am," the sergeant said, "but we are not permitted to give out any personal information over the telephone about anyone on the force."

"Will you at least tell me what hospital a wounded officer would be taken to in an emergency?"

"That would depend upon the severity and condition of the wounded officer. Most likely the closest one to where ever the incident would have occurred."

Jessica had reached the point where she wanted to scream. Her brain searched for a name. What was it? Knowles? Noll? Novacek? Novack? "Detective Novack! Is he there?"

"No, ma'am. Detective Novack and several of the other detectives are at the Milwaukee County General Hospital." He paused long enough for her to grasp the meaning. "I'm sorry I can't be of more help, ma'am."

"Thank you, Sergeant. You've been a big help." He had given her the name of the hospital without disobeying a rule. Now there was no doubt in her mind that the wounded detective was either Doug or Vic.

Jess hung up and immediately dialed Liz. She found out she had only one session scheduled for the afternoon, so she told Liz if the news was bad she'd have to cancel it, and promised to keep her informed.

Jess finished dressing and within minutes was en route to the hospital. When she arrived, this time, determined not to be turned away because she wasn't family, Jess walked boldly up to the reception desk.

"Where can I find Detective McGuire?"

The receptionist fell for it. "He's probably up on the 4th floor with the other detectives."

"Thank you." Jess turned and headed for the elevator. It had worked—and the good news was that obviously Doug wasn't the patient. As selfish as it might be, she was relieved to find out that the man she loved was not the injured detective. However, the bad news was that most likely it meant that Vic was.

There were several detectives from the First Precinct in the hallway and a few others in the waiting room, plus a captain, and the chief of police. A young girl was sitting on a couch cuddled against an older woman, and looking lost and desolate. Two young boys were squeezed in beside them. These had to be the Peterson children. There was no sign of Doug or Beverly Peterson.

Jess suddenly felt like an intruder. She just couldn't barge in. She didn't know whom to approach, or what to say. The fact that the Peterson children were there left no doubt that Vic was the injured detective, but what could she say to them without knowing his existing condition? Was this a death vigil? Dear God, she prayed not.

Fortunately, the chief of police recognized her and came over. "Judge Kirkland," he said solemnly.

"Good morning, Chief. What is Detective Peterson's condition?"

He put a hand on her elbow and guided her out of the room. "He's hanging in there. The doctor said that normally a single dose of insulin wouldn't be fatal, but he obviously received an excessive amount."

"Has he regained consciousness at all?"

The chief shook his head. "No, he's still comatose, and his vital signs are still at critical levels. At least they haven't worsened."

Jess didn't know what to read into that. Negative or positive? Was the glass half-full or half-empty?

"And how is Beverly holding up?"

"She's a cop's wife. Inflexible inner strength and infinite faith. An inspiration to all of us. Detective McGuire is at the bedside with her."

"Was Detective McGuire harmed at all in the incident?"

"No. From what I understand he and Peterson were answering a distress call. McGuire was checking out the backyard and Peterson had gone to the car to get a flashlight. That's when he was attacked."

"The news report indicated the suspect was apprehended."

"Yes, by Detective McGuire."

"Well, I won't intrude. If you have an opportunity, please convey my sympathy to Beverly, and tell her I'll contact her later."

"I will, Judge Kirkland. I'm thinking of asking the other officers to leave, too. I understand how they feel, and they're here to support a fellow officer, but there's not anything any of us can do."

Jess went back into the room and offered a few words of reassurance to the two boys. When she attempted to do the same to Andrea, the young girl turned away and burrowed deeper into the older woman, who introduced herself as Beverly's mother.

Just as Jess was preparing to leave, Doug came into the waiting room.

"Vic's going to make it. He's coming out of it. His

vitals are stabilizing and he's beginning to show some motor control.''

There were murmurs of relief all around, and the chief and captain immediately started to shuffle the detectives and their wives out.

When Doug saw Jess, he came over to her. ''Have you been here long?''

''No, I just arrived a few minutes ago. I'm glad to hear the good news. Will you give Bev my regards?''

''Yeah, I will. I'll call you when I leave here.'' For a long moment he gazed at her. ''Thanks, Jess, for coming.''

The strain of the ordeal showed on his face. His normal tan appeared paler, and dark circles had formed under his eyes. She wondered how many hours of sleep he'd actually had since these murders had begun.

She wanted so badly to put her arms around him to comfort him, but this was neither the time nor place with all the curious stares on them.

''Yes, call me, Doug. I'll be waiting.''

And waiting is precisely what she did. By seven o'clock that evening she was pacing the floor of her apartment—still waiting for his call.

Where was he? What was he doing? Had Vic taken a turn for the worse? Had Doug had an accident?

He'd made no attempt to contact her. What could be responsible for his not calling?

For the sixth time that day she picked up the telephone intending to call him, and for the sixth time she slammed it down before doing so. No, she wasn't going to track him down like a jealous wife. He'd said he would call, didn't he?

He didn't call, but showed up at her door a short time later.

The instant she saw him, she broke out in tears. It was

ridiculous of her, but she couldn't control herself. From the time she'd first heard the news report that morning, she'd been on tenterhooks. Every little incident, whether at home, the hospital or court had only added to her anxiety.

"Doug, how could you do this to me?" she accused. "You promised to call. I've been a nervous wreck worrying about you."

"I'm sorry if I've upset you, Jess. I was tied up all day."

"No one is *that* busy that they don't have a few seconds to pick up a telephone. That's all it would have taken—a thirty-second phone call—to keep me from going nearly crazy worrying about you. Even this morning, until I walked into that waiting room, I didn't know if you were the wounded officer or if Vic was. I wasn't even sure if the two of you were even involved."

"Things were moving pretty fast."

"I realize that. But once you got to the hospital, I'm sure one of those other detectives would have made a call for you, if you'd have asked him."

"I suppose so. I guess it's better if I leave. You're upset, and I'm responsible, but I don't need this right now, Jess. I've got enough on my mind."

She realized she should have given him a chance to explain rather than attack him verbally the instant he stepped in the door. "Vic didn't have a relapse, did he?"

"No, he's doing fine. They're keeping him overnight just to make sure there are no complications. Captain's ordered him to take a three-day medical leave."

"I think that will do you both good. Ever since these murders, the few hours the two of you have had to sleep or relax is ludicrous. Your suspect's behind bars now, so you should relax, too."

"Tate was released a couple hours ago."

"I don't understand," Jess said. "Why?"

"He has an airtight alibi. He lives two blocks from the scene and he and his neighbor jog every night. We're got a sworn affidavit from the neighbor that he and Tate were jogging at the time Vic was attacked. And Harry Rhodes couldn't ID Tate as the guy who's been stalking him."

"Then who attacked Vic?" she asked.

"Obviously the perp. He probably hadn't intended to, but Vic must have gotten in the way. Vic said when he went back to the car he saw a gray or light blue Toyota parked a short distance away. A General Investigative Unit from that precinct checked it out and nobody on the block has one. The GIU team said that Tate drives a white SUV, and his wife drives a red Acura."

"Oh, Doug! What a disappointment."

"You've got that right."

"I'm so sorry. I've been so self-absorbed. So now you're back to where you started from."

"Except it's not my problem anymore. I'm off the case, and I've been suspended without pay for thirty days."

"Why?" she asked, aghast.

"Jess, don't you ever watch the news or read the paper?"

"I try not to, in order to keep an open mind in court."

"Well, every channel's carrying it as well as the front page. It seems one of the gawkers last night had a camera and the good citizen snapped a picture of me hitting Tate."

"Oh, Doug, you didn't." She sat down in despair.

"No lecture, please. I've already heard one from the chief. The paper's crying police brutality, and the mayor's calling for my badge permanently. He claims I'm an embarrassment to the city."

She looked up on the verge of tears. "You know it's all

just posturing for the camera, Doug. It will all blow over. Darling, we've had our differences in court, but there's not a judge on the bench who doesn't agree that you're an outstanding homicide detective. Nobody's going to take away your badge.''

"Frankly, Jess, I don't give a damn if they do. I'm sick of the whole thing. They can have the badge.''

"You don't mean that.''

"My best friend was almost murdered last night, and I have to take heat for taking a swing at the guy whom I thought did it. I'm telling you, Jess, any cop who walks into a dark alley and takes a bullet, any fireman who walks into a blazing house or any guy who puts on a uniform and goes into combat is a fool. There'll always be some big mouth out there pointing a camera or guilty finger to tell the poor sucker—who was willing to put his life on the line—just what he did wrong.''

"Don't say that, Doug. I know you're bitter right now.''

"Why shouldn't I be? The finest man I know almost was killed last night in the line of duty. It was worth one line in the newspaper and on television. But my throwing a punch at Tate got a full-size picture on the front page and the lead-in report on all the local news channels. The damn job sucks.''

"Doug, you wouldn't be in law enforcement if you didn't believe in what you're doing.''

"I'm in law enforcement because I like to solve puzzles,'' he lashed out. "The biggest puzzle though is why I was stupid enough to join the force in the first place.''

She stood up and went over to him. "Why don't you take a shower and climb into my bed. You need a good night's sleep, Doug. I'll unplug the phone, smash that cell phone of yours into pieces and sleep in the other room. Tomorrow we'll talk about this. As long as you're on suspension, maybe we can think about going away for a couple of weeks. I'm sure I can shift my cases around. How about it, McGuire?''

''Sounds good, but not tonight. I've got some serious thinking to do, so I'll call—''

She put a finger over his lips. ''Don't say it. Promise me you'll get some sleep.''

He tried to grin. ''Probably more than if I'd stay here and think about you lying in a bed in the next room.''

She slipped her arms around his neck. ''I love you, Doug.''

His kiss was hard—almost desperate. Then he left without another word.

Her heart ached for him.

Despite all he had on his mind, Doug couldn't forget Jess's stricken look when he'd walked in tonight.

He's seen it on Bev's face during her vigil through the night at her husband's bedside. He'd seen it in the eyes of Vic's children.

And Lord knows, he'd seen it enough times on his mother's face through the years not to recognize its meaning. In these past couple weeks he had shoved that memory to the back of his mind. Being with Jess had made him forget the many nights he had watched his mother walking the floor, but keeping up a brave front for his sake. The funerals of the officers killed in the line of duty and the looks on the faces of the loved ones left to mourn them. He had vowed he'd never put a woman he loved through that agony.

And, yeah, he loved Jess. When or how—or what—it was it had happened to him. But when he walked into that waiting room this morning and saw her standing there, he realized just how much he loved her.

Why had he let it happen? His eyes had been wide open when he first got involved with Jess, but he was cocky enough to think he could walk away any time he was ready. He sure had to eat those words. But thank goodness today made him spew them back up. Tomorrow he'd make it clear to Jess he wasn't in for the long haul. Maybe love belonged in her world, but it was a luxury that had no place in his.

The answering machine was blinking away when he walked into his apartment. He figured it was Jess, punched the button and listened to the message.

His face was grim when he turned it off and reached for the telephone.

Chapter 17

Jess had spent a restless night fretting over Doug. He was so bitter and unhappy. It broke her heart to see him that way. At least it was Saturday and she didn't have to go to court. Maybe the two of them could get away for a couple of days. Some place peaceful and quiet. Leave the rest of the world—and his cell phone—behind. She would pamper him, make love to him, and try to convince him there was another world out there, a world in which courts and murderers did not exist. With buoyed spirits she took a shower, and when she came out there was a message on her answering machine.

"Jess." Her heart automatically skipped a beat when she heard Doug's voice. "I have to go out of town for a few days. I'll call you when I get back."

Stunned, she stared at the machine, waiting for the message to continue. That was it?

Figuring the tape was stuck, she rewound it and played the message again. That *was* it!

Nothing more than those few terse words. No why or

where. Not even a goodbye. For all the intimacy in the message, he might just as well have been calling the corner laundry to check on his dry cleaning. She wanted to bawl, but knew that tears wouldn't be of any comfort.

As if in commiseration, the angels did it for her. The sky opened up in a downpour and rained steadily all day. She turned down Liz's suggestion to go to a movie in favor of cleaning out her closets.

By the next morning the rain had reduced to a nonstop drizzle. Surprisingly her father called her—which he never did on weekends. She declined his Sunday dinner invitation, opting instead to clean her oven, and then feast on a bowl of Campbell's tomato soup.

By evening she couldn't bear it any longer. Surely Vic would know where Doug had gone.

Bev's cheery greeting only added to Jess's depression. Bev went through the nitty-gritty of how Vic was feeling, and although Jess was sincerely glad to hear he was fine, she almost dropped the telephone when Bev said, ''It certainly was a shock about Doug's father, wasn't it?''

Jess offered a mumbled reply, wanting, instead to cry out, What about his father?

''It's unusual for a police chief to put himself in the line of fire,'' Bev rambled on. ''But Doug always said his father never gave up a connection with the cop on the beat. But shot down responding to a robbery—that's a real shocker.''

''Yes, it certainly is,'' Jess replied, managing to find her voice.

''And coming on top of Doug's suspension... I feel for him, Jess. Vic's more worried about Doug than he is his own health. He said Doug's thinking about quitting the force.''

''He's bitter right now, Bev. He just needed to vent. But I'm afraid after this latest tragedy he just might decide to do it.''

"At least Chief McGuire died with his boots on, so to speak," Beverly said. "He wanted to go out in the line of duty. Well, thank God that didn't happen in the Peterson house. I don't have to tell you, Jess, I'm going to be mighty relieved when Vic retires in six months."

Jess tried to swallow the lump that had formed in her throat. "I didn't realize Vic was that close to retirement."

"Yes, ma'am. Amen! We're thinking about selling the house and moving where there's no snow and ice in the winter."

"Yes, that sounds like a good idea, although I wouldn't mind some of that snow and ice right now. This heat and humidity is devastating."

"I'll remind you of that next winter. Besides, gal, you've got it good. It's always about ten degrees cooler near the lake."

A few minutes later Jess managed to end the conversation and hang up.

She was crushed to hear that Doug had left without even mentioning his father's death to her. She was so emotionally attached to him that she couldn't fathom how he could do that to her. Excluding her from such a tragedy in his life made her realize that his feelings for her certainly didn't run as deeply as her's for him. And as the evening wore on, she began to doubt that he had any deep feelings for her at all.

She shared Doug's grief over his loss—she knew how she'd feel if, God forbid, she lost her father—but when she cried herself to sleep that night, the real cause of her tears was a broken heart.

Doug entered his apartment and the hot air smacked him in the face like a blast from hell. He tossed his keys and mail on the table and turned on the air conditioner. Why had he turned it off before he left? Now after five days in this heat, it would take a whole day to cool the place down again.

He stripped down to his boxers, and then plopped down on the chair in front of the conditioner to let his pores suck in the cool air.

He had a lot of serious thinking to do. A lot of decisions to make—and they all centered around Jess and his job.

His answering machine was flashing like red lights at a three-alarm fire. He felt like pulling the damn thing out of the wall and smashing it on the floor. Instead he got up, went to the kitchen and popped a Miller, then he came back, sat down and pushed the message button.

The first message was from the precinct captain. "Doug, I'm sorry to hear about your father. I had the pleasure of meeting him once when I was a patrol officer. He was the guest speaker at a seminar I attended. Law enforcement has lost one of its most dedicated servants."

Doug raised his beer can in a toast. "Right, Captain Collins. Here's to those dedicated law enforcement servants. May they rest in peace." He polished off the beer.

"On a different note, Detective," Collins voice droned on. "I would like you to report in when you return. You've been taken off suspension."

"Screw you, Collins. I'm taking the thirty days. Sorry, your two minutes are up." He cut off the message.

The next several messages were from wives of other detectives who called to express their sympathy over his father's death. He lifted his head when a new message clicked in.

"Detective McGuire, this is Sherilyn Matthews." Her voice sounded better on the telephone than it did in person. "Would you be interested in coming to the studio? I'd like to interview you for our Sunday night *Best of Milwaukee* show."

"Not interested, Ms. Matthews." He moved on to the next caller.

"Doug, call me when you get back."

He played it over and over, just to hear her voice. He finally shut it off and leaned back in the chair.

I need you, Jess. Lord, how I need you.

For the first time in his thirty-six years he was at a total loss what to do with his frigging life. He crushed the beer can in his clenched fist and let it drop to the floor. Then he buried his head in his hands.

Doug still hadn't budged when the telephone rang a short time later. The answering machine clicked on and Vic's voice shouted, "Pick up the damn phone, Doug. I just talked to your mother so I know you're home."

Doug sighed, and reached for the phone. "What?"

"Well, hello. How are you doing, partner?"

"Trying to get some sleep."

"Did you hear we're back on the case?" Vic asked.

"Screw the case."

"The chief took you off of suspension."

"Screw the chief. He can take my damn badge and shove it up his—"

"Hey, cool it, Doug. At least for six months. I don't have the patience to break in a new partner."

"So what brought about this change of heart?" Doug asked.

"The morning after you left, Ron Tate called an interview and said he's not filing any charges against you. He said you are an excellent detective and the city needs more like you. When you hit him, he had not been arrested. It was between you and him. And you were reacting as a private citizen who thought his best friend had just been killed. He said he would have done the same thing in your place." Vic started to chuckle.

"So is this a joke?" Doug asked.

"No. You should have seen the chief and the mayor scrambling around trying to save their butts. The editorials are running ten to one in your favor. Most of them calling for the mayor's resignation for that crack he made about you being an embarrassment to the city.''

''What?'' Doug asked when Vic started chuckling again.

''I can't figure it out, Wolfman, but that 'go to hell' image of yours has grabbed the public. They've even formed a fan club for you. And this will crack you up, McGuire. Guess who's the organizer?''

''Britney Spears,'' Doug said sarcastically.

''Close. The chief's sixteen-year-old daughter. She and Justin are schoolmates, and they've set up a fan club on the Internet. Glamour shot and all. They've had hundreds of members.''

''Thank God I don't have a computer.''

''Bev thinks what's really helped is that Romeo and Juliet romance you've got going with Jess. The women are really into it.''

''Yeah, well that story ended in a tragedy, too.''

The remark changed Vic's tone. He came back subdued. ''The two of you bust up?''

''I'm no good for her, Vic.''

''Why don't you let her be the judge of that. Have you called her since you've been back?''

''Not yet.''

''Doug, I was out of line about Jess. I should have trusted your instincts. For the record, there were no large withdrawals from her bank account.''

''I didn't believe there would be. But that has nothing to do with it.''

''Why don't you call her, Doug? She's been worried sick about you.''

''It's not your problem, Pappy.''

''Is it ever going to sink into that thick skull of yours that it's not you against the world? There are a lot of us who love you. I'll see you at the precinct tomorrow morning. We've got a murder case to solve, partner. In the meantime, call her.''

As much as he would have liked to talk to Jess, he wasn't ready yet. It seemed that every time he was consumed with guilt, he took it out on her. So this time would be the last time.

He'd figured that out these past few days. That was how he punished himself. Jess was the only person he could draw comfort from by just being with her. And he didn't deserve to be comforted. He ought to even turn off the damn air conditioner just so he could punish himself more.

Lord, he hated self-pitying whiners. That's what he'd become. Everyone had to pay the piper eventually. His mother called it the Lord's retribution. To him it was just plain what goes around comes around; but okay maybe giving up Jess was his *retribution* for a damn lot of guilt.

He jumped to his feet. He had to get out of there or he'd end up calling her for sure. He'd do it tomorrow and try to make her understand. He pulled on jeans and a shirt, and headed for The Precinct.

The usual group of guys were there, and the usual card game in progress. His rotten life was being turned upside down and...life went on.

After a perfunctory greeting to Ski and the other guys, Doug went over and sat down at the corner table. His and Jess's table. There he went again! What in hell was he thinking? He'd been in and out of the joint more times than he could remember. Sat at the same table. He'd only been there a couple of times with Jess, but thought of it now as *their* table.

Kate came over and put a hand on his shoulder. ''I was sorry to hear about your father, Doug.''

''Thanks, Kate.''

''So what's it going to be? Suds or sandwich?'' she asked.

''Suds.''

"You've got it, honey." She came back with a pitcher of beer. "You've become our local hero, Doug."

"Yeah, Vic clued me in earlier."

"You've always been a hero to me."

"I'm not a hero, Kate. You of all people know better than that. You've lived with heroes."

He killed half the pitcher of beer and it wasn't helping. He went over and punched in "Crazy." And thought of Jess. He leaned his head against the jukebox in frustration.

"I believe this is our dance."

Doug spun around and there she was.

He stood there and just looked at her. She was manna to his senses. His eyes breathed in the sight of her, his nose the fragrance of her.

Jess clasped his hand and led him to the small dance floor at the rear. And then she was in his arms. That indescribable feeling of being alive when she was in his arms.

Dear God, he couldn't let her go. No matter what he'd resolved. He litcrally clung to her as they moved to the music and let Patsy Cline tell it as it was.

As soon as the song ended, he said, "I've got to get out of here." Like the cowardly bastard that he was, he left her standing in thc middle of that dance floor and went back to his apartment to sulk in the dark. Hc might have known she'd follow—or maybe that's what he hoped for.

He opened the door in response to her knock, and walked back and sat down. Jess came in and closed the door quietly.

"Don't you think we need to talk, Doug?"

"Yes we do, but I'm not in the mood right now. It would be better if I call you tomorrow."

"Tomorrow? Why put off until tomorrow what you can do right now. Can't you face me and say what you have to say?"

"I thought it would be easier on both of us if I called."

"It's not going to be easier either way, Doug. I know what you have to say, but I had to hear it from you. That's the only way I'll know for sure and can quit fooling myself."

"Jess, we're both adults. We knew this couldn't last when we started. But it was a great ride while it lasted."

She took it without even flinching. But like he'd always said, she had a lot of class.

"Well, that's what I came to hear. Sorry to have bothered you." She turned to leave.

She didn't deserve this. Not Jess. Not this way. He couldn't let her walk out of there without an explanation.

"Wait." He was on her before she could take two steps, and made the mistake of putting his hands on her shoulders and turning her around. Then it was too late.

Pulling her into his arms, his mouth swooped down and captured hers with a hunger that made mockery of the words he'd just spoken to her.

"How can I let you go, Jess?" he murmured when he broke the kiss. "I can't," he repeated over and over as he covered her face with a multitude of rapid, insatiable kisses. It took a long moment before he realized he was tasting her tears.

Doug picked her up and carried her over to the chair and sat down, holding her on his lap. "There are some things I can't have, no matter how much I want them. It tears me up to know I'm not good enough for you, that's why I have to let you go. But I can't do it by myself. You've got to help me. It's got to come from both of us."

"How can I? I love you, Doug. And I don't understand why you keep saying you're no good for me. Is that an excuse to avoid commitment? I've tried to understand, but the more we're together, the less any excuse makes sense. Why let whatever baggage you're carrying from the past destroy our future? I can't help you if you're going to keep it all inside."

She was right. It was show-and-tell time. "I don't know where to begin."

"How about why you shut me out of your life when you're facing a crisis. You did it when Vic almost died, and again with your father. Am I just someone to be there for the good times, Doug? Don't you see, I want to be there for you through the bad times, too? Did you stop to think how badly I want you to need me then?"

"Jess, I made a conscious decision to become a cop. But when I did, I also decided I wouldn't put a woman I love through what my mother went through. I grew up watching her heartache every time my dad went out the door."

"There are many professions that involve risk-taking. And men die every day of heart attacks or traffic accidents. But no one can go through life wondering if this is the day they'll die. But if you feel that strongly about it, what's stopping you from quitting the police force if that's what is preventing you from having a normal life—whatever a normal life is?"

"Easier said than done. There are deep hang-ups we often develop as a child and carry into our adult life. And they're a lot deeper than disliking liver or asparagus."

"And you have such a hang-up."

"I grew up resenting my father for what he put my mother through."

"That's common, Doug. A lot of children grow up resenting their mother or father. You've studied enough psychology to understand that."

"But we were never able to bridge the gap. He was a strict disciplinarian whose son couldn't do anything right in his eyes."

"So you got even by becoming a rebellious teenager, right? That's textbook, Doug."

"Yeah…but I wasn't as bad as some, but not as good as others. I smoked a little pot now and then, got drunk a few times and my buddies and I went for a couple of joyrides in cars we hot-wired. I never got pulled in, but I knew it annoyed the hell out of my dad. By the time I left for college, I knew I was leaving home for good.''

"But surely your father must have been pleased when you joined the police force.''

"At first, but then the rift widened when I became a homicide detective. He had no use for homicide detectives. He scoffed at them being called the *elite* of the force. He believed the true police force was the officer on the street. And when I told him that I went into it for the puzzle-solving and not for justice to be served, it only aggravated him more. We've rarely spoken in the last ten years.''

"I'm so sorry, Doug.''

"When I went back for his funeral, I had a long talk with my mother. We spoke of the same things I've just told you, and she got very upset with me. She told me how much she loved him through all those years of putting his interests above her own. She said I didn't understand the depth of love. That when you really love someone, that person's loves and interests will always come first. It doesn't matter if that devotion isn't reciprocated. What matters is *your* love for that person. She said she has never regretted one day of her marriage that I considered to be painful and heartbreaking to her. That she'd give up everything she possessed if she could have one more day with him. She told me I should be ashamed of myself for resenting my father all through the years, instead of embracing him with the same pride and devotion she felt.''

"Oh, Doug.'' She hugged him. "I'm sure she didn't mean to condemn you. She was grieving the loss of the man she loved.''

"I understand that, Jess. But you see, I did love him. All I ever wanted from him was a word of approval. Some sign that he loved me. And because I didn't get it, I let him go to his grave believing I didn't love him. Guess it's too late to tell him now."

"How can you be so certain he didn't know?" she asked. "You respected his profession enough to choose it for your own, didn't you? What better way of showing your love? And if solving puzzles was your only motive, there are a dozen federal agencies you could have selected, but you chose a city's local police force. Don't you think that's quite revealing? Since you're such a puzzle solver, it shouldn't be too difficult to put *those* pieces together, Detective McGuire."

She stood up. "But why do you think a penance of making our lives miserable will appease the guilt you're feeling now."

"Jess, right now I'm exhausted, grief-stricken and guilt-ridden. I need your understanding."

"Doug, I understand your exhaustion, your grief and your guilt. I don't understand what it's got to do with us and our feelings for each other."

"I thought I made that clear. My mother said when you love someone you put that person's interests above your own. That's what I'm doing. I won't let you live under the same strain she did."

"Fine. There's an easy solution. Quit the force. By your own admission, you're not a dedicated lawman like your father was." She sat back down on his lap. "So you admit you love me?"

He'd come this far, so what would be gained by holding back. "Yes."

"Then trust me on this. I can handle anything that comes my way as long as you don't shut me out. Do you still want me to leave?"

"You haven't heard a word I've said, have you?"

"Not true. You admitted you loved me, Doug. That's all I need to hear. Anything else we can work out together."

He wove his fingers through hers, then raised it and kissed her palm. "You make it sound easy, Jess. I wish it were."

"It will be, my love. I'll be there to help you through it," she murmured softly.

"Your father is right. You don't listen."

"I'd be a pretty poor judge if I didn't listen. My job depends upon it. I've learned to tell when someone isn't being honest. That's why I know you aren't when you say you want me out of your life."

"I never said I *wanted* you out of my life, Jess. I'm saying it's for your own good."

"That's very noble of you, Doug, and I love you more for it, my darling, but I'm not a Dresden doll that will crack when dropped. I'd never have chosen law if I was that fragile."

"Just why *did* you choose it?"

"Actually, I intended to pursue a career in teaching."

"What changed your mind?" he asked.

The laughter left her eyes. She leaned her head against his chest. "My sister's death."

"You want to talk about it?"

"I've never discussed it with anyone except my dad and mother."

"So like me, you've held the pain inside for too long. You made me get mine out, Jess. It's time you get yours out, too."

She began hesitantly. "Karen was only seventeen when she died. Two years older than I was. She was a freshman at UW up at Madison. She was so beautiful, Doug. Blond hair, bright blue eyes."

"Yes, I've noticed. That's her in that picture with you, isn't it?"

"But that's just external. Her real beauty came from within. To know her was to love her. She loved life…and people. One night on the way back to her dorm, she was raped and murdered. They've never found the man who did it.''

He pressed a light kiss to her forehead, and wished he hadn't forced her to stir up these painful memories. He'd already upset her enough this past week.

Jess took a deep, shuddering sigh. ''So that's why I went into law. It angers me, as much as it hurts me, to know that whoever did it might still be out there.'' She raised her head and looked up beseechingly. ''You understand, don't you, Doug?'' Tears were streaking her cheeks.

His own problem was of no consequence. Jess was hurting. She looked so heartbroken that he was overwhelmed by an urge to protect her. He loved her and wished he could absorb her pain and bring the laughter back into her eyes.

She was struggling to force back her tears. ''I'm sorry. I didn't mean to cry. I thought I could get through this without tears.''

''Let them out, sweetheart.'' Tears were a cathartic, and she needed to purge herself of the pain she had held in for all those past years. ''It's okay, honey,'' he whispered over and over into her ear, and pressed a kiss to it.

He kissed her gently on the lips and he felt her quiver, then arch instinctively against him. She parted her lips and kissed him back. They were soft and he felt them tremble beneath his. He drank in the sweetness of them, and then traced his lips along her cheek, tasting the salt of her tears. The tears of his precious Dresden doll, too tough to crack. This time the thought made him smile.

He raised a hand and slid his fingers along her jaw, then buried his fingers under the silky thickness of the hair at the nape of her neck. The usual serenity of her gaze now glistened with tears. When he tenderly placed a kiss on each eyelid, she slipped her arms around his neck.

The moment was one of intimacy and need that had

nothing to do with the lust of passion, yet the urge to hold and make love to her was just as great.

He carried her into the bedroom, laid her down gently on the bed and slowly undressed her. She made no sound as he shed his own clothes, and then he lay down beside her. Their gazes locked in understanding. The need was to soothe the ache in their psyches, not their bodies. As they lay in the sanctuary of their shared love, the tempestuousness of any of their previous lovemaking had been replaced by a peaceful rhythm of light touches, tender caresses, gentle kisses until they reached that sublime moment that bound their bodies together.

And after, holding her snuggled against him, they drifted into sleep.

Chapter 18

Doug woke up in the middle of the night and turned over in bed. Jess lay asleep beside him. For the longest time he just lay watching the even rise and fall of her breathing.

The air conditioner had finally cooled down the apartment, so he got out of bed and put on his boxers, and then covered her with the sheet. Still he couldn't pull himself away from the bedside. He would never tire of just looking at Jess.

It gave him a strange feeling to see her sleeping peacefully in his bed. She looked so natural there. Certainly more so than he did among her silk sheets.

But it touched something deeper within him. It made him feel she was safe—protected. The world could no longer hurt her as long as she was there. He'd see to that.

They were a pair all right. Both carried baggage that could destroy them if they let it. Like he'd almost done. But she wasn't going to let that happen to him—and he, for damn sure, wasn't going to let that happen to her. And it felt damn good knowing this.

Unable to sleep, Doug went out to the kitchen. Since he was officially back on the case, he gathered together his working file of the murders, copies of reports and notes from the case file that he'd been accumulating since Gilbert's murder. It was time he put all of the puzzle pieces together his way.

There was nothing unique about his approach. His formula for a murder case was to set up a table with four columns: Motive, Opportunity, Means and Connection to the Victim, and plug in a name. He'd then analyze the final result for whoever's name appeared the most often on the chart. Up to now he had completed the chart through Bellemy's murder, but had not had time to approach it since.

To date, Liz Alexander's, Ben Kirkland's and Jess's names appeared most often—their motive being their devotion to Jess, who had been publicly condemned for throwing these cases out of court. Although he believed Jess had nothing to do with the murders, he had to include her name in order to tie the other two to the case. Thank goodness she hadn't presided at Sanderson's trial, because it helped to knock all three out of the running.

He picked up the additional information he'd accumulated on Marcus Sands, aka Mark Sanderson. It was the first time he had the chance to go over it because of the interruption due to his father's death.

It was simply a brief report relating to the arrest of the suspect, his subsequent incarceration and the chain of events leading up to his trial. From what Doug read, he saw nothing that linked Ben Kirkland or Liz Alexander to Sanderson. Maybe Vic was right, Sands's murder might have been a copycat killing.

He started to put the paper aside when one line in the last paragraph caught his attention. The hair at his nape stood on end.

Originally assigned to the court of Judge Jessica Kirkland, she recused herself for prejudicial reasons because of the similarity between the decedent's murder and that of her sister's.

Doug groaned. Dammit, not one stinking break in the case. He entered Jess, Liz and Ben in the motive column.

"What are you doing at this late hour?" Jess had approached from behind him. She slid her arms around him, leaned over and nibbled at his ear.

He hadn't even heard her approach. He was really slipping. He turned the chart over and put it facedown. "Just catching up on my homework."

"Aha! So this is how the fabulous Detective McGuire solves his cases," she teased. Before he could stop her, she snatched it up.

"Jess, give it to me."

Too late, she had already started to read it. "Motive, Liz Alexander. Ben…Kirkland…Jess." She looked at him, stunned. "These names are your suspects?"

"Jess, you don't understand."

"You're right, Doug. I don't understand. How could you make love to me, tell me you love me and consider me a possible murderer?"

"Believe me, Jess, I've *never* considered you one. I rule people out with this method as well."

Still visibly shaken, it was as if she wasn't even listening. "And you've made my father and my best friend suspects as well." She looked at him like a wounded deer. "How could you?"

"It's a giant puzzle, Jess. This is how I put the pieces together until the puzzle is completed."

"A puzzle! You're talking about people. People I love dearly. Someone you claim to love. We aren't puzzle pieces to be moved around. We're human beings." She picked up the paper he had just read, and paled after reading it. "You even knew about Karen and you pretended not to. You let me run on about it. What were you hoping for, Doug? That I'd trip myself up somewhere along the way, and you'd have your murderer." She ran out of the kitchen.

Doug followed her. "Jess, I just read that myself. I didn't know how your sister died. I swear it."

She wouldn't even look at him. She finished dressing, and grabbed her purse. "Goodbye, Doug. I never want to see or hear from you again. Good luck on finding your killer. I can only suggest you come up with some new suspects because the ones you have aren't murderers."

"Jess, for the love of God, please listen to me."

She was already out the door. He was in his boxers and couldn't chase after her. By the time he got into a pair of shorts and got downstairs, she had gotten into her car and pulled away.

Doug went back upstairs and dialed Jess's number. He left a pleading message on her answering machine to call him. He knew she wouldn't, but he was desperate.

He sat down on the edge of the bed. He'd really screwed up this time. There was no turning back. She was through with him, and meant it. She never wanted to see him again.

Picking up the pillow, he buried his nose in her scent, then reached for the phone and dialed her again, hoping against hope, she'd answer. He left another message.

It was useless to go back to the chart. He'd never be able to concentrate, so he reached over and turned on the lamp. In her haste to leave, Jess had left her earrings behind. With a shuddering sigh he picked them up, and as he stared at them, the detective's memory for details kicked in and penetrated the haze of his misery. He's seen one like it before.

Doug bolted off the bed and hurried into the kitchen. Shuffling quickly through the papers, he found what he was looking for: the photos of the four earrings he'd found in Marcus Sands's locker. One of the photos matched the gold and pearl earrings he held in his hand.

Adrenaline pumped through him in a flood tide. Galvanized into action, he wrote down two addresses, and then went back to the bedroom and put on a suit.

Before leaving, he called the number of the security desk at Jess's condominium. Charlie answered.

"This is McGuire. Did Judge Kirkland get home okay?"

"Yeah, she pulled in about five minutes ago. What happened, McGuire, you two lovebirds have a spat?"

"When I write my memoirs, pal, you can read all about it." He hung up.

Doug knew he'd get nowhere trying to get Jess to even listen to his questions, so he'd have to make a couple more enemies that night. He checked the address he'd written down and drove to Liz Alexander's house. She lived in a small ranch house in the residential section of a northside suburb. He wasn't surprised to see the black Cadillac parked in the driveway.

Her irritation at being awakened at two in the morning quickly changed to concern when she recognized him. "Did something happen to Jess?"

"No, that's not why I'm here. May I come in?"

"Is this an official visit, Detective?" she asked, stepping aside for him to enter.

"I need an immediate answer, and I know I won't get it from Jess."

"Then you're wasting your time, Doug. Jess is my best friend. I'm not about to tell you anything she doesn't want you to know."

Doug reached into his coat pocket. "It has nothing to do with the personal relationship between Jess and me. I'm hoping you might know where she got these earrings. They look expensive."

Liz examined them. "They are expensive. I've seen

them on her many times, but I have no idea where or when she got them.''

''You think your houseguest might know?''

Her eyes rounded in surprise. ''I don't know what you're talking about.''

''Let me see them,'' Ben Kirkland said, entering the room. When Doug didn't even raise a brow, Ben laughed. ''You aren't surprised, Doug.''

''No, I figured it out a couple weeks ago.''

''What gave us away?'' he asked.

''I'll be straight with you. You two are the only possible suspects we've been able to come up with on these murders.''

''You suspect us?'' Liz groped for a chair and sank down in it.

''Good Lord, Doug! I've never even met any one of those victims,'' Ben said.

''And neither have I,'' Liz interjected. ''I've only heard of Gilbert and Bellemy because they were two of Jess's cases. This Sands fellow I'd never heard of before until I read about him in the paper. Why in the world would you suspect us?''

''I won't go into the reasons why you're considered suspects at this time.''

Ben Kirkland seemed more amused than shocked. ''What does that have to do with figuring out Liz and I have a relationship?''

''As suspects, we've done some checking up on you and discovered both of your absences were unaccountable on the day Liz was a no-show at the courthouse. Which happened to have been the same morning we found Bellemy's body. So we checked back further. You'd be amazed what turns up when you start checking credit cards, gasoline charges and telephone calls. The two of you left a paper trail as wide as the Mississippi.''

''I suppose I should be indignant for such an invasion

of my privacy, but frankly, Doug, I've always been impressed with your detective skills.''

''It wasn't difficult to put the pieces together. I should advise you that although they explain your whereabouts, they don't rule out the possibility of the two of you being conspirators in these murders. Especially the way you've been pussyfooting around.''

''As much as I admire your tenacity, Detective, the only crime Liz and I have committed is deceiving my daughter.''

''Which is a part of the puzzle that doesn't fit. Why the deceit? Jess is a big girl.''

''It was my idea, Doug,'' Liz said. ''Jess had just broken up with Dennis Wolcott. Ben and I got together to discuss her situation and found ourselves attracted to each other. We didn't want to say anything to her then, and the longer we put off telling her, the harder it became.''

He never understood why people made things difficult for themselves by avoiding simple explanations. ''Well, that's your business. Mine are homicides. What about these earrings?'' He handed them to Kirkland.

''Yes, I recognize them. I had identical pairs made for Jess and Karen as birthday gifts. They both were born in June, and pearls are their birthstones. It had to have been—''

''At least eighteen years ago,'' Doug said.

Ben looked at him, surprised. ''Yes, before Karen was…before she died. What do these have to do with the murder cases you're working on?''

''I can't tell you that, sir. It's just a hunch at this time.'' So Kirkland hadn't gotten over Karen's death, either. What is it about people that they continue to carry baggage around that fouled up their lives? Lord knows he was a shining example.

''Do you think the same man who murdered these men was involved in Karen's death as well?'' Ben asked.

"No, I don't." Doug walked to the door. "Sorry to have bothered you so late. I'll get in touch with you if my hunch pans out."

Doug drove straight to the precinct. It was a quiet night, and the shift on duty welcomed his requests. One of the detectives got on the wire to check out unsolved murders similar to that of Karen Kirkland's: Caucasian, blond, campus student. Although not all cities report this information to the FBI, their database came up with eight identical cases: Berkeley, California; Gainesville, Florida; Carbondale, Illinois; Duluth, Minnesota; two in New York at Buffalo and Albany; the University of Wisconsin-Madison, which was Karen Kirkland's; and the University of Wisconsin-Milwaukee, the case that had involved Mark Sanderson.

They, in turn, transmitted copies of the earrings found in Sands's locker to the FBI and the police in those targeted cities for the possibility of recognition among the families and friends of the decedents.

Doug then put in a call to Vic, and as soon as his partner showed up they headed for the Property and Evidence Bureau warehouse where the file cabinets removed from Sands's locker had been stored.

With cities and dates to go on, they had a starting point. Marcus Sands's meticulousness and color-coding made it easier. His records did not go as far back as the New York slayings, but since Sands's roots had been in New York, Doug called Phil Evans at the precinct and asked him to check to see if Sands might have been a student at those colleges at that time. He also told him to check out the other colleges for the same thing.

It was a tedious job reading every paid receipt or bus ticket Sands had saved. By four o'clock they had established that Sands had been enrolled in state universities in Madison, Duluth and Carbondale at the time of the murders, but found nothing in his files that could link him to Berkley or Gainsville.

When they returned to the squad room they were met with interesting news. Evans had found out that Sands had been a student at the Albany and Buffalo universities at the time of the respective murders.

"Well that explains what Sands did during the day—he enrolled at colleges to stake out his victims."

The local detective bureau in Duluth had immediately gone to work on Evan's request, and interviewed a woman who had shared a dorm room with that decedent. She recognized one of the earrings as belonging to the victim, because she had often borrowed them from her.

Vic gave Doug a high five. "Good detective work, partner. Thanks to your lead, Sands is definitely tied to the Duluth, Madison and Milwaukee murders, and he can be placed in Albany, Buffalo and Carbondale at the time of those murders. With a little more police work, I bet you the local departments will turn up an identification of the other two carrings. You've uncovered a serial killer, Doug. The department should give you a medal."

"A dead serial killer, Vic," Doug said. "We still have to find the live one we have on our hands."

Reality had crashed back down on him again. Jess.

He hoped Ben Kirkland and Liz Alexander weren't involved in the murders. He liked them both, and he knew what they meant to Jess. His gut feeling was that they weren't. But as Vic said, he couldn't let his emotions cloud his judgment.

He dialed Jess's number again and left another message. Then on a hunch, he dialed the security desk.

"Charlie, McGuire. Did you see the judge leave?"

"Yep, earlier this morning with suitcase in hand."

"Did she tell you where she was going?"

"Nope. Most of the people usually don't, unless they want me to take in their mail or water their plants. I figure she was going off with you. You know, a little lovers' tryst for the weekend.''

"Nobody can pull anything over on you, can they pal?'' Doug hung up.

I listened to his message, Jessica. McGuire sounds pretty desperate. I wish you wouldn't go away like this, Jess. I'm very lonely when you go away. At least you're not with him. If that McGuire has upset you again, he's going to have to pay for it. I won't tolerate him making you unhappy. Detective McGuire is living on borrowed time right now.

Doug left the precinct, drove home, shucked the suit and tie for jeans and a T-shirt and then tried Jess's cell phone. He slammed the phone down and tried the courthouse but got Liz Alexander's answering machine, so he dug through his files and came up with her home phone. Same result. Next he dialed Ben Kirkland's number. When he struck out there he left his apartment and drove to the Water Street Bistro.

Ben and Liz must have decided to come out of the closet about their relationship, because they were having dinner together and smiling at each other like two people in love. At least some relationships were going smoothly.

"Well, good evening, Detective, would you like to join us for dinner?'' Ben asked cordially when Doug approached their table. "Or did you come here to make an arrest?''

Doug wasn't amused. "Where's Jess?''

He shrugged, "I really can't say.'' It was clear the news that she was gone didn't come as a surprise to him.

"Can't or won't, Kirkland?'' He turned to Liz. "Is that your story, too, Ms. Alexander?''

"She didn't tell me where she was going,'' Liz said.

"And you didn't ask, of course. You're her secretary.

Do you expect me to believe she went away without telling you where she was going?''

"It's the truth, Doug. I'm as upset about it as you are. Jess left me a note that she'd cleared her docket and would be back Sunday." Liz dug in her purse and handed him the note Jess had written. "I thought she'd probably gone away with you."

"At least sit down, Doug, and have a drink or are you still on duty?"

He sat down, and a waiter immediately appeared with a glass and a menu. Doug waved aside the menu as Ben filled the glass. After taking a drink of it, he was no wine connoisseur but had to admit that something could be said for the taste of hundred-dollar bottles of wine.

"What's going on between you and Jess?" Ben asked. "The last time I saw the two of you together, you looked pretty cozy."

"You missed the last time Jess and I were together, Kirkland. It was anything but cozy."

"So you had a lovers' quarrel."

"Jess never wants to see me again." Ben and Liz exchanged surprised glances. "She didn't take the news too well when she found out the three of you were our leading suspects on these murder cases."

Ben's gaze sharpened. "Are you saying you suspect her, too? Dammit, Detective, that's carrying suspicion too far."

"Now I understand why she doesn't want to see you again," Liz said. "I'd feel the same way in her place."

"Ms. Alexander, you *are* in her place. As I told you before, you are a suspect, too."

Irritated, Liz spoke up, "And as a woman, McGuire, it would be too shattering to hear from the man I loved that he suspected I was a murderer, much less a serial killer on top of it."

"I don't give a rat's behind what you two think of me personally. For the record, I never considered Jess a suspect. But that's my personal opinion. Others will until I can prove to them otherwise.'' He shoved back his chair to leave.

''Doug,'' Ben said, ''the only place I can think where she might have gone is up to Rhinelander. We have a cottage up there.''

Doug pulled out his notebook. ''Write down the address and directions.''

''Wouldn't you be better off letting her cool off?'' Ben suggested. ''Jess has a level head, Doug. Once she has a chance to—''

''The address, Kirkland,'' Doug said. Ben sighed and wrote down the directions. ''Off the record, Ben, I have some information that is of concern to you. Since you are one of our suspects, you may have known this long before I did.''

Ben looked quizzical; Liz appeared engrossed in what he was saying. ''You understand, this is off the record and not to be repeated beyond this table until it becomes official.''

''For heaven's sake, man, what is it?'' Ben asked.

''We have a positive identification on the man who murdered your daughter.''

''Oh, dear God,'' Ben murmured. Tears moistened his eyes.

Liz Alexander reached over and clutched his hand. ''Oh, Ben.''

''Who is it?'' Ben asked, swiping the moisture out of his eyes.

''Who *was* it,'' Doug said. ''Marcus Sands.''

Ben frowned. ''Wasn't he the dead man pulled out of the lake?''

Doug nodded. ''In going through the locker he rented, we discovered an earring identical to the pair Jess has. It seems Mr. Sands was a trophy killer.''

''Trophy killer?'' Liz asked.

"Collects an item belonging to his victims," Doug explained. "So we checked him further and came up with a lot more evidence that links him to other murders."

"I don't know what to say," Ben said. "All these years, knowing Karen's killer was still out there unpunished has been eating Jess and I alive. The heartache of it killed my wife."

"I know Jess would like to know this, that's why I have to talk to her."

"I suppose you've tried her cell phone," Ben said.

"She's not answering it."

"Well, if you get going now, it's a little over a four hour drive. You can still reach there before it turns dark."

Doug stood up. "I'm not afraid of the dark, sir."

Chapter 19

Jess sat on the front stoop, her head bowed, her shoulders slumped in despair. The heartache of her misery was so acute it felt like a vise squeezing the breath out of her. The pain in her chest burned like a fire, searing her very soul. She closed her eyes and leaned back against the railing post.

She felt so betrayed. She loved him so much—and he'd betrayed her. If he'd become bored with her, or even preferred another woman, she might have understood it. But his deceit was such a cruel violation of trust. Had she been so blinded by passion that it clouded her thinking? She'd always heard that no one knows a man better than the woman who shares his bed. How could she have misjudged him so terribly? She sighed and drew a deep breath. It even hurt to breathe.

Jess stood up. She had to stop rehashing these same questions again and again. It was over between her and Doug. She'd have to accept it and get on with her life.

Jess drew another deep breath. Pretty soon it wouldn't

hurt. Pretty soon the hurt would go away. *You'll get through this, Jessica. Just don't make the mistake of wallowing in self-pity. You went into it with your eyes wide-open—trouble was, your heart was wide-open, too. If only you could hate him. That would make it easier. So much easier.*

Ben Kirkland had not exaggerated the remoteness of the cottage. Dusk had descended by the time Doug turned onto the dirt road Ben had indicated on the map he'd drawn. Cut through a thick forest of pine and birch trees, the narrow road was barely wide enough for the width of a car. After a quarter of a mile of cursing the bumps and ruts he came to an abrupt halt at a cottage. The last rays of the setting sun glistened on the waters of a small lake that lay beyond it.

Doug was relieved to see Jess's Park Avenue parked near the entrance. He pulled in beside it, and then removed his gun and shoved it and his cell phone into the glove compartment. As he walked to the door, he could feel his heartbeat quicken in anticipation of seeing her. He'd always felt it from the time they started going together and knew it took about thirty seconds for his hormones to stop hopping around. Then she'd smile at him and they'd kick into overdrive again.

The front door was open, but there was no light in the house, so he knocked on the screen door. Unlatched, it bounced each time he rapped.

"Jess," he called out, but sensed a stillness and knew the house was empty.

He opened the screen door and stepped inside. After a quick check, he went out the back door to find her. There was no sign of her outside or on the pier. A small boat was still tied to it, so he knew she wasn't on the lake, either.

"Jess," he called out again, and was answered with the cry of a loon.

The shed was padlocked. Which was the only thing he'd found locked up till then, because her car was unlocked when he'd checked that out.

Doug went back into the house. Jess's purse lay on the kitchen counter and her car keys tossed beside it. He checked out the purse and her wallet was untouched. There clearly was no sign of robbery or foul play, but the detective in him didn't like it. She was too damn trusting. How could she wander away and leave the house wide-open, and car keys and money as an invitation to anyone wandering by.

He sat down to wait. The longer he waited, the angrier he grew for her being so careless. And the angrier he grew, the more worried he became. What if she'd had an accident, or been attacked by some wild animal? And God knows who might be lurking in those woods.

He bolted to his feet just as the back door slammed.

Jess came into the room and gasped in alarm. When she recognized him, alarm changed to contempt.

"Get out of here, Doug. I made it clear to you that I never want to see or hear from you again. If you continue to follow me and break into my residences, I shall have you arrested for stalking."

"I don't have to break into your residences. Any fool and his brother can walk through the open door."

"I didn't realize you had a brother."

"What have I told you about not locking your doors?" he demanded. "For a person who is a felony judge, and has to deal with scum daily, you walk around like Pollyanna acting as if there's no evil in the world, even though you're torn apart by the heinous murder of your sister. If I live to be a hundred, lady, I'll never understand you."

"I'm not asking you to."

"Furthermore," he continued to rant, "what are you

doing walking around in the woods without anything to protect you? You could have encountered a wild animal.''

"The only wild animal I've encountered since I've been here is you, McGuire.'' She was so angry she felt wilder than any animal she might have encountered.

"I bet you don't even own a weapon, and if you did, it would be as worthless to you as door keys, door chains or car keys.''

"Or as worthless as you, McGuire. If you don't get out of here, I will.'' She stormed out the back door and ran to the pier.

Doug chased after her and caught her before she reached the boat. He grasped her by the shoulders and turned her around. His expression was so thunderous that he looked mad enough to hit her, but she knew he wouldn't. "I've been up all night and just drove four hours to talk to you. If you don't cool down and listen to me, Jess, I'm tossing you into that lake to cool off.''

"Then that's what you'll have to do.'' She stomped on his foot and when he winced, she shoved him away as hard as she could. He fell back, but the trouble was he was holding on to her when he did. They both toppled into the water.

Jess broke the surface and saw that Doug had just done the same a few feet away. The water did feel good, and it cooled her anger. The fight was out of her; she just wanted to be left alone.

Doug hoisted himself up on the pier and reached out a hand to help her up. When she felt the warm, secure grip of his hand, she knew how much she would miss that touch. It seemed to embody every sentimental moment they had shared.

Once on the pier, he didn't release her. She felt numb, and couldn't bear to start arguing with him again. She looked down at their clasped hands and then up at him.

"Let me go, Doug," she said softly. Both knew she meant more than just a hand clasp.

The water seemed to have had the same effect on him. His touch was gentle when he put a hand on each of her shoulders, and gazed tenderly down at her.

"I can't, Jess, I love you."

Drops of water clung to his forehead and glistened in his dark hair. She turned her head away. It was too painful to look at him and not succumb to the temptation to reach up and run a finger along that rugged jaw or press a kiss to those sensual lips.

"Please, Doug, just go away." She began to shiver and slumped down on the pier and folded her arms across her chest to try and stop shivering.

He walked away without a word, and she hugged her knees to her chest and let her tears mingle with the water running down her cheeks from her dripping hair.

Jess was unaware he'd returned until he knelt beside her, wrapped a blanket around her and began to dry her hair with a towel.

"Let's get you out of those wet clothes before you catch a cold," he said. He removed her shoes and socks, then pulled the blouse over her head and off her arms.

The movement snapped her out of her apathy. "What are you doing?"

"I'm trying to get these wet clothes off you, Jess."

"Stop it. Stop it," she shrieked, and began to flail out at him with both hands.

He hugged her, pinning her arms to her sides. "Jess, honey, I'm not going to hurt you."

She tried to struggle out of his grasp, and his body forced her down until her back was against the pier. Then he stretched out on top of her, holding her down with his body and using his hands to pin her arms to the pier as well.

"I'm not going to hurt you, Jess," he repeated. "I just

want to talk to you. I have some news about Karen's death.''

Jess was fully alert now, and stopped struggling. It was useless against his strength anyway.

"What about Karen?"

He released her arms, but didn't budge. "We know who killed her."

She tried to comprehend what he was saying as she listened to him explain about matching earrings, a locker and campus murders. After all these years—it couldn't be possible. It finally sunk into her muddled mind that Karen's murderer was no longer out there. His life had been extinguished with the same violence and lack of dignity as his victims'.

Nothing could ever bring Karen back again, but Jess felt a tremendous sense of closure to her sister's death, though there would never be closure on the loss of her.

She threw her arms around his neck in an unbridled feeling of gratitude. "Thank you, Doug. Thank you so much." Tears of joy replaced the ones of despair she had shed only moments earlier.

It was instinctive—inevitable—that a kiss would follow.

They reached the point of no return the instant their lips joined. His firm mouth hungrily seeking the response she couldn't deny. Her urgency matched his as her body and senses soared to life again.

That's what this man's touch could do to her. For the past twenty-four hours she had agonized, trying to deny her need for him; a need that went far beyond the physical demand her body now sought. The core of her soul cried out for the solace he brought to it just as fervently as the core of her body demanded the same succor.

Their hands moved with speed and wildness as they struggled to remove each other's wet clothing. And then they were free—mouth on mouth, flesh on flesh, their love flowing between them with the same intensity as their passion.

And as they loved, her arms enfolded him, her body welcomed him, her soul absorbed him.

Later they swam in the isolation of the quiet lake, and then wrapped together in the blanket they returned to the house. They showered together—which had become a ritual with them—and then went to bed, made love again and then, overcome by exhaustion they fell asleep.

Jess awoke a few hours later and lay watching him sleep. She savored the comfort of his nearness. Even in sleep he was compelling, exuding masculinity. His unshaven jaw was darkened by a light dusting of whiskers, and to her loving gaze his face bordered on beautiful, were it not for the tiny lines that crept from the corners of his eyes and mouth. She smiled, knowing she dare not call him that or Lord knows how he'd react.

Unable to resist the sensuous draw of his lips, she pressed a light kiss to them. He opened his eyes.

"I didn't mean to wake you," she murmured.

The gleam in his eyes was as seductive as the smile on his lips, coaxing her nearer until their breaths mingled.

"I'm glad you did, Angel Face," he said in a husky whisper, and pulled her even closer.

They lay contentedly for a long moment before he asked, "Are you ready to talk about it now?"

She knew what he meant. Would it rekindle all the pain again? No matter how often she had told herself she could give him up, she'd crumbled the moment he appeared. It was foolish to go on thinking she could leave him; she loved him too much to walk away. But would his betrayal always be a painful memory between them?

"I don't know, Doug. I feel betrayed. I trusted you, but you didn't—"

"Jess, I tried to explain this to you last night, but you wouldn't listen. I do not consider you a suspect."

"Then why am I on your suspect list?"

"In order to tie your father and Liz to the crimes. We could hardly do that without adding your name. And just because their names are on the list doesn't mean I personally suspect them."

"Why, Doug? Why in the farthest reach of your imagination would you want to link them to these crimes?"

"Honey, the day Gilbert was released you made an urgent plea on the steps of the courthouse that these killers must be brought to justice."

"All of Southern Wisconsin heard that. Why try to link it to Dad and Liz?"

"Because we have to start somewhere—and that would be directly connected to you."

"So you *did* suspect me in the beginning?"

"With Gilbert, sure in the beginning before I got to know you." He grinned. "Deep down I hoped that a babe with legs like yours wasn't guilty."

She gave him a swat in the arm. "So when did you rule me out."

"The first time I kissed you, Angel Face."

"I thought this was supposed to be a serious discussion, Doug. This isn't a laughing matter."

"All right, I'll be serious. That same afternoon, practically right after the television incident, Vic and I got a tip from one of our stoolies that somebody was trying to put out a contract on Gilbert. It crossed my mind that you were the only person who knew in advance that he was getting a walk, so maybe you were making the contract. I swear that was the only time I even remotely considered you a possible suspect. By the time Bellemy was murdered, I knew you could never murder or sanction one. Trouble was, these were both cases you threw out of court, so others did."

"You mean Vic."

"Vic's my partner, Jess. He's a damn sharp detective. It also increased the suspicion against your father and Liz, if someone was knocking off these guys for your sake."

"Thank goodness you didn't approach my bench with that half-baked theory," she grumbled.

"After Bellemy's murder I added Ron Tate to my suspect list. Bellemy had killed Tate's daughter and got a walk. Honey, I was even scared that if it was someone out for revenge you might be in danger for letting the perp go."

"So that explains all those locking doors and fastening the chain lectures from you, McGuire."

"Not entirely. For safety sake, I wish you would learn to lock doors, Jess. Anyway, Sands's death eliminated any motive or connection with you, or any motive for your father or Liz to be involved. Then the attack on Vic eliminated Ron Tate. So we were back to square one until I read you had recused yourself from the Mark Sanderson trial—aka Marcus Sands. It put your father and Liz back on the list as suspects."

"Well, you're wrong. Neither one of them is capable of murder."

"Your father is quite amused that he's a suspect."

"You told him?"

"How do you think I found out about this place?"

"Why would you suspect Liz? These were big men. Physically, how would she ever overpower them and dispose of their bodies?"

"We suspect the killer uses a wheelchair after murdering them. We checked out medical supply companies but couldn't turn up any recent purchases that didn't check out. We even tried hospitals and nursing homes to see if any had a wheelchair missing or stolen. No luck there, either."

"I don't care. You're wrong about Dad and Liz, Doug. You're so wrong."

He hugged her closer. "I hope you're right, honey. I like both of them, and I hope neither is guilty. But trust me, Jess, guilty or not, we will solve these murders."

I wished I hadn't followed him to the cottage. I saw what the two of you did. It was so disgusting I had to leave. How could you lay naked on that pier and let him do those things to you? He's turning you into a harlot, Jessica. Can't you see he's no good for you? He's pulling you down to his level? I can't stand by and let it happen. I'll have to put a stop to it. And soon before he ruins you more.

Jess woke up early the next morning and before she could become distracted by the sleeping figure beside her, she got out of bed and retrieved the wet clothing they had left on the pier last night. She had them washed and in the dryer by the time Doug woke up and showered. She'd found him shaving supplies in the other bathroom, but none of her father's clothing was large enough to fit him. He padded barefoot into the kitchen with only a towel wrapped around his hips.

"Have you ever considered becoming a male model, Doug? You have a beautifully proportioned body," she commented, with an appreciate glance.

He measured her with a withering look. "Yeah right. I thought I would as soon as you do a *Playboy* spread, Judge Jess."

By the time they ate a breakfast of bacon and eggs, Doug's clothes had dried and as soon as he dressed, he went out to his car and returned with his gun and cell phone. Unfortunately, his wallet had been in his jeans pocket, and anything that wasn't plastic or laminated was soaked.

"Next time you get a notion to go swimming, warn me

in advance, lady,'' he said, spreading his currency out on the kitchen counter to dry.

"I'm sorry, Doug."

He slipped his arms around her waist and grinned. "I asked for it, Angel Face." Then he kissed her, and as always past grievances were forgotten.

"So what would you like to do today?" she asked. "Should we play tourist and go sight-seeing?"

"What's wrong with just relaxing?"

"I like that idea. You need a quiet day off."

She beat him unmercifully in a game of *Scrabble;* he tromped her in a game of backgammon. Then they went swimming. Afterward, they stretched out on towels on the pier and as they soaked up the sun they talked about their pasts. This time they shared the fondest memories of their childhood, chuckling with delight at the pleasant ones, laughing out loud at the awkward ones. Blissfully happy, indescribably in love.

Neither one wanted the day to end. They ate a late dinner, took a midnight swim without suits, came back inside, showered together and made love.

Later, cuddling next to him, Jess murmured, "This has been the happiest day of my life. I wish it would never end."

He kissed her forehead. "So do I, but tomorrow we go back to the separate worlds waiting for us."

"They aren't separate, Doug."

"Jess, from the beginning neither of us have been playing by the rules."

"What rules?"

"You're a judge. I'm a detective."

"Yes, our friend Ms. Matthews has pointed that out. So what?"

"As a detective I've crossed a line as far as my duties and responsibilities are concerned. I'm in the middle of a murder investigation, yet yesterday I not only left town to follow you up here, but against everything I've been trained to do, I left my weapon in my car overnight because I wasn't thinking of anything except making love to you. And my worst violation is that I'm in love with my partner's prime suspect.''

She refused to let his words stir up old uncertainties. ''Let him and the whole city of Milwaukee think what they want. What *we* think is what matters, Doug.''

''Yeah right! You know as well as I do, that if I suddenly backed off this case, or quit the force, it would only make people more suspicious of you, your father and Liz. The best thing I can do is stick with it and hope for the right ending.''

''Furthermore,'' she declared, ''I don't want to hear another word from you about our separate worlds. I'm a judge, you're a detective. So what? Can't you see that it's never been your world or my world? It's *our* world.''

He rolled over and stretched out on top of her. ''We can't run away from reality. My point is if this case doesn't turn out the way we'd like it to, where will that leave us?'' His face was lined with tension awaiting her answer.

Yesterday that question would have ripped her apart internally, but since then she had come to understand the position he was in. Given the chance to think clearly, and use her common sense rather than her emotions, she had the confidence and peace of mind that her father and Liz were not involved.

''Where we are right now. Two people in love. Nothing can change that.''

He kissed her and their love swirled between them, firing their bodies as always with the heat of their shared passion.

Chapter 20

The telephone was ringing when Jess opened the door to her apartment late the next day. It was Liz and they chatted for a few minutes, and when she hung up, Doug had just finished a conversation on his cell phone.

"That was Liz," Jess said. "There's a rescheduling snag, so I told her I'd come in and work it out."

"Yeah, I have to go into the precinct, too. Why don't I drop you off at the courthouse, pick you up when I'm through and then we'll grab something to eat."

"Just let me…" Jess halted what she was about to say when she noticed the picture of Karen and her had been moved again. "Doug, why do you keep moving this picture?"

"What are you talking about?" he asked.

"This picture of Karen and I." She picked up the framed photograph and returned it to its rightful spot.

"I've never touched that picture."

She scoffed. "Yeah right! Doug. I don't care if you

came in here while I was gone. That doesn't matter any-more.''

"Jess, I said I have never touched that picture."

She frowned. "Really." Confused, she shook her head. "I know I didn't move it."

"Maybe your cleaning lady did," he said.

"No, Sarah's been away all month visiting a daughter in Maine. She isn't due back for another week."

Doug was now clearly concerned. "I never told you, Jess, but I thought I heard someone in here one night. Who else has a key to this place?"

"Ah, besides Sarah—who's been with me for ten years by the way—my father has one, Liz keeps one at the office, and Charlie, the doorman, has a key in the event of an emergency such as fire."

"What about Wolcott?"

"Dennis returned it to me when we broke up." She opened a table drawer. "It's still here. I should have given it to you a long time ago."

"That still doesn't mean he couldn't have had a dupli-cate made."

"No, these keys cannot be duplicated without the au-thorization of the owner."

"Dammit, Jess, you're the most naive person I've ever met. There's nothing easier than to have a duplicate key made. Nine out of ten locksmiths don't give a hoot about any restriction on the key. Do you mind if I have the pic-ture and a couple other things here dusted for prints?"

"Doug, there's nothing missing."

"Jess, please. Humor me. If someone's coming in here without telling you, I want to know."

"All right, if it'll make you happy."

"That's my gal." He kissed her lightly on the forehead. "I'll send someone from Forensics over tomorrow."

"*Now,* Detective McGuire, may I get to the court-house?" she asked.

"We're on our way, Angel Face."

*   *   *

Doug dropped Jess off and said he'd be back to pick her up. Vic was waiting for him at the precinct with the news that another victim's earring, similar to the picture they'd put on the wire, was among the remains of the decedent in Carbondale, Illinois.

The slayer of Marcus Sands had murdered a serial killer of at least four women.

"And who knows how many others." Doug sat down at his desk and picked up a videotape. "What's this?"

"Your favorite female reporter dropped that off for you," Vic said.

There was a note attached from Sherilyn Matthews saying that she thought the Mr. Law and Ms. Order would enjoy showing the tape to their grandchildren some day.

"Why doesn't that barracuda find someone else to chew on?" Doug grumbled.

Vic chuckled. "She's got the hots for you, partner. By the way, how did you make out with Jess?"

"We settled a lot of things between us. Vic, we've got to solve this case. There has to be something we're not connecting. As long as it's open, it's a wedge between Jess and me. I can only hope her father or Liz Alexander's not involved."

Vic's grin dissipated, replaced by a grim frown. He slapped Doug on the shoulder. "I hope for your sake they aren't, either, partner. Well, I'm out of here. See ya in the morning."

Doug popped the video in the VCR and sat down to watch it. The tape was from the day he and Jess had the argument on the courthouse steps—the day Gilbert had been released from jail.

Doug leaned back to enjoy just looking at Jess. He couldn't get enough of looking at her. He wanted to spend the rest of his life with her, and wondered if she'd ever consider them getting married. It had taken seven years for her to decide not to get hitched to Wolcott, so she sure as hell wasn't one who rushed into marriage.

Yeah, but who was he to criticize. Doug McGuire, the confirmed bachelor. That would be a good laugh to the guys in the locker room.

He grinned, watching the two of them go at each other on the tape. God, she was beautiful when she was angry. She was beautiful any time.

The camera spanned the spectators. He'd been so engrossed in their argument at the time that he hadn't realized what a crowd they'd attracted.

He suddenly sat up and leaned forward, then backed up the tape and froze it on the awestruck face of one of the spectators, staring at Jess with devotion. The hair at his nape stood on end, and he realized with the sixth sense that had guided him throughout his law enforcement career that he had found the perp.

He reached for the telephone and dialed Vic's cell phone. After a short conversation, he then dialed Jess.

It was nine o'clock, and despite the incessant phone calls they were close to finishing their revision of Jess's schedule. When the phone rang again, Jess snatched it up impatiently. "Hello."

"Jess, I think I just figured out who's responsible for these murders."

She gasped in surprise. Doug sounded apprehensive. Despite her confidence that those she loved were not a part of it, Jess couldn't help but feel uneasy.

"Doug, I'm sorry, but we're almost through here. You can tell me when I see you."

"Okay, I'm on my way over."

Jess hung up the phone. "That was Doug. He said he's figured out who's responsible for the murders."

Both Liz and Stanley's heads popped up in surprise.

"Did he say who it was?" Liz asked. She and Jess exchanged a meaningful glance.

"No, I didn't give him time. Are we about through?"

"Jess, are you sure this is what you want to do? You can see the turmoil it's created already."

"Yes, I've thought it out clearly and made up my mind. Two weeks from today I'll be a free woman. So, can we wrap this up?"

"Yes," Liz said. "Stanley and I just finished." Liz glanced at her watch. "And not a minute too soon. I have to leave. I have an engagement."

Jess winked at the young man, who had been such a valuable help to them. "That sounds intriguing, doesn't it, Stanley? Do you know who Liz's mystery man is?" Stanley grinned and shook his head.

"You'll find out soon enough," Liz said. She pulled out a compact, checked her makeup, then stood up. "You coming, Stanley?"

"Would you like me to drive you home, Judge Kirkland?" Stanley asked.

"Thank you, but that won't be necessary. I have a little more to finish up here, and Doug said he would pick me up."

"Well at least lock up after we leave. Everyone's gone on this floor," Liz said.

"Yeah, I will. Shut off my phone, Liz. These phone calls are too disruptive." She arched a brow. "And enjoy your, ah…engagement. Thank's again, Stanley, for your help."

As soon as the two left, Jess resumed reading the transcript that had been assigned to her from another court. With luck, she would finish it before Doug showed up.

"Judge Kirkland, I have to talk to you."

Startled, Jess looked up to see Stanley in the doorway of her chambers.

"Stanley, you startled me! I thought you left with Liz."

"I did, but I came back. You didn't lock the door like she told you to do. But I locked it now. No one can get in."

Jess began feeling uneasy. He appeared agitated and not himself. "Sit down, Stanley. What is the problem?"

"I did what you asked me to, didn't I?"

"Yes, you did, Stanley, and I appreciate it. Liz and I would still have hours to go if you hadn't helped."

"I don't mean tonight. I'm talking about those men."

"What men, Stanley?"

"Those dead men. I killed them just as you asked."

Jess was horrified. She wanted to run, but knew she'd never make it out of her chambers before he'd catch up with her. Obviously he was disturbed and she didn't know what to believe. She had to keep him talking until Doug arrived.

"I don't understand what you mean, Stanley."

"You know, those evil men. Gilbert, Bellemy and Sands."

"Stanley, surely you can't believe I asked you to kill them."

His eyes flared in anger, and now she could see the gleam of insanity in them. "Yes, you did. Why are you denying you asked me to do it? You said something has to be done about these criminals getting off on technicalities. You asked me for a solution. I did it for you, Jessica, because I love you. I thought you would be so pleased." His last sentence came out in a whimpering sob.

She wanted to scream for help, but no one would hear her. What was keeping Doug?

"But, Stanley," she said gently, trying to calm him, "surely you must know I would never ask you to murder anyone. I meant we needed a solution to these criminals being able to escape being punished for their crimes."

"And thanks to me, they didn't, did they? And now nobody can blame you for releasing them. I have a list from other cases, but now I won't have time to bring them to justice.'' He grimaced in a flare of anger again. ''Thanks to Detective McGuire. I liked him at first, because he wanted them punished, too, but now I hate him for those vile things he's done to you.''

''What vile things, Stanley? Detective McGuire hasn't hurt me.''

He pounded his fist on the desk. ''He has, too. Don't try to deny it, Jessica. I've seen the way he touches you. What he does to you. He treats you like a harlot. I've watched the two of you, squirming and rutting together like animals. In your apartment. At the cottage. It sickened me.''

''In my apartment! How did you get in my apartment?''

His chuckle was more deranged than amused. ''It was so easy. I took the key out of Ms. Alexander's desk and had a duplicate made. I used to watch you sleep, Jessica. You always looked peaceful.'' His face contorted with hatred. ''I even watched you sleeping with Detective McGuire.'' His eyes gleamed with madness. ''I planned on killing him tonight. He's as evil as the others I've killed. Now it's too late. I waited too long. He knows I'm the executioner.''

She stared, horrified, when he drew a hypodermic needle out of his pocket. Oh, God, she had to get out of there. He had snapped completely, and was now beyond any hope of understanding reasoning.

''This won't hurt, Jessica. I'd never hurt you. All you'll feel is a little needle prick, then you won't feel anything else. Then I'll do it to myself. When they find us, we'll be together. Romeo and Juliet. Together in eternity, too.''

She tried not to show her fright. ''But I don't want to die, Stanley. You said you loved me. Why do you want to kill me?''

''I can't leave you to his vulgar pawing, Jessica. This is an extra-strong dosage, and by the time they find us, it will be too late to save us like they did Detective Peterson. I'm glad he didn't die, though. I really didn't want to hurt him.''

"But we don't have to die to be together. We can go away. Someplace where they'll never find us.''

For an instant his eyes gleamed with hope, then he shook his head. "No, Detective McGuire would find us. He'd never give up until he found us.'' His mouth curled in bitterness. "He's like a relentless bulldog. I'm afraid there's no other solution, Jessica.''

Just then her cell phone went off, but it was in her purse in a desk drawer. She knew it was Doug. He'd probably tried the office phone, and when he couldn't get through on it, he most likely tried her cell phone. Knowing Doug, when she didn't answer either phone, he wouldn't let it rest. But what was keeping him?

As soon as he took Jess home, he'd have to go back to the precinct. He hated to break their dinner date, but he had to check out his suspicion about Stanley Haley. There was no doubt in his mind that Haley was the culprit.

As he approached the courthouse, Doug saw there had been an accident that was tying up traffic. He couldn't get near enough to park there, so he pulled into the court-house's parking structure and drove up to the level where Jess had a reserved spot.

At this time of night, there were only a couple cars remaining. He saw that one of them was a gray Toyota. Curious, he walked over to it. Ever since Vic's incident, he automatically checked out gray or light blue Toyotas. Doug pulled out his cell phone and called the precinct. Vic had arrived and Doug told him to run the license plate number.

Vic was back a few minutes later. "Looks like your hunch might be right, partner. The license is registered to Stanley Haley. Where are you now?''

"On the third level of the courthouse's parking garage. Get over here with a search warrant. I'm going to pop the trunk."

"Wait until I get there," Vic said.

"No. The bastard could drive off by the time you get here. I'm doing it now."

"Dammit, Doug, wait and do it legally," Vic shouted. "Don't give the perp an excuse to walk."

"Hold on for a minute," Doug said. He'd already gotten a crowbar out of his car and proceeded to pry Haley's trunk open. When he raised the lid, he hit pay dirt.

"Vic, bring an arrest warrant, too. There's a wheelchair in the trunk, and I bet there'll be enough prints and DNA on it to keep this guy locked up for a century. There's rope and a plastic bag, too. Looks like he's got big plans for tonight."

"Well, stay put until I get there with the warrants. It shouldn't be more than fifteen minutes."

"I'm not budging. This guy's not slipping away this time."

"Just watch your back, partner," Vic said.

As soon as he hung up, Doug dialed Jess. When she didn't answer he figured she'd gone outside to wait for him, so he dialed her cell phone. He let it ring until the answer message clicked in.

He didn't like it. Not at all. He dialed the office phone again. She or Liz would have answered the office phone unless... He looked around at the other couple of cars. None of them was a Ford. Liz drove a Ford Thunderbird. That meant Jess was alone. What if Haley was with her? He dashed to the door and raced down the hallway to Liz's office. The lights were out and the door was locked.

Doug felt a little relieved, but couldn't figure out why Jess would leave with Liz without calling him. Unless she tried and someone didn't give him the message. He dialed Jess's home phone. No answer. He was getting more nervous by the minute. He dug out Liz's number and tried her. She answered on the fourth ring.

"Liz, this is Doug McGuire. Is Jess with you?"

"No. She said you were going to drive her home."

"How long ago was that?"

"About twenty or thirty minutes. Doug, what's wrong?"

"She's not answering the phone."

"Oh, is that all? I turned off her phone before I left."

"Liz, she's not answering her cell phone, either. I'm outside of your office right now and the lights are off and the door's locked. Was she alone when you left?"

"Yes. I told her to lock the door after Stanley and I left because there was no one else on the floor."

Doug's stomach flipped into his throat. "Stanley Haley?"

"Yes, he was helping us."

"Did you see him drive away?"

There was a short silence, then Liz said, "Come to think of it, I didn't. He was unlocking his car when I pulled out."

Suddenly Ben Kirkland's voice came on. "Doug, what's this about Jess? Are the two of you quarreling again?"

"I wish that's all it was. I've gotta go."

Doug tried the door again. He pounded on it, and shouted her name. Then he tried to unlock it using a credit card.

Suspecting the worse, he was becoming desperate. He looked around and saw a fire extinguisher attached to the wall. He ran down to it and snatched it off the wall, and then he hurled it as hard as he could against the door of Liz's office. The glass shattered and he kicked out the rest of the glass and crawled through it.

"It's time now, Jessica," Stanley said. He extended his hand. "Come over here and lie down on the floor. We'll be lying side by side when they find us. I hate to part with you even for a little while, but we'll be together again soon.''

"You'll have to come and get me, Stanley, because I'm not going to come over there."

"Don't make this harder for me than it is already. I don't want to hurt you."

A metal statue of the blindfolded Themis, Protector of Blind and Swift Justice, holding the scales of justice set on the credenza behind her desk. Jess picked it up when Stanley started to approach her holding the hypodermic needle.

"Put the needle down, Stanley. You're ill, dear. You need help. I'll see that you get the proper medical attention you need. Trust me, Stanley."

"It's too late. I told you, Jessica, I can't desert you and leave you to the mercy of Detective McGuire."

He turned his head in surprise at the sudden crash of glass shattering in the outer office.

She swung the statue and hit him in the head. Stanley staggered back just as Doug burst into the room.

"Look out, Doug, he's got a needle," she cried out.

Driven by madness Stanley leaped at Doug and tried to drive the hypodermic needle into him, but Doug was too quick for him. He gripped the man's arm and the two men struggled for what seemed an eternity to Jess. Finally the needle flew out of Stanley's hand and Doug delivered a blow to the chin that sent Stanley sprawling to the floor, unconscious.

Doug came over to her and took her in his arms. "Are you okay, baby?"

"Yes, just hold me, Doug, until I stop trembling."

She closed her eyes and reveled in the feel of his arms around her. Her world was secure again.

Stanley was still dazed when Vic and several patrol officers rushed into the room. Vic cuffed him and bagged the hypodermic needle. They were just preparing to lead Stanley away when her father and Liz came rushing in.

"I'll bring her in for you to get her statement," Doug said to Vic.

Vic nodded. "Let's go, pal," he said to Stanley.

"Oh, Stanley," Liz said sadly, wiping the tears from her eyes.

Mollified, the madness no longer in his eyes, the young man looked pathetic and scared. He stopped in front of Liz. "I only did it because I love her, Ms. Alexander." He turned his head and looked back at Jess with the same worshipful glance she had always seen in his eyes. The officers nudged him, and he moved on.

Doug drove her to the precinct and as soon as Jess finished giving a statement of what occurred in her office, they joined her father and Liz at the Water Street Bistro. While Jess and Doug ate a late-night sandwich, Doug filled them in on the minor details.

"Haley confessed he killed Sands because he'd been the court reporter on that trial."

"Where did he get the wheelchair?" Ben asked. "You said you and Vic couldn't trace it."

"It belonged to his mother. She died several years ago and he had never disposed of it. That's how he got the insulin, too. He kept forging her doctor's name from an old prescription of hers."

"Well, wouldn't the similar name ring a bell with you?" Jess asked.

"His mother had remarried—her name was Kensington. When her husband died, Stanley had moved back in to take care of her."

Liz sighed. "I still can't believe it. I loved that boy. I hate the thought of him locked up in prison the rest of his life."

"He's a sick man, Liz. He's killed three men and would

have killed Jess, too. Don't ever lose sight of that," Doug said.

As they lingered over cups of coffee, Liz and Ben told Jess that they were in love and intended to get married.

Jess was flabbergasted, but delighted. As much as she'd loved her mother, it made her happy to think that her father was ready to get on with his life. Considering how she and her father had lived so long with the grievances of the past, it was good to know these ghosts had been put to rest. She looked at Doug with love and pride. And most of it was due to him.

Her father must have been on the same wavelength. He filled their glasses and raised his in a toast.

"To the best damn detective in the state. Thanks, Doug, we Kirklands owe you more than we can ever show."

Jess winked at her father. "Oh, don't underestimate me, Dad. I'll give it my best shot."

Doug grinned, and before kissing her behind the ear, he whispered, "No time like the present. Let's get out of here."

Later, as she brushed out her hair before retiring, Jess said sadly, "I just don't understand it. Stanley was always such a gentle young man. It seems impossible he could have committed such crimes. What do you think really made him do it?"

Doug was stretched out on the bed. "I think I understand, honey. Love for a woman can often make or destroy a man. I know how he felt. Both of us knew we weren't good enough for you, but neither of us could deny our feelings. Unfortunately, he channeled his destructively."

"Are you suggesting that your love for me has or will destroy your life, too?"

"On the contrary...I think I'm a better man for loving you. You showed me how to open up my heart with love and trust. Are you coming to bed, Angel Face?"

Jess put aside the hairbrush and crawled across the foot of the bed up to him. "What's missing in your theory, Detective, are my feelings. You see, why it worked for you and not poor Stanley is that this woman loves this man," she declared, poking a finger at his bare chest. "And those are the operative words."

He grinned and tried to sound flippant, even though his insides were revving up like an eighteen-wheeler. "And like the song says, 'Woman needs man, and man must have his mate.' Which reminds me, we haven't watched that tape for a couple weeks. How about it?"

"Not a chance, McGuire. I'm going to burn that *Casablanca* tape. Dammit, Doug, I'm serious." She shoved him down and straddled him. "You lie there and listen, because I've got something to say."

"Should I get your gavel, Judge?"

"I don't need a gavel. I never have. That's my point— a point that I've neglected to remind myself of for the past several weeks. For most of my thirty-four years I've prided myself on being a pretty independent, self-assured person. I admit I was devastated by Karen's death, but it made me more determined to set my goals and go for them. And, frankly, I think I did pretty damn good until I fell in love with Detective Douglas I.—for intractable—McGuire. Then overnight I became a spineless wimp vacillating between he loves me, he loves me not, like petals being plucked from a daisy. I swore I never wanted to see you again one minute, and vowed I couldn't live without you the next. I was flooded with such insecurities that I couldn't make a rational decision and stick to it. It was easier to rule on the worst case I've ever had to face in court, than to cope with the uncertainty of my relationship with you. Well, in the past few days I've done some serious thinking. I suffered mood swings from one end of the spectrum to the other, and I finally came to one irrevocable conclusion—I know who I am, I know what I want and I will *not* settle for anything less. I'm so in love with you, Doug McGuire, that there's no way I'm going to let you go. As one of my final official acts, I sentence you to life, Detective.''

"You saying you're retiring from the bench?"

"To quote my favorite detective, 'You've got that right.' Actually, I've resigned already. Two more weeks and I'm through.'' She sighed deeply. "Oh, Doug, I'm so tired of courts and criminals, I'm getting out. I only went into this because of Karen's death. My biological clock is ticking away. I want to have a baby. Your baby.''

He couldn't believe it. Nothing in his life had ever worked out this perfect. He pulled her down to him. "Fine. Let's make a baby. There's no time like the present.''

"We might have done that already. I didn't take any pills with me when I went up to the cottage.''

He chuckled. "Then I guess we better not waste any more time. Can a judge officiate her own wedding?''

Tears glistened in her eyes. "Do I detect a marriage proposal somewhere in that?''

"You've got that right.'' He dumped her off him and rolled over, cradling her in his arms. "Will you marry me, Jess? I can't figure out why you'd even consider a bum like me for the father of your child, but I swear there isn't anything in life I want more than to marry you.'' He cupped her cheek in his hand and gazed into the eyes of this woman he worshipped beyond reason. "I love you, Angel Face.''

He wanted to say so much more. Not only that he loved her, but how much she'd changed his life, his attitudes. Given him a belief in a better life. How he wanted her physically—would always want her physically—but now he wanted the house and picket fence, too. The two-car garage. The His and Hers towels. And he wanted a couple kids, at least a little girl with auburn hair and brown eyes like her mother's. But he'd settle for whatever she wanted.

Just as long as he had Jess. He could make it—get through anything thrown at him—as long as there was Jess.

Yeah, there was so much he wanted to—*should*—say to her, but he couldn't now. He had to learn how. And he would. It would come in time. She had the love and patience to teach him how.

So, instead, in his best Bogie imitation, he said, "Of all the criminal courts in all the towns of the world, I walked into yours."

"McGuire, that's the worst Humphrey Bogart impersonation I've ever heard." She moved in closer and their bodies melded like a kidskin glove to a hand. That was another thing he loved about Jess.

Jess slipped her arms around his neck. "But as your man Bogie said," she murmured, her lips so near he could taste them already, "'Louie, I think this is the beginning of a beautiful friendship.'"

* * * * *

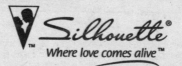

If you enjoyed what you just read,
then we've got an offer you can't resist!

Take 2 bestselling
love stories FREE!
Plus get a FREE surprise gift!

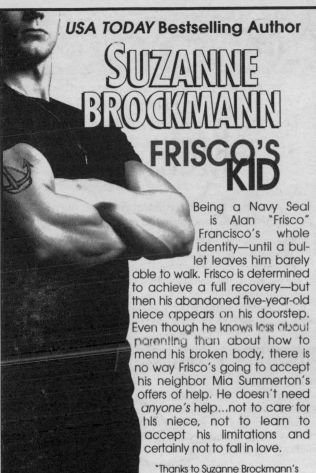

From *USA TODAY* bestselling author

EMILIE RICHARDS

**comes the story of a woman who has played life
by the book, and now the rules have changed.**

Faith Bronson, daughter of a prominent Virginia senator and wife
of a charismatic lobbyist, finds her privileged life shattered when
her marriage ends abruptly. Only just beginning to face the lie
she has lived, she finds sanctuary with her two children in a
run-down row house in exclusive Georgetown. This historic
house harbors deep secrets of its own, secrets that force Faith
to confront the deceit that has long defined her.

PROSPECT STREET

"Richards adds to the territory
staked out by such authors as
Barbara Delinsky and Kristin Hannah....
Richards' writing is unpretentious and
effective and her characters burst with
vitality and authenticity."

—*Publishers Weekly*

*Available the first week of June 2003
wherever paperbacks are sold!*

MIRA®

MER693

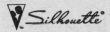

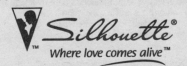

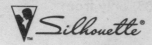

COMING NEXT MONTH